ATONEMENT

TORI FOX

Erica—

Dying isn't fun.
or so I heard.
I don't know.

XO Tori Fox

Editing/Proofreading by Ellie at My Brother's Editor

Cover Design by Juliana at Jersey Girl Design

For Tom Ford.

PROLOGUE

BASTIAN

I slam closed the file in front of me. "Fuck."

"I assure you everything in there is true, Mr. Montford. When it was brought to my attention, I made sure to fact-check it all. The photos aren't edited."

I slide my fingers along the back of my neck. "Make the call then."

"Sir, are you sure?"

I look up from my desk and glare at my assistant. "Make the damn call."

His hands shake before he shoves them into his pockets. "You know what this will mean."

I clench my fists that are laying on top of the file that will crush my entire world. "I'm not an idiot, Parker. Make the call. Consequences be damned. I should have known this would happen."

He stutters, something I haven't seen him do in years. "But you'll go to prison."

I glare at him. I know he can see the anger, the fire,

the betrayal burning in my eyes. "I am quite aware of what will happen. I should have known sooner or later I would."

He nods at me and heads toward my office door but stops suddenly before he opens it. "She will never forgive you."

I sigh as my eyes scan across the window to my left, looking over the sea I believed would bring me peace. "She already hates me. But it's time she learned the truth. I would be a fool to think she would give me her forgiveness."

"As you wish, sir."

I don't look at him as he walks out of my office. Instead, I look at the sea. At the calming blue of the water. The water that reminds me of her and I know always will. But where it once brought me peace, I know now it will only bring me pain.

I don't know how long I sit there. I can only tell it's been hours since I watched the sun set below the horizon.

The sound of footsteps in the hall does nothing to make me move. Or make me regret my decision.

I don't even look up when the detectives walk through my office door without a knock.

The Interpol agent doesn't say a word to me.

What could he possibly say?

What's done is done.

I stand when he places his hand on my shoulder.

I don't even wince when he places the cold cuffs on my wrist.

"I'm sorry, Bastian. I didn't want it to end this way."

I close my eyes, letting the image of her flash behind

them. Her blonde hair flowing in the wind, the curve of her body as she stood on the spot just outside on the terrace of my home in Deià, the sparkle in her eye as she gave me that smile she saved just for me.

I did this for her.

To save her.

Just one more secret I will keep buried.

1

CAM

"Paris!" I yell at my boss in disbelief.

He looks at me with disdain.

I settle down in my seat and try to remember how to breathe. "I'm sorry. I just... I thought I was interviewing for a position here. In *New York*."

He runs his hands over his bald head, the sweat forming over the wrinkles that protrude from the back of his scalp. He sighs. "Well, you were. But we had a few more qualified applicants."

"So you are sending me to Paris? How am I even qualified for that?"

He clears his throat. "Well, you did get a minor in French at NYU. They are in desperate need of help. They asked us if we had any promising candidates."

Promising candidates, my ass.

I know they have been trying to find a way to get rid of me for months. Not because I can't do my job but because I am too good at it. They know I am asking for a lot of money but I feel like I am worth it. And if I learned anything from my father, I know it's to demand your worth.

"They are willing to pay you twenty thousand more than you are asking of us here."

My ears perk up at that. Twenty thousand more? That is a hell of a lot of money. "Twenty thousand dollars or euros?" I ask.

Demand your worth.

"Ugh, I would have to check," he says as he rubs the back of his neck.

"If it's euros, I will take the job. If not, you can expect my resignation."

His eyes bulge out as I say the words I was surprised even came out of my mouth.

Damn, girl, you still got it.

"I'll be sure they mean euros."

"Well, then, I guess I am moving to Paris." *What?* I shriek in my head. Paris! This has to be a dream.

He gives me a weak grin. The sweat on his forehead is more prominent than before.

"We have an apartment for you already. The company will pay for it until you find more suitable accommodations. You leave in a week." He grabs some papers from my desk and hands them over to me. My fingers avoiding his chubby ones.

"A week? But that gives me no time—"

"Do you want this promotion or not, Ms. Wilder?"

I hate when he calls me that. "I do."

"Then I suggest you leave early for the day and start working on the arrangements for your belongings. Every-

6

thing regarding your relocation is in there." He gestures to the pile of damp papers he handed me. "There is a list of moving companies we suggest but you are free to use whomever you wish as long as it stays within the budget. Your flight information and apartment information are in there as well. I will talk to HR over in the Paris office to update your offer letter and have them email it to you by the end of the day."

"I—uh. Thank you, sir."

"Ms. Wilder, you deserve this promotion. I only wish we could have you stay in New York and be a part of our team. But I know you will do great things in Paris."

Yeah right. The man despises me. But not that I can say much. I despise him too. He creeps me out. I always worried about working late and being left alone with him. Fortunately, the only thing he ever did was look at me.

"Thank you, Mr. Banks, for this opportunity." I shake his hand and head to his office door. "Paris!" I shout again as I walk out with a pep in my step.

"Paris!" Tacoma yells into the phone. "What am I gonna do with you so far away, Cam?"

"Pssh," I say as I flip through the papers Mr. Banks gave me earlier as I talk to my best friend. "You already moved away from me and fell in love and got married. So don't get mad at me that I'm moving a little farther away."

"Cameron, I'm in New Orleans. It's a couple hour flight to New York. Not an extra five thousand miles."

"How do you even know that?"

"I Googled it."

"T, you know I love you but you left me first by moving home to BFE, Tennessee."

Tacoma, my best friend from college, left New York two years ago to find herself back at home in her small town of White Creek, Tennessee. Instead she found her high school crush and fell in love with him all over again. Now they split their time between White Creek and New Orleans.

"Don't blame me for you moving across an ocean!"

I slump onto my couch. "I'm not. I just wish I could see you before I go."

"Maybe I can fly out there. When are you leaving?"

"In a week," I whisper.

"A week?! Damn, they are wasting no time getting you over there."

"I know. I was really hoping I could see you before I go. Maybe make one last trip to Dollywood."

Tacoma snorts into the phone. "Ryder would kill me if I dragged him there with you again."

"Oh you know he had more fun than I did."

"Cam, I don't think anyone has ever had as much fun as you did in Dollywood. Like ever."

She makes a good point. I love Dolly Parton. My grandmother loved her and I would always listen to her records as a child. When I found out Tacoma's hometown was only a few hours from Dollywood, I forced her to take me. She dragged her dreamy husband with us

8

and we all had a blast. Well, maybe me more than them since I snagged myself a cowboy just like I always dreamed.

What a weekend that was.

I twirl my ponytail in my fingers as I picture Clayton and his six-pack.

"Earth to Cameron!"

"What? I was thinking about that happy trail."

"You are hopeless."

"Not as hopeless as you were with Ryder."

She groans into the phone. "Well, it all worked out in the end, didn't it?"

"Somehow."

"I would strangle you if I was there right now."

"No, you would be accompanying me to the nearest bar and celebrating my promotion with martinis."

She laughs. "Ugh, why do I need to be responsible and have a job when I could jump on a red-eye and come see you."

"You said it."

"Oh Cam, you know I wish I could but we are moving back to White Creek this week. I wish you had just a little bit more time."

I sigh as I stretch my legs and look out my window to the lights of Manhattan. I really am going to miss this view. "Me too, T. Me too."

We spend the next hour going over everything I know about my job which isn't much but she doesn't really even care about the job. She has been telling me for years I deserve a promotion and now I finally have it. I tell her about the apartment the company has for

9

me in Paris and the stress I am already feeling from moving.

She reassures me it will all be okay. I am a spitfire. I take life by the balls and there is no way I am going to fail in my new position. I can't help but laugh as she says it even if it brings tears to my eyes. I am going to miss New York. I am going to miss Tacoma more than I already do. And I'm going to miss my family even if we don't always get along. They've always been here, always been close. And for the first time in my twenty-eight years, I am finally going to do something I've always dreamed of doing.

2

CAM

I sip on my café au lait and bite into a croissant as I make my way through a park to the Paris offices of Hidings, Sloan, & Dubois PR.

I love summer in Paris. Every time I came here as a child, I was in awe of the city. And I am grateful I got this position. Paris has always been a far-fetched dream of mine. I wanted to do a semester abroad here but the opportunity never came about.

But now I get to live here. Yes, I am thousands of miles from my friends and family but it's Paris! The city of lights! The food, the wine, the romance! This is truly a dream.

I mean, except for the fact the apartment the company is paying for is a four hundred square foot studio and I barely have room for all my clothes, let alone my shoes and my makeup collection. What can I say? I am a girly girl that was raised with the upper elite of Boston and then moved to the upper west side of New

York. Even my dorm room at NYU was bigger than the shoebox I have now. I need to find somewhere new, stat. But the view is to die for. My lone window looks out over the Seine River and I can see the Eiffel Tower in the distance. The very far distance but I can see it no less.

I am not a hopeless romantic. Far from it. In fact, I prefer one-night stands over relationships any day. Just ask me about my damn golden rule. But there is some kind of magic in Paris. Something that makes me yearn for romance. And maybe I will find it. Someone to change my mind, even if just for a night.

I stroll across a bridge over the Seine and watch a few boats float down the river. My heart skips a beat, the excitement of being in Paris yet to settle down as I cross the bridge and into the sixth arrondissement and into Saint Germain des Pres, the home to my new offices. I find the building on an older tree-lined street filled with coffee shops, bookstores, and vintage clothing stores. The complete opposite of downtown Manhattan.

I open the door to the sleek offices of my new home. I eagerly climb the marble staircase to the third floor and pull open the glass doors embossed with Hidings, Sloan, & Dubois Public Relations on it.

"Bonjour," I say as I approach the reception desk.

"Bonjour," the young girl with silky dark black hair and blunt bangs answers. "Avez-vous un rendez-vous?"

"No, mademoiselle. Je m'appelle Cameron Wilder et aujourd'hui c'est mon premier jour."

"Cameron!" The girl bounces out of her chair and walks around the desk. "I am so excited to meet you!" she says in English, although her accent overpowers her words. "From New York! My dream is to go to New York."

I giggle as she boasts about the city. I could be doing the exact same thing as her right now except talking about Paris.

"Oh my, I am so sorry for my outburst. But we are so excited for you to join us. Well, at least I am. And no need to speak French here. Most of us speak English as we have so many international clients. But it's good to know you speak French. We once hired someone from South Africa and they couldn't speak a word. It was quite a challenge."

"I bet."

She grabs my hand and pulls me into the large room to the right of her desk. It's completely open with ornate wooden desks along the wall facing a large round table in the center.

"This is you," she says as she points to a desk in the corner of the room. "The big table is where everyone goes to discuss ideas for clients. The conference room is through those doors and the bosses' offices are in the hall to the left. I am sure HR will come by to see you after the morning meeting which is in" —she looks down at her watch— "ten minutes. We always start the week with a meeting in the conference room and HR would never get here early enough to have you finish whatever paperwork you need to finish. Anyway, I am Sophia. It's so good to meet you but I should get back to my desk just in case a client shows up unexpectedly."

I watch her as she twirls away. She seems even more of a whirlwind than I am.

I set my purse in a drawer of my desk and grab a notebook and pen and make my way to the conference room.

I am the first to arrive but I know French customs and usually nothing ever starts on time.

Within fifteen minutes, people start filing into the room. A few give me strange looks while everyone else just ignores me.

"Bonjour," an older woman says as she walks into the room in a sleek black power suit. Her dark mahogany hair pulled into a low chignon at the base of her neck. Her lips painted a deep shade of red as she starts speaking quickly in French. "We have a busy day ahead of us today and an even busier week. Four new clients signed contracts over the weekend. We need to secure the Hall account by end of day, and that damn Bernard account by the end of the week. We are not losing that one. Tom and Abigail, I need you to do whatever it takes to secure that account. A case of Dom, dinner at Le Meurice, I don't care, just do it. We need to move forward with the—" She stops and pauses as I am trying to keep up with her quick French. When I look up, I realize she is staring at me. "You are new."

I set my pen down and stand up with my hand out, of course I turn to a dumb American custom. I quickly drop my hand. "I'm Cameron Wilder."

Her stern mouth slips into a smile "Ah yes. The Montford account."

"The huh?"

"The Montford account? Were you not told why you

were transferred here?" she asks as she crosses her slender arms over her chest.

"Um, no?" I say as a question.

She drops her arms and sighs. "Oh very well. Moving on," she continues like my presence was just a blip on her radar. Although she does switch over to English.

I listen to the woman ask about the current state of every account and then list off assignments for the week. She walks out of the conference room without a dismissal and I look around the room and see everyone else grabbing their notebooks and heading out.

"You're the American that transferred here?" a young man a few years younger than me with a strong French accent asks me as we walk out the door.

"I'm sure that's obvious."

He snorts then runs his hand through his platinum blond locks. "I like to state the obvious."

I smile at him and walk to my desk.

He follows. "You were given the Montford account?"

I look up at him and he has a look of pity on his face. "Yeah. Why the look?"

He sits on the corner of my desk. "You don't know?"

"Obviously."

He smirks. "Hmm. Well considering Montford Hotels are only in Europe, I am guessing news didn't reach the other side of the ocean. At least the juicy details. My guess is they only hired you on so you would take the account. No one here wants to work for him."

"Why?" I ask curiously as my thoughts sway back to the words Mr. Banks said about promising candidates. I knew he was lying by the sweat on his forehead. It's because they couldn't get anyone to take this account.

"Oh Jacques, will you stop spreading gossip around. I need a copy of the Maison contract and a cup of coffee."

Jacques slides off my desk and gives the woman from the conference room the fakest smile I have ever seen. "Tout de suite, madame."

The woman rolls her eyes and hands a thick file over to me. "I'm sorry no one gave this to you sooner. I thought I asked Mr. Banks in the New York office to make sure you had a copy before you moved here. Give you the weekend to digest everything." She adjusts her suit jacket down over her hips. "Anyway, I am Caroline Dubois. I wish I could say I was your boss but my father hasn't yet decided to retire. But I am the senior publicist here. If you have any questions about the file, please don't hesitate to reach out to me."

"Thank you, Ms. Dubois."

She turns her nose up to me. "Well, I have to finalize that Maison contract. Good day."

I watch as she walks away with a bit more of a goodbye than she did in the conference room. I flip open the file and barely make it through the first page, detailing the client, when Jacques slithers back up to my desk.

"That woman needs to learn to get her own coffee," he humphs.

I snicker. "The woman I can only assume is your boss."

"Who knew you needed experience to be a publicist. Now I am stuck being a lowly PA."

I purse my lips. "I'm sure you will get there."

"Oh who cares! Now, where were we? Oh yes, Bastian Montford," he snorts. "The guy is a dick. He runs Montford Holdings with a noose around everyone's neck. Which is probably why it's so successful but no one wants to work for him."

"I find that hard to believe. Doesn't matter how tight that noose is, people work for people. It's probably only the ones who couldn't take the heat that spread the rumors."

Jacques raises a brow at me. "I can see why they chose you. You are feistier than you look."

"Qui se soucie si je suis." *Who cares if I am?*

"And you speak French."

"And I'm smart too. I don't think I will have a problem. Not to mention I'll be working for Montford Hotels. Which from what I read isn't run by Bastian Montford but by Matías Montford," I say as I look down at the first page of my brief.

"Maybe you should read the rest of the file," he says with a gesture of his hand.

I look at him curiously. I would rather him just tell me than have me read whatever it is that he knows. "Tell me."

"Matías Montford is in prison for money laundering and Interpol is investigating possible human trafficking. Hell, it's the reason Montford needs a PR company. They need to dig out their prestigious name from the gutter."

"What?"

"I'm guessing you didn't read far enough. You thought that one of the most prestigious hotel groups in the world just wanted you to run their PR?" He laughs as he says it. "Bastian Montford fired their entire PR staff after what his brother did. He needs the name to be recouped. You pretty much need to build it back up from nothing. The casino has been temporarily closed. Sales have dropped catastrophically at the hotel. No one wants to stay at a hotel they may get arrested at or worse caught up in an underground sex world. Montford Holdings is at risk of losing billions in real estate if you can't pull them out of the gutter."

"Well, I have done a lot in my last five years with HSD. This is nothing but another challenge."

He snorts and mumbles something in French slang I can't quite decipher. "He's been through three PR companies in the last two months. And has fired every single one of them for not making progress fast enough."

"I've worked with celebrities with horrible reps. I can handle this."

"Well, good for you. But Bastian Montford is not like a celebrity being carted off to rehab. He's a brutal Englishman. He gets what he wants or he will get rid of you. If you fuck up this account, you will surely be fired."

Oh. I don't say it aloud. This must be why they sent me here. They didn't think I could handle this account and it was an easy way to get rid of me.

"Look, I don't mean to be rude. I actually feel bad for you. Ms. Dubois tried to get every single person here to take the contract, but they all found excuses why they couldn't take on another client. I'm sorry you got coerced into moving to Paris just to be fired."

"It won't happen."

He shrugs. "I hope not. I like you. You have spunk. The only other person I like here is Sophia."

"Jacques! The contract!" We both hear Ms. Dubois yelling down the hall.

He stands from the corner of my desk. "You should get a move on. Don't want to leave Mr. Montford waiting. I'm sure he will fire you and the company on the spot if you are late."

I flip through the file, skipping over everything Jacques just told me. I see the address for Montford Holdings offices in Paris and while I might not have been here in a few years, I know the general area it's in. "His offices aren't too far from here."

"You didn't get the memo then."

I try to keep my cool, already feeling overwhelmed as I flip through the file.

"Montford is on his yacht in Saint Tropez. He is returning from some meetings in Spain and is expecting you to meet him there. At the Montford Hotel offices."

"What?" I shout then look around trying to act professional.

Jacques grabs the file out of my hand and pulls out a flight itinerary.

"How do you know so much?"

He laughs at me. "Caroline's assistant, remember? I put this together. Sorry, maybe I should have started out with you have a flight to catch." He looks down at his watch. "Shit, in three hours. You should probably get a move on, considering you will be working from there. Not here. You may want to pack quickly."

"Jacques!"

"And I should probably get her that contract. Good luck!" he says with a weak smile as he heads toward his boss' office.

I try to analyze everything I just learned in the last twenty minutes about my account and try not to think about failing. Because I have no idea what I agreed to.

One thing is for sure though.

I think I'm screwed.

———

I exit the cab and am greeted with a humid breeze. It's warmer in the south of France but the salty air of the Mediterranean is a welcome escape. I sling my oversized purse onto my shoulder and head down the cobblestone steps to the dock, my suitcase rolling behind me.

I reach into my bag and grab the file I was given this morning. I managed to make the most of my time and thoroughly read the entire contents on the plane and do a bit more research when the Wi-Fi worked. And I uncovered a lot more than was in the file in the few hours I had to research. Thank god I took those journalism courses at NYU. And binge-watched true crime, I swear I learn everything from those shows.

I shuffle through the pages until I find the dock number I am looking for.

Thirty-six.

I walk along the boardwalk in awe of the boats I pass. Not that I would call them boats. Most are yachts and from my experience with yachts, which isn't much, I would say they are all well over ten million dollars.

My parents never bought one, saying it was a waste of money with the upkeep, but plenty of their friends had them. But none of them were ever this nice.

I see the dock number I am looking for and start to walk down the pier, head down due to the blinding summer sun.

But when I look up, I nearly stumble in my Louboutins.

A gorgeous man is stepping onto the back sitting area, phone to his ear. His skin is perfectly olive, bronzed and glistening in the afternoon sun. I study the way the sleeves of his white dress shirt are rolled up to his elbows exposing his strong forearms, the sinewy muscles causing my thoughts to spin. My eyes move up his chest, where you can tell he no doubt spends a lot of time in the gym from the way his shirt is just tight enough across his chest until it splits open exposing the finest trail of hair on his tanned skin. My eyes continue their gaze upward until I hit his face, and dear lord this man should not be allowed to leave the house. Sharp-cut cheekbones make his square jaw more pronounced. A jaw with the finest bit of stubble on it. You aren't sure if it's there on purpose or not. His lips are full, much fuller than any man I've ever kissed, and while some might find it unattractive, I curse myself for staring at them for too long. My eyes make their way up to his eyes, which are covered in aviator sunglasses. His hair blows slightly in the wind, the black almost as dark as night. I can tell his hair is longer on top than on the sides and the breeze is close to winning a battle to let it blow freely in the wind.

He finally turns to face me straight on as he hangs up

21

his phone. Someone else must finally notice my presence as a large man whom I can only assume is a bodyguard jumps onto the dock and steps into my face.

"Pas de journalists," he says sternly. *No reporters*.

I take a step back. "I'm not… Désolée, je ne suis pas une journaliste. I'm from HSD PR. I was hired by Mr. Montford."

"Credentials?" he asks in a thick French accent, although the man looks anything but French. More Sasquatch.

I hear a throat clear behind the beast of a man in front of me. "Lucas, Mr. Dubois did agree his employee would meet us here."

Lucas steps out of the way rather reluctantly. The man I assumed was Mr. Montford, from the second I saw him, steps off his boat, slinging his suit jacket over his shoulder like he is some kind of model. I bite my lip to hold back the groan I know is ready to slip.

"My apologies, Miss…"

I blink a few times, forgetting that he is talking to me and grateful I have my damn Prada sunglasses on so he can't see my ogling. "Wilder. Cameron Wilder."

"Cameron Wilder." The way he says my name almost drips seduction. He has the strangest accent, like a melting pot of cultures blending his voice into his own distinct timbre. "My apologies. I thought Mr. Dubois was sending a man."

My hand goes to my chest and I take a step back. "Are you saying that a woman can't save your company?"

He smirks. "My company is not in need of saving. But the public image my brother left—"

I cut him off. "Yes, I know all about what happened. I read your file. I know what you hired me to do. And I also know the effect your brother's indiscretions have had on your own company. Don't pretend that nothing is wrong with Montford Holdings. I looked at your financial statements. I saw that some of your shareholders have been worried and started selling your stock. I mean, can there only be one bad apple in the bunch? Or is this a pattern? And sooner or later, Montford Holdings will fold just like Montford Hotels is on the cusp of doing."

Mr. Montford removes his glasses and steps into my personal space, even more so than Lucas did. I'm surprised to find gray eyes underneath the aviators. Gray eyes that darken with every word he speaks. "Ms. Wilder, while I appreciate your thorough initial investigation into my company, none of what you say is true. Montford Holdings is prosperous and will not fail. Montford Hotels has had a minor setback but will surely recover. As for your accusations that you say I don't think a woman knows how to save my company the answer would be yes. I don't think you could save my company because you know nothing about my company. Whatever petty things you read on the internet or find in interviews is just the surface of the iceberg. The workings of my company go deep, deeper than you could ever imagine and there is no way I could fail. I don't care if you are a woman or a man. This company will prevail."

"Then why hire us?"

He steps even farther into my space. Farther than I thought someone could. "Montford Hotels is the epitome of luxury. I need you to fix our image. Quickly. I know in time we would recover but I don't want to lose any profit now. Not with our expansion. And I don't have the time to do the work myself.

"I need someone who can turn things around quickly. Now excuse me for speaking the truth but I've had three other firms say they can do it. Three firms. Three women. And every single one of them failed. When Mr. Dubois said he had a Cameron Wilder, I assumed you were a man. I was wrong. But here is your chance to prove me wrong."

He steps away from me so quickly I nearly fall over.

"Lucas, call for the car. We need to head to the office so *Ms.* Wilder here can get to work and I can head back to Paris."

3

CAM

M y heels click across the boardwalk as I follow Mr.
Montford, Lucas, and another man who I am
guessing is Montford's assistant from the way he is
rattling off an agenda to him. I try to keep up but
walking on a boardwalk in a pair of Louboutins is not
the easiest task. I grunt as I bend over and rip my heels
off. When I look up Montford is looking at me over his
shoulder. His aviators are back on so I can't read his
expression.

When we make it to the end of the dock, Lucas
opens the door of a black SUV. Mr. Montford and his
assistant climb in and I take a deep breath before getting
in. Mr. Montford has a presence about him, an air of
power I felt before I even saw him on his yacht. I can't
imagine how that power will feel in an enclosed vehicle.
Lucas grabs my luggage from me as I climb into the
vehicle.

"Shoes optional for you, Ms. Wilder?"

I look up to meet stormy gray eyes. I purse my lips before letting out an exasperated sigh. I lean over and put my heels back on my feet. "When you decide to walk at a pace faster than my legs can keep up with while wearing four-inch heels then you better believe I am going to take the damn things off." I smile at him, in a feline way. "I assure you, Mr. Montford. I am quite civilized. Even if you think I am not because I am a woman. And from the look on your face, I'm guessing because I am also an American. Ne vous méprenez pas, je suis plus forte que j'en ai l'air."

Don't get me wrong, I'm tougher than I look.

Montford's assistant starts to snicker next to me and Montford shoots him a glare before turning back to me. "Just because you speak French doesn't make you more civilized. There are plenty of Frenchmen that are not."

"Like you?" I can't help but provoke him even though I know he isn't French.

"I'm not a Frenchman. I'm an Englishman."

"I thought you were Spanish?"

He leans slightly forward to ensure he has my attention. "I see you've read all about me Ms. Wilder. You know I am."

"So is that where your temper comes from?"

His assistant gasps beside him as he leans back in his seat, a smug look taking over his face. "You should know from your research, my temper is from my English side. You won't learn what comes from my Spanish side."

He stares at me and I stare right back, not letting him intimidate me even though I know that's what he is trying to do.

He already thinks I am bound to fail. He walked up to me with that mindset and I have no problem proving to him I won't. And it all starts with not letting him have the upper hand. I will stand my ground no matter if it seems foolish or not.

The tension in the air grows thick. His assistant adjusts his tie as he looks back and forth between the two of us but neither one of us moves.

Eventually, he clears his throat, clearing out the tension in the SUV. "We are on our way to the Montford Hotel offices. We can discuss what needs to be done in more depth. I will clear up some of the accusations you have no doubt been told. And you can begin working on your plan. Parker can assist you with anything you need until I need to return to Paris and then he will be returning with me."

I turn to Parker. "Nice to meet you, Parker. I am Cameron Wilder. But you can call me Cam."

"Parker Brown." He turns to face me with his hand outstretched. "Pleasure to meet you, Cam."

I turn back to Montford and the scowl he's had on his face is still there. "You are going to need to find a new PR team. I'm sure it's in the file that you *so thoroughly* read that the team that worked for Montford Hotels is no longer with us."

I nod and hold back any comments.

"The last company we hired started the process but did not get very far before I terminated our contract."

"And why have the last three firms not worked out for you?" I ask curiously.

He looks away from me and gazes out the window.

One of his hands glides over the top of his hair. "That's not really any of your business, Ms. Wilder."

I shift in my seat, uncrossing and recrossing my legs. "I believe it is my business, Mr. Montford. If I know what they fucked up on then I assure you I won't make the same mistake."

His eyes flit back over to me as I curse. The exact reaction I wanted. "You have a death wish, Ms. Wilder? I don't appreciate being talked back to."

"I don't have a death wish. But if you cannot open the lines of communication, you surely have a death wish for your own company." I pause, giving him time to digest my comeback. When he goes to speak, I cut him off, the devil in me patting me on the back. "Now I cannot fix something when I don't know what isn't working. So please elaborate on what the other companies did to fail."

The tension in the SUV returns but I ignore it as I study Montford. His lip curls up like a dog ready to attack. But before he can bite me with his words, Parker cuts in. "I will get you all that information tomorrow, Cam. Let's just go over the plan today." He pauses as the car comes to a stop. "And look, here we are."

The door to the SUV opens when we reach our destination on the east side of the peninsula. Lucas reaches his hand out for mine so I can step out. I nearly stumble as I take in the hotel in front of me. The pictures of this place do not do it justice. My breath is taken away by the sheer luxury of the building and I haven't even stepped inside yet. How have I never stayed at one of these hotels?

The building is white marble, pristine and sparkling. Different from the old French villas that pepper the coastline. The roundabout drive is obsidian, dark as night and the perfect contrast to the white building. A fountain sits in the middle of the roundabout, more white marble cast against the black. Tropical foliage is sprinkled around the small outdoor landscape, bringing a feeling of comfort to the otherwise stark exterior.

"This way," Montford commands as he exits the vehicle, buttoning his suit jacket as he heads through the front door. A doorman already holding the door open for him and nodding as he passes through.

I follow him and try to take everything in without looking like a child in a toy store. The inside is more magnificent than the outside. The reception desk sits to the right of the entryway, tucked into a corner as to not take away from the grand staircase leading up to the second floor. A chandelier of crystal hangs above another fountain in the center of the lobby. This fountain black to contrast against the white marble floors. I look up at the crystal chandelier, the size and opulence of it astounding. The ceiling is grand, at least thirty feet tall, the chandelier taking up over half the height.

Gold accents highlight the white marble walls. Gold sconces, gold picture frames, gold railings. As I look up toward the second floor, huge arched windows frame each side of the hall that no doubt leads to a ballroom. I can't even imagine what the chandelier looks like from that view.

I look ahead of me to the outdoor terrace that sits at

the end of the hall. A turquoise blue pool looks off the cliffside into the Mediterranean Sea.

From the corner of my eye, I see Montford head to a bank of elevators to the left. I quickly follow him, Parker and Lucas right behind me.

Montford scans a key card and presses the elevator button. Once it arrives, we all step inside. The opulence still present. White marble, gold accents. He swipes his key card again and hits the button for the fourth floor.

"I have a key card waiting for you in the offices. It is what you will use to get in and off the elevator. The offices take up the entire fourth floor of this side of the hotel and only these black key cards will get you onto the floor."

When we get to the office my breath is taken away from the view. Floor-to-ceiling windows overlook the crystal blue water. I immediately weave my way through the desks and look out the window.

The hotel sits on the edge of a cliff and I can see the walkway down to the beach from the sundeck. A few guests lie out by the pool that is surrounded by greenery and shrubs, making the pool look like an oasis.

"Quite the view, isn't it?" Mr. Montford asks as he steps beside me.

It's the most civil thing he has said to me. "Yes."

"Let me show you to your office," he says as he clears his throat.

I follow him as Parker follows behind me. We walk into a corner office made entirely of glass windows. In fact the five enclosed offices are all comprised of glass except for the walls dividing the offices. The rest of the office is open much like the HBD offices in Paris. The views from this office even better than the view from the common area. I didn't think that was possible.

"This was my brother's office. Not that he spent much time here. But I figured you could work here."

I nod. "Do you have a new CEO for Montford Hotels? Maybe the CFO or…"

He clenches his fist as he stares at the bookshelf along the one solid wall in the room. "I am in charge of the hotel group until I find someone fit to run it."

"So you don't want this office then?"

"I prefer to work from my own office. Not this one that has been tainted by poor decisions."

I am ready to make a snarky remark but I hold my tongue. I can only hope this place has been cleaned after the stories I've heard.

Mr. Montford unbuttons his suit jacket as he takes a seat on a chair in a small sitting area of the office and gestures for me to take a seat across from him. Parker stands in the corner, tablet in hand.

I take a seat as he elaborates on everything that has happened. The cancelations, the stock value decrease, employees leaving. He lets me in on little details of the truth of what really happened. He said earlier not to believe everything I hear but yet he won't expand on what the truth really is. I figure in time I can get more out of him. Once I gain his trust that I know what I am doing. And I will need more in order for me to fix the reputation of this hotel.

He lets me know that he fired the entire PR team. At least he gave me a reason for that. Some were involved in letting the raid reach the news level and none of the team worked to put out the fire. The last company that he had hired narrowed down candidates. He vetted them and Parker says he will send me the list.

"You can do final interviews. Anyone on this list you deem worthy enough to fix this nightmare, go ahead and hire. The team in this office was only three people but the other office in Paris has ten. My team is working on Paris, you just need to fill the positions here."

"Two offices? I thought there was only the office here."

Mr. Montford nods. "With the expansion coming up, I opened a second office in my building back in Paris. The expansion is my project. I knew my brother was struggling enough to run this office and the five properties we have."

"Why don't you just use your team to fix the situation?"

"They couldn't do both. I already put enough workload on them as it is."

I skim through the list of candidates. "So three people. What about a head of PR?"

Mr. Montford uncrosses his legs and leans his elbows on his knees. "That's you. For the time being. Once everything is back in its proper order, I'll promote someone or hire someone to fill the role."

"Fair enough."

"Now you have two months to get this office in order. I've managed to get rid of everyone here that played a role in—"

"Did you just say two months?" I cut him off.

His eyes turn dark and I can only guess it's because he doesn't like to be interrupted. "Yes."

"Why two months?"

He leans back into his chair. "Because the expansion I have invested well over a billion dollars in is set to be announced to the press in two months. Now if I had chosen the right person to begin with, they would have had more time to set things right. Now it's up to you. Two months. If I am not happy with what I see in the next month, you will be fired." His eyes get even darker and I can tell he is enjoying this and I can only guess it's because I interrupted him. "And you can kiss any dream you have of being a publicist goodbye."

"Are you threatening me, Mr. Montford?"

"No. I'm just telling you the truth."

We stare at each other and the tension from earlier returns to the room. Neither of us backing down from the other.

Parker speaks up. "Sir, you have a meeting in thirty minutes."

Mr. Montford cuts his gaze away from me. "Thank you, Parker." He stands, buttoning his jacket. "Everything you need should be on the tablet Parker will give you. If you have questions, Parker can answer them for you. He will show you where you'll be staying. I'll check in on your progress in a few days."

With that, he exits the office.

Parker watches him walk away before walking over to me.

"I wouldn't step on his toes too much. He doesn't like to be questioned."

I snort. "Couldn't tell."

Parker smirks and walks over to the desk. "Here is the tablet with all the information you should need. If you need anything, please don't hesitate to ask me. I will get it from Bastian."

"On a first name basis with the boss?"

He actually chuckles at that. "If I called him by his first name in front of him, he would probably fire me."

I laugh too. "Good to know."

"Let me show you to your room," he says as he pulls the black key card off the desk. "Bastian said this key gets you onto this floor but it pretty much gives you access to the entire hotel including your room."

"I'm staying here?"

He nods and pinches his brow. "Where else would you stay?"

"I just imagined in some old beat-up flat on the outskirts of town."

"You are a funny one."

I shrug.

"Bastian may be a ruthless businessman but he wouldn't put you in a cheap rental. Besides, he wants you close to the job in case of an emergency."

"I wish my company felt the same way."

"Did they not give you somewhere to stay?"

"Temporarily until I find my own place but there is no rush. I only moved to France a few days ago. But they put me in a tiny studio in Paris. It's not terrible but I am used to a thousand more square feet."

"Well, then I am sure you will find these accommodations suiting to your taste."

I follow him out of the offices and past the original elevators. He scans the key card and we walk into a vestibule with two more elevators.

He nods to the one on the left. "That goes straight to the penthouse." He swipes the key card next in front of a black panel to the elevator on the right. "This one leads to the top three floors. You can access your floor from the lobby but this makes it convenient when you are working."

The doors open to the elevator and I follow him in. This elevator is smaller than the others and I can tell it is used very infrequently. He presses the button for the fifteenth floor and the elevator rises quickly.

When I step off into the hall, I only see two doors.

"The main elevators are down that hall. Again only with your key card can you access this hall to the executive rooms. The guest rooms on the other side do not have access."

He scans the card in front of the door and it beeps, he gestures for me to go in first and I cannot believe this is where I will be staying.

I grew up with the upper elite of Boston. Lived on the upper west side of Manhattan for the last five years after graduating from NYU. But this place has nothing on those. The foyer to the room is just like the lobby. White marble and gold accents. A table of tropical flowers sits in the middle of the foyer. I walk past it and into the open concept room. A large sitting area sits off to the right and a small kitchen to the left. I am drawn to the floor-to-ceiling glass windows that seem to be a staple of this hotel. My room looks off to the sea just as the offices did but from this height the view is even more incredible. And it has a private deck with a small eating area and sun loungers.

"There are two bedrooms and an office in this suite. If I were you, I would choose the bedroom to the left. I believe your luggage has already been dropped off."

I turn to Parker. "This is too much."

"Don't tell that to Bastian."

"I don't need an executive suite."

"Once you check out the rest of the place, I am sure you will be singing a different tune. You have full access to all amenities. The fitness room is next to the pool house. Room service will be covered by Montford Holdings. And if you want groceries delivered just call the concierge." He hands me over the key card. "Well, I will be on my way. If you need anything, my number is listed in the contact sheet on the tablet."

"Thank you."

"Not a problem."

I watch as he leaves and let out a squeal. I kick my heels off and run and jump onto the huge lounging couch. I sink into the soft leather and kick my feet in the air.

I jump off the couch when I remember Parker saying something about taking the room on the left. I wander over to the other bedroom. It looks out over the pool and has a modest white marble bathroom with a glorious walk-in shower and a separate soaking tub.

I skip across the suite and make my way over to the other room. The first door leads to a small office. I open the door across the hall and I cannot believe this is where I will be staying the next two months.

The bed is massive, larger than a standard king, with a tufted headboard built into the wall. Pillows upon pillows are stacked at the top of the bed and I want to jump into them. A small sitting area sits off to the side of the television next to sliding glass doors that lead to another terrace. As I walk outside, I realize it actually wraps around and is connected to the front terrace.

I head back inside and walk through the doors leading to what I thought was the bathroom but is a massive walk-in closet. The closet is almost larger than the one I had back in New York. Almost.

I step through the closet into the massive bathroom. A two-person shower sits behind an island with double sinks. Off to the side are more glass windows leading to yet another terrace. This one completely separated from the other with a wooden lattice privacy screen covered in ivy. Tropical plants take up all the corners of the balcony and a giant bathtub sits in the open, facing toward the endless sea beyond.

Holy hell. I cannot wait to sit in that tub after a long day with a martini!

I decide to unpack and get to work. I have a few hours before dinnertime and I would like to dive into as much information as I can so I can start tomorrow off on the right foot.

I yawn as I rub my temples and finally look at the clock. It's just past eight at night and I haven't moved from my office in five hours.

I've been reviewing candidates and immersing myself in all the work the previous PR companies tried to do and come up with a brief overview of a plan.

I crack my back as I stand and head into the kitchen to look at the room service menu when my phone rings.

"Hello?"

"How was your first day? How is your boss? What's your office like? Tell me everything!" Tacoma shouts into the phone.

I laugh into the phone as I flip through the menu. "You won't even believe me."

"Did you already get fired or did you get promoted to CEO?"

"Neither."

"Well I guess that's a good thing on the not being fired."

I shake my head at her. "Yeah, T. A very good thing." I hear commotion in the background. "Are you working right now?"

"Define working." She yells at someone in the background. "I mean, I am sitting on a stool behind the bar at Sawyer's but I wouldn't call it working. More of telling the other bartender what to do. I worked a double yesterday and Ryder is out of town and I am horny and grumpy."

"Well, you definitely don't want to hear about my day then."

She says something loud to someone, her southern

accent coming out and I can't help but laugh. "Sorry, but my sister's stupid husband just showed up with his stupid friend and they are already being obnoxious."

"That's fine. Can you hold on a second? I just need to order some room service."

"Room service? Did you upgrade your apartment to a hotel?"

"Just you wait." I set my cell down and pick up the room phone and quickly order dinner. I glance around the room and find the minibar that really isn't mini and more a full-size bar with a wine refrigerator. I find some champagne and pop it open as soon as I get back on the phone with Tacoma.

"Are you ordering room service and drinking champagne? What the hell, girl?"

"Are you still sitting down?" I ask her.

"Yes?"

I laugh as her answer comes out as a question. "Well I am in a hotel. Because I was immediately given a client and the offices aren't in Paris."

"Continue," she commands.

"The office in Paris is amazing. I love it. But I only spent about an hour there because I had to pack all my shit back up, which thankfully I barely unpacked because that flat is smaller than my closet in New York—"

"Just tell me! I am dying from anticipation over here!"

"So I packed my suitcases and jumped on a plane for Saint Tropez."

"Saint Tropez? As in the French Riviera?"

"The one and only."

"Shit. How the hell did you get an account where you get to live in paradise?"

I take a sip of champagne and wander over to the terrace. The warm breeze calling to me. The glitter of stars reaching out to me in the night sky.

"No one wanted it."

"Who the hell works for that company that wouldn't want to go to Saint Tropez?"

I sigh as I settle into one of the couches on the terrace, my elbow propped on the back as I look out into the dark sea. "It's more like no one wanted to work for the client. He runs a multibillion-dollar real estate and investment firm and isn't the easiest man to work for."

"Not really an excuse in my opinion."

"Tacoma, the guy is a total asshole. He has this air about him like he thinks he is the best there is. That he knows more than everyone else. Hell, one of the assistants at my office in Paris warned me about him." I sip my champagne and think about my first encounter with Bastian Montford. "God, T, he has such an arrogance about him. He's cocky and rude. He talked down to me like I had no idea what I am doing. A total fucking prick."

She laughs out loud. "Well, I'm guessing you talked right back to him because I know how you are, Cam."

I grin into the phone. "You bet your sweet ass I did. He didn't like it very much."

"I bet he didn't. The cocky ones never do. So is he old and gross like Mr. Banks? Did he get all red-faced and sweaty?"

"I wish," I mumble into the phone.

"What do you mean?"

"You know those romance novels you read? The billionaire ones? He's like that."

"How would you even know? You don't even read them."

I snort. "Yeah, because I prefer to keep myself prepared for serial killers. But T, remember when we lived together all you did was talk about them. I have a pretty clear idea of what they look like from your overactive imagination. Seriously, Google Bastian Montford."

"My imagination is not that overactive. And there is no way he is. There is no man on earth that is as hot as those… oh my god…" She trails off.

"God T, he is so fucking sexy. Like I could barely take it. I had to keep squeezing my thighs together as we argued because all I could picture was him dragging me onto his yacht and taking me on the deck or pushing me up against the glass windows of his hotel and having his way with me. And I would pretty much do anything with that man." I groan into the phone. "I'm so fucked. And an idiot. I researched so much in those four hours I had before meeting him but never did I think to look at a picture of him. I should have prepared myself. I just hope he doesn't stay here too long and goes back to Paris. I can't deal with looking at him all day and dealing with his grumpy ass."

"Sorry, Cam. But I would not mind looking at that all day even if he is an asshole. Do you think he has a six-pack or an eight-pack underneath that shirt?"

"Don't you have a husband with an eight-pack? Stop drooling over my boss!"

"Oh honey, I am going to keep drooling over him. You will have to keep me up to date on all the sordid details of your relationship."

"Really, T? He's my boss. There will be nothing dirty happening between us."

She makes a noncommittal noise into the phone. "So where are you staying, and how long? And can your boss buy me a plane ticket to come see you?"

I laugh into the phone and tell her all about the hotel and my job and the intensity of what I have to do. She gets mad when I tell her there is no way he is buying her a plane ticket.

We laugh and joke around until my dinner shows up and the butler brings it out onto the terrace.

"I'll talk to you soon, T."

"Bye, Cameron. I miss you so much. Keep me posted on all the dirty things you do with your boss."

"You're ridiculous."

"You love me."

"I do."

I hang up the phone and sit down to eat. The flavors of the amazing food melting on my tongue.

Despite Bastian Montford being an asshole, I could get used to this, I tell myself as I settle into the outdoor sofa and sip on champagne, watching the night sky.

4

BASTIAN

I hang up the phone, walk over to the bar in my office and pour myself a drink. The last few months have been a constant headache since Matías got caught sticking his hand in business he shouldn't have been. I told him time and again to stay out of the underground. Step away from the darkness. But he was too eager, too curious and now he is paying for crimes he shouldn't be paying for.

I sip on my Dalmore scotch and step out of my office and across the dark hall to the terrace. My need to smell the sea vital after my last phone call. I barely make it past the floor-to-ceiling curtains when I hear Lucas say my name.

"Bastian."

I turn to face him, stepping back inside. "I thought you would have retired for the evening. It's been a long day."

"I wanted to check in on you after I heard that call you were on."

I sip my scotch, watching him over my glass. "Eavesdropping?"

"Looking out for your well-being, sir."

I pinch my brow. "Don't call me sir, Lucas. I need at least one person to treat me like a normal man."

He chuckles at that. "You are far from a normal man."

I look at him, training my eyes to not give away the pain. "And most days I don't mind that. But days like today," I sigh as I turn toward the open balcony doors. "Weeks and months like the last few, I wish things were different. I wish I was just a businessman running a business."

Lucas clears his throat. "As far as I am concerned, that's all you are."

I nod even though my eyes are trained on the endless sea in front of me.

"You gave her your brother's office."

"Yes," I respond nonchalantly.

"All the other PR companies you hired, you had work from the conference room."

I take another sip of my drink, letting the flavors of oak and vanilla slide across my tongue.

I hear Lucas take a few steps closer to me. "You have a different feeling about this one?"

I look over at him. "Like what?"

"That perhaps she might work out."

I sigh into my glass. "I'm not keeping my hopes up."

"Then why give her an office?" he questions me.

I take another sip of the amber liquid, swishing it around my mouth.

Lucas folds his arms over his chest. "I know you find her attractive."

I don't answer him because we both know it's true. Cameron Wilder is gorgeous, wild, enticing. And very dangerous.

"You could fuck everything up if you fuck her."

I stare out into the ocean, my voice stern. "You are out of line, Lucas."

"I'm just saying what needs to be said, sir. We need her. The missing piece to get—"

"I'm well aware."

"Sleeping with her will—"

I turn to him, my jaw tight. "I just said I am well aware, Lucas."

We stare at each other. Two strong-willed people facing each other down. I know he's right. He always is. Part of the reason I keep him around.

"I just want to make sure we are clear on everything."

"Crystal. You can go now." My voice is stern, rough.

"Sir, I—"

"Leave."

He nods and heads to the door.

"I have a meeting at eight in the morning tomorrow. Please be here by seven."

He nods once more before leaving.

I refill my scotch before I make it out to the terrace and take a seat in the dark, my eyes flickering to the stars.

I need to listen to Lucas. He is not just my bodyguard

but my right hand. My eye of reason. The one who will take a bullet for me. And he has.

I know he is right. I need to be careful around Cameron Wilder. She has the power to destroy everything.

But for some reason, I cannot get her out of my mind. When I first laid eyes on her I knew she was trouble. The way her sheath dress clung to her body, the skirt bordering on being almost too short for business. Her long, lean tan legs, striking in the heels she wore. Her platinum hair pulled high into a ponytail. I pretended I wasn't thinking about wrapping it around my wrist and controlling her head as she sucked on my cock. And then when she stepped into the SUV and took off her sunglasses, her striking blue eyes reminded me of home.

But that wasn't what made me realize how dangerous she was. It was her bite. Her energy. Her confidence.

No one has ever talked back to me the way she has. Interrupted me. Questioned me.

She walked a very thin line by being so reckless.

But I am on the other end, taking the bait.

I sip my scotch, willing my mind to stray from her. But it's impossible when I hear her laughter on the wind.

5

CAM

I turn up my music as I dance around the office barefoot. I've been here five days. Five grueling days of recruiting and interviewing while I still made broad plans of how we can tackle this project and get Montford Hotels on the right page.

Luckily, I've been able to concentrate since I haven't seen Bastian Montford since the first day. And ever since Tacoma put those thoughts in my head all I can think about is if he does have a six or eight-pack underneath those formfitting suits he wears.

I've talked to him on the phone twice. His voice enough to make me lightheaded. I am getting closer to nailing his accent down. I think. Somewhere between French, British, and Spanish. Although, I try not to think about his voice because it's just as sexy as his face. Especially when he gets angry, which I think I have made him more angry over the past week than pleased. But I am doing my damn job so he can suck it.

I interviewed all the people on his list and I found a few promising candidates. But I felt like I needed someone stronger. Someone that could learn from me and take over as head of PR for the Montford Hotel Group when my assignment is over.

So I searched high and low. Found some potential people and flew them out for interviews. I narrowed down the ones I liked then told Bastian to interview them. He was pissed. Said he didn't have time in his busy schedule and that I was supposed to stick to the list he gave me. I told him that we needed someone better. He growled at me, literally growled at me then hung up. Parker called me back a few minutes later with a few times Bastian was available. And as I knew it would turn out, he thought my candidates were a better fit for the company.

I've also been calling him Bastian in my head all week. The way his name rolls off my tongue is like sex. It feels too stuffy calling him Mr. Montford in my head.

I shuffle some papers around on my desk and go to grab a file from the cabinet along the wall when "9 to 5" comes on.

I pump my arms toward my legs as I dance around the office singing along, "working nine-to-five, what a way to make a living…"

I twirl around and stumble over my feet when I see Bastian standing in the doorway. The door I had locked. I was smart enough to find the switch that blacked out the glass so no one could see me dancing around.

He steps into the office, shutting the door behind

him, a look of derision on his face. I ignore him and skip around the desk, still humming along to Dolly.

"Is this what I am paying you for? Dancing and singing when you should be working?"

I stop dancing and look him in the eye. "You aren't paying me. My company is."

"But I am paying your company for your services."

I put my hands on my hips. "And my company pays me enough to let me dance and sing when I want to."

He steps toward my desk and walks up to me. I forgot how tall he was and since I am not wearing shoes, he towers over me. He leans into me, his body too close to mine as he reaches behind me. My breathing picks up at his proximity. Our chests are almost touching and his intoxicating scent of earthiness and sea is making me dizzy.

The sounds of Dolly are cut out abruptly and I realize he leaned over to shut my music off. He steps back as quickly as he stepped into my space.

"Do you remember why I hired you?" he asks me, the grit in his voice even better in person than on the phone.

I fold my arms over my chest and snort. "You did not hire me. You hired my company. And from what I recall you were not happy I was yet another woman that came in to save your ass."

His lip curls at my words and I can't help but smirk. I find too much entertainment in pissing this man off.

"You are not saving my ass—"

I hold up a finger, cutting him off. "Mmm. I kind of am."

He brushes my hand away and steps into my space.

49

"I do not appreciate being cut off." I go to speak, but he takes another step toward me. "You think you can come in here and take over. Run this company how you best see fit but remember you still work for me. I am your client and what I say goes. Any decision you make needs to be approved by me. I don't care if you think it's what's best for the company. It gets run by me."

"I did run things by you. Yes, I did go outside to find talent, but I still ran it by you, Mr. Montford."

He runs his hand through his gelled-back hair, disheveling it in the process. He walks over to the window and looks out over the sea, sighing. "I expect a report on my desk on Monday morning with your weekly strategy to get this company back into a positive light."

"I don't have a team yet and I would prefer if I had a team to review it with and bounce ideas off of."

He turns toward me, his hands sliding into his pockets. "Then I suggest you see if they can start tomorrow."

I open my mouth but can't find the words.

He walks to the door. "We have an open-door policy here, Ms. Wilder. I suggest you don't lock the door unless you are in an important meeting."

I glare at him.

"And one more thing. No country music."

I laugh. "Are you telling me what I can and cannot listen to?"

He nods. "I despise country."

Well, I despise you.

"Excuse me, Dolly isn't just country. She is a queen and should be respected like the royalty she is."

He shakes his head at me as he opens the door. "Monday, Ms. Wilder."

I collapse on the outdoor terrace with a martini in hand. It's been a long weekend. I think I've slept four hours since Friday. It's nearly midnight on Sunday.

Parker came into my office on Friday afternoon asking how he could help after Bastian went on a tirade in his office. He laughed when he said he's never seen Bastian get so worked up over someone before. And told me that maybe I should keep stepping on his toes because he finds it entertaining. When I said it will end up with me being fired, Parker just shook his head saying that Bastian couldn't fire me. It's too close to his deadline and I've done more work in the last week than anyone else and that he couldn't afford to lose me.

I did go to Bastian, despite not wanting to cave to his demands, to ask for sizable signing bonuses for the PR team. He approved and it helped me get the three people I hired in the office the next day.

We spent the weekend tirelessly working out a strategy that would make the biggest impact on Montford Hotels. And it's a solid plan. One that Bastian cannot say no to. Even Parker read it over and said Bastian would approve.

I learned that Parker has worked for Bastian for the last ten years. He's spent more time with him than he did with his ex-wife. I felt bad when I asked about her and learned he got a divorce because he spent too much time with Bastian. But he said it was for the best. He still gets to see his daughters every weekend when he isn't traveling with Bastian.

I look up into the sky as I sip on my martini. It's nice to see stars again. I only imagined the stars when I was in New York. The city lights too bright to see anything besides smog. I miss New York. I miss the sights and sounds. The life you could hear beating through the city at all hours of the day. But I know I am making the right move for my career.

My whole life I've battled with myself. I've always been the pretty face in the family not the brains. When I was younger, I didn't care so much but then my dad spent so much time focusing on my sister as she got her law degree I felt left out, pushed aside. My mom didn't care what I did, she was always supportive of any path I took. But as I grew older, I realized she was more than happy with me being a housewife. She really meant a trophy wife. For the last ten years, since I was eighteen, she has been trying to match me up with sons and cousins of her socialite friends.

I don't want to be the pretty face anymore. I want to be the one my parents talk about in praise for my personal successes. That's why this job is so important to me. I need to prove not just to my parents but to myself that I am worthy of success.

Now I need to prove it to Bastian too.

"Cheers!"

I knock my martini glass against those of the PR team I hired and Parker's. It was a long grueling weekend for all of us and we all felt the need to celebrate. Since Bastian approved the strategy we proposed, we all decided to go out for a drink.

Well, he approved almost all of it except for the gala I threw in. He said no galas. But I will find my way to get the gala approved. He needs to be more present. The public needs to see the responsible brother. The one who will revive the appeal of Montford Hotels. I just need time to get under his skin. Although, I don't know if that is a good idea with Bastian Montford.

We are sitting in a swanky bar in downtown Saint Tropez. The revelry in the city picking up as the sun sets along the harbor. As the night goes on the lights in the bar dim and the bass of dance music starts to hit my ears.

"Is there a club around here?" I ask Parker.

He points upstairs. "It can get pretty wild up there. But it's a Monday. We all work tomorrow."

I smirk at him and down the rest of my martini. "Wild is my middle name."

Andrew, one of the guys I hired for the team, laughs out loud. "I would never have guessed."

"What?" I ask, bringing my hand to my chest in an overexaggerated flourish at his sarcasm.

"Don't get me wrong, you are one hell of a hard worker. But even in the last three days of working with you and the way you seem to go against everything that Mr. Montford would approve, I could only imagine you are a bit more free-spirited."

I look around the table at the others I hired, Celine

smiles over her wine glass. She is the one I think could be head of PR for Montford Hotels. Marie blushes as she nods at me.

"Well then, let's move this party upstairs."

Andrew lets out a woot while Celine and Marie laugh. Andrew leads the way to the back of the bar, where the staircase leads up to the club. We climb the steps and enter through a doorway where the beat of the music gets louder.

"I'll grab a round of drinks," Celine says, and Marie follows her to the bar.

"I'll grab the table," Andrew says.

I go to follow Andrew, but Parker's hand lands on my arm. "You sure this is a good idea? There is a lot of work that needs to be done. And even though you may have the work ethic to work through a hangover, I don't know about them."

I shrug him off. "Parker, we are here for a few dances. Not to get shit-faced. Besides, these guys signed up for this last minute. Quit their current jobs to come work for an asshole who probably knows nothing about work-life balance. Let them blow off some steam. They worked far too many hours in the last three days."

His gaze wanders over to a roped-off VIP area before looking back at me. "I'm just letting you know I don't think it's a good idea."

"If you don't like it, you can leave. You don't need to stick around. It's early. I'll make sure the kiddos get home before eleven." I tap his cheek with my palm.

His face grimaces at my sarcastic comment.

"If you think you need to babysit me you don't." I

study his face. "Oh my god, Bastian does have you babysitting me."

Parker's face fills with shock. "No, he doesn't. He just uh—"

I shake my head at him. "If the man doesn't trust me, then why doesn't he just fire me?"

"It's not that at all," Parker answers quickly. His eyes flick back over to the VIP section. I go to follow his line of sight but he starts talking again. "Just be responsible. Bastian won't be happy if you are all hungover tomorrow. I need to go though, I have an early morning meeting with him."

I watch Parker head out then look back over at the roped-off area. I let it go and turn to head toward the table Andrew found.

We spend the next few hours dancing and enjoying ourselves. It's the first night I've let myself be the girl I was in New York. Carefree, wild. I let the energy of the night release all the stress that is resting on my shoulders.

When I notice Celine and Marie yawning, I give them money for a cab to get back to the flat Bastian rented for them. It didn't go past me that he put the team in a flat and not the hotel.

Thirty minutes after they leave, Andrew calls it a night. He asks me if I want a cab, but I tell him I am going to finish my drink and head out.

I let myself get caught up in the music, my ponytail swinging freely when I feel a pair of hands grab my waist. I turn around and see the goofy grin on the young man's face. He's younger than me. He asks me to dance.

So I do. I let myself be Cameron Wilder for a night. Wild and free.

I let him kiss me.

I let his hands roam my body.

And I let him take me home for the night.

I could use the release.

6

BASTIAN

I hate this club as much as I hate this town. But for some reason Kilian always wants to meet here. It's because he will always find a willing piece of ass to take home and have his way with.

It's also loud here. And although it's one of the busiest nightclubs in Saint Tropez, the booths in the VIP section are private. The noise of the club drowning out the conversations that take place. Conversations that the wrong ears should never hear.

I sip on my second glass of scotch, waiting for the man who is always notoriously late. He told me to meet him at eight. I showed up thirty minutes later, knowing I probably still beat him here. And I did.

I hate the man as much as I love him. Kilian Bancroft was born a businessman. Cruel, charming, dangerous. I guess we were cut from the same cloth but whereas my family ran a clean business, his family has always been deeply seated in the darker side of things. But it's made them enough money that they could buy me out more than twice. And I am worth billions.

A glimpse of platinum hair catches my attention. My eyes focus in on her. Just my luck that I would see her here. She is talking to Parker and from the looks of the conversation, she is arguing with him. I'm not surprised, she argues with everyone. He stomps off and she walks over to a table with one of the guys from the PR team.

I suck in a breath as I watch her. She has on a tight white dress that makes her tan look even darker. I wonder if she has been making use of the outdoor terrace of the room I gave her. Her ass looks amazing in the dress and it's not just that. Every curve of her body is accentuated in it. I like how the top comes all the way up to her neck. Giving her a bit more class than the dress the other patrons of this bar have on.

I'm mesmerized by her as she dances with the others on her team. No doubt celebrating that I approved her proposal. She whips her long ponytail back and forth as she dances with the girls.

I don't even see Killian approach; my mind caught up in the view of Cameron.

"You finally looking to take someone home?"

I blink and then look up at Kilian. "No."

"Well, something caught your eye."

"It was no one."

He snorts. "Right." He takes a seat, unbuttoning the jacket of his custom-made Italian suit. He crosses his leg and runs his hand through his blond hair. "It's not like you would act on it anyway. Tell me, when was the last time you got laid, brother?"

"I don't see how that is your concern."

"Oh come on, we always tell each other everything."

I sip my Dalmore. "It's been years since we told each other everything."

He laughs at me as a waitress comes over to take his drink order, he touches her as she leaves and she gives him a sultry smile.

"If you keep fucking around like that, it's going to get you into trouble."

He grins at me. "More trouble than I already get myself in?"

He has a point.

"If I remember correctly, you weren't much different from me."

"That was before I was married."

The waitress comes back with his drink, setting it on the table, her cleavage on full display for him, but he ignores her this time.

"And now you are divorced."

I run my hand through my hair. "Kilian, just because I don't tell you I am getting laid, doesn't mean I am not getting laid. But you need to watch yourself, fucking a different girl every night. Nothing good is going to come from that."

"I didn't come here to talk about my sex life with you."

"You brought it up."

He sips on the whiskey he ordered, then rests the glass on his knee. "Fair enough."

"Did you find anything out?" I ask him, dropping my voice low as I change the subject.

"I dug as deep as I could without raising any red flags. I couldn't find shit," he mutters before taking a large sip of his drink.

"Merda."

"I called Tomas."

My eyes snap up to Kilian. "I told you not to use him. I don't want to owe him any favors. Not after last time."

Kilian's green eyes darken. "I owe him the favor. Not you."

"He will know this is about me."

He shrugs. "Sure, but I'm the one who called it in."

"I know how that man's circle runs. He will want a favor from both of us."

"I'm taking care of it, Bastian." His voice grows quieter, deeper. "You need him. Before you get caught up in something worse."

"Fucking Matías," I groan into my palms as I scrub them over my face.

"Has Interpol questioned you again?" he asks me, a look of concern on his face.

I shake my head. "No. But I know they are following me, watching my every move."

"Then don't do anything stupid."

I throw my head back in laughter at that. "Thanks for the advice, Kil."

He grins at me. "Anytime."

We talk shit for another hour. Reminiscing on the days when our lives weren't as dark as they are now. When we were two kids at Oxford just wanting to get laid. Or traveling the world once we graduated before we took our rightful chairs in each of our father's companies.

I call it a night when I glance at my Audemars Piguet watch and see it's after ten. Kilian nods at me and gazes toward the crowd of young men and women dancing the night away.

"Don't get in too much trouble tonight," I tell him.

He pats me on the shoulder. "I'd be more worried about the woman who gets this tonight," he says as he gestures at his body. "Poor girl will be fantasizing about me for years."

I shake my head at him. "Keep telling yourself that."

He heads over to the bar as I make my way over to the exit. Not before I notice Cameron dancing very close to a young man, someone too young for her and from the looks of him probably too stupid. She passes in front of me, not even seeing me as the two of them leave the club together hand in hand.

I clench my fist as they pass.

7

CAM

I slam the phone down on the receiver. Starting the morning with Bastian's voice in my head is not the way I want to start the day.

Today has been a pain in my ass and it's only nine in the morning. I don't need him making it worse.

It all started when I woke up at ten after seven this morning in some stranger's hotel room. I never would have spent the night. I never let myself do that. But with the number of hours I put in over the weekend I was exhausted and after a horrible round of sex where I didn't even get off, I passed out.

To make matters worse, my phone died. Which is why my alarm didn't go off. I scrambled around the stranger's room and found a charger. Luckily with a five-minute charge, it was able to power back on. I rushed out of the room before he woke up and was able to snag a cab immediately.

I had fifteen emails from Bastian. Fifteen! Some came

from late last night. Others from five in the morning. I groan as I read through them. Some asking more details on the proposal he approved of. Others on a few articles from the media I needed to control the story on.

Twenty minutes later I was rushing through the lobby doors. I saw Lucas on the phone and nearly collided with a hotel guest as I peered around the corner to see if Bastian was anywhere in sight. I didn't want to have to deal with him after a bad one-night stand.

Fortunately, he was nowhere to be seen and I made it back to my hotel room ten minutes before I needed to be in the office. I stripped my clothes off as I ran through my living room, took the fastest shower I have ever taken in my life, and somehow made it into the office at eight oh two.

I spent the first forty-five minutes answering emails, then Bastian called. He told me I needed to be more available. That I needed to respond to his emails when he sent them.

I, of course, gave him my opinion, letting him know in the kindest voice I could manage that I would not be answering emails at midnight if I was asleep. He then told me spending nights in the club and going home with strange men didn't count as an excuse for not answering emails.

I then gave him a nice long string of curse words before I hung up the phone.

I take a few deep breaths and smooth the hair back on my ponytail when I look up and see Parker walking into my office.

"You're a snitch," I bark as he takes a seat across from my desk and turns on his tablet.

"What are you talking about?"

"Mr. Montford made it very clear to me that he knew we were out last night."

Parker's face breaks into a small smile. "Was that who you were on the phone with then?"

I ignore his question. "I told you not to say anything."

"I didn't, Cam. I mean that. I met him at six thirty this morning for an early briefing before we met a client. He was already in a crabby mood. So I think he might just be taking it out on you."

"Well then how did he know we went out last night?"

Parker shrugs. "Maybe he was there."

I snort. "At a club? Please, Bastian is wound tighter than a clock. There is no way he was at the club."

Parker taps his stylus against his lips. "He has been known to go there to meet clients. Or friends."

"Friends? I highly doubt that man has any friends. But—" I think back to how Parker kept looking toward the VIP section last night. "Wait a second, you knew he was there."

He sighs and leans forward. "I—he might have told me he had a meeting there last night. But I don't know if he was there. The person he was meeting isn't always reliable."

Well, this all makes sense. He probably saw me. And fuck if he knew I left with someone he definitely saw me making out with said someone before that happened.

"I'm not hungover."

"You don't seem like you are."

"Then why is he so pissed at me."

Parker opens his mouth to speak but shuts it. I wait for him to say something but we are interrupted by Celine.

"Hi Cameron. We are all set up in the conference room and are ready to go over a list of media outlets to reach out to."

"Perfect. I will be there in just a minute." I turn back to Parker. "Now, did you come here for a reason or to spy on me some more?"

He clears his throat and stands. "No. Mr. Montford just wanted me to see if you needed assistance with anything while he handled some phone calls."

"I think we are all good," I tell him as I escort him out of my office.

8

BASTIAN

I grab a cup of coffee as I make my way to the Montford Hotel offices. I had no intention of stopping by here today but after seeing Cameron leaving with a man from the club two days ago, I cannot get the sight out of my head.

It shouldn't bother me. I have strict rules about interoffice relationships. And she is the last person I need to be involved with. Regardless if she works for me.

I get off the elevator and nod to the team working. I see the three people she hired deep in conversation with the head of marketing.

When I make my way to her office, I hear two people laughing. I open the door that I told her not to shut and find Kilian leaning on the edge of the desk. The smile on Cameron's face the biggest I've ever seen.

I clear my throat as I walk farther into the office.

Kilian turns to look at me. "I like your new assistant."

I shoot a glance at Cameron who glares at Kilian when he says assistant.

"She's not my assistant. She is the consultant from the PR company I hired to clean up Matías' mess."

Kilian gives her a look, a look I know too well when he wants to make a move. "Then she's free game—"

"She's got a job to do."

"Well enough. I'll leave." He stands up from the desk and walks over to me. "I just came by to drop off the file you asked for. Tomas works fast."

I grab it from him and walk him to the door. "Keep your slimy paws away from her."

He grins at me. "You getting on that? I thought you said no interoffice relationships."

I pinch my brow. "I'm not getting on her or anyone. I just don't want a bigger mess than what she's dealing with. And you would cause a mess."

He shrugs. "At least you know I'm good at something."

I push him out the door and slam it shut.

"I thought you said to keep the door open."

I growl as I turn to face her. "What was that?"

"He came in here looking for you. I told him you weren't here."

"Stay away from him."

She walks toward me. "You know I can stand up for myself."

I look at her quizzically. My mind wandering to the man she left the club with the other night.

"He's not my type if that's what you're thinking."

I push off the door and head to her desk, slinking into her chair, my hands steepled in front of me.

"And what is your type, Ms. Wilder?"

"None of your concern."

I don't miss the blush that barely hits her cheeks or the way she shifts her thighs together.

You are walking a very dangerous line, Bastian.

"What are you doing here, Mr. Montford? Checking up on me? I think your assistant already has the job down pretty well."

I smirk at her. She caught on quickly that I am keeping tabs on her. It's really just my need to have control over this shitshow of a situation.

"I'm assuming everything is coming together as planned."

She nods. "Yes, in the last ten days I have been here we are making great progress."

I don't miss the sass in her voice.

"Did you take care of those press releases I asked about?"

She folds her arms across her chest, giving me a tease of her cleavage that's peeking up from her blouse. "Did you really come here to ask me questions that I could have easily answered in an email or over the phone?"

"No," I answer as I sit up straighter in her chair. "You need to come to London with me."

"Excuse me?"

"The board of directors for Montford Holdings wants you at a dinner tonight. They want to hear what your strategy is to ensure we are paying you for the right reason."

"And can't you tell them my strategy? You approved it. You know it as well as I do."

"I could. But they asked for you."

She throws her hands up in the air. "I can't just drop everything and go to London. I have work to do here."

"It's only for the night."

"And that is twenty-four hours I won't get back."

I stand abruptly and step into her space. "That's why you have a team."

She glares at me. Her aqua-blue eyes turning darker. "Mr. Montford, you can't—"

"I'm your boss," I cut in. "We leave in four hours. I suggest you inform your team and find something nice to wear."

I know she is ready to explode on me much like she did at the beginning of the week or the first time I met her. But I don't let her. I grab the file from Kilian off the desk and walk out of her office.

When I get up to my office, I call the restaurant in London to add one more to the reservation.

The board never asked for her to be there but for some reason I do not want to let her out of my sight. Especially knowing Kilian is still in town.

9

CAM

I storm into my hotel room. I have approximately thirty minutes to pack for this impromptu trip to London. I lost track of time in the office as I finished up a few story angles I want to pitch to the media.

I run into my closet and look through the formal dresses. I knew I would probably need some so I brought a few with me. The others are still hanging on my shower rod in the bathroom at the shoebox apartment in Paris.

I grab a floor-length burgundy dress and throw it onto the bed next to my carry-on. I grab my skincare and makeup essentials and dump them into the bag, along with some jewelry, shoes, and pajamas.

I look at the clock just as my phone rings and see I still have fifteen minutes. Damn, that is the fastest I have ever packed.

I pick up my phone, half expecting it to be Mr. Montford, telling me I need to meet him now. But I see my sister's name pop up on my screen instead.

"Hey, sis!" I say way too overenthusiastically into the phone.

"Hi Cameron. How are you? How's Paris?" Natalie asks me.

"Great," I say.

Natalie sighs. It didn't take as long as I thought it would. "Cam, that was your favorite city to visit as a kid. I know you must really be enjoying yourself there."

I pick at the comforter on the bed. "Well the apartment the company gave me is small—"

"We both know you have the means to afford a better place. Companies never spend money on temporary living arrangements. If you don't have money, you can always call Dad—"

I cut her off. "I know I can call Dad. And I know he would give me what I want. You do remember I lived on the upper west side of Manhattan. Did you really think I could afford that place on my assistant salary?"

She sighs into the phone and I know it's the beginning of many. The thing about my sister is that she is the picture-perfect specimen of what my family has envisioned both of our lives to be. She is an accomplished corporate lawyer, she made partner last year, she is married to the perfect Upper East Side man, and they have two doting children.

She is everything that my parents wanted their children to be. My mother would have been happy with just the husband and the two point five kids for me. She never thought I was smart enough to succeed in the business world. She thought my efforts would be best spent on finding a man to take care of.

But I had other plans. I wanted to prove to my dad that I could be as successful as Natalie. She's six years older than me. She was accepted into the top three law schools while I was goofing off in high school. I saw the difference in the way my parents treated her from how they treated me. And I wanted that. I wanted to prove to them I could be just as successful and smart.

"Are you even listening to what I am saying?" she asks me.

"Hmm?" I ask back as I get off my bed and walk into my living room.

"I said I can have my friend look for some apartments for you in Paris, if you have been too busy. I am sure it's hard and stressful starting a new position in a new city."

I still have ten minutes until I need to head downstairs. I glance over at the bar and say screw it. I can drink a martini fast. I let her drone on about apartments and the best places to live in Paris, as if I don't already know while I quickly mix up a drink. I slide open the door to my terrace and take in a deep gulp of the salt air and watch the mega yachts float by in the water.

I sip my martini. "You can stop, Natalie. I know where to live in Paris. And I actually am in a good spot. Just tiny. I'll look when I am back there."

"Back there? Have you already frolicked off on some vacation instead of committing to your job?"

I roll my eyes and sit on the couch, resting my elbows on the edge of the balcony. "No, I am not gallivanting around. Why do all of you just assume I am fucking up and making bad decisions? I wouldn't have gotten this job if I am as terrible as you all think I am. Hell, Mom is probably banking on the fact that I will screw this job up just so she can say I told you so."

Natalie sighs into the phone. "I am sorry for jumping to conclusions. And you know Mom doesn't want you to fail, she wants you to succeed."

"She wants me to find a husband and settle down and stop dreaming about being successful."

"That's not true, Cam."

I down half my martini. "Yes, it is."

"So where are you if not in Paris?"

"The client that I am working for has their main offices in Saint Tropez."

"Oh wow. That place looks so beautiful in pictures."

"It is beautiful, Nat. In fact, I am staying at one of the hotels the company owns and it's luxurious. Like nothing we have ever stayed in traveling with Mom and Dad."

"You'll have to send me pictures," she says, less mom-like and more sisterlike. I like it when she acts like my sister. "What hotel?"

"Montford Hotel."

"Wow. I've looked at those when we have traveled to Europe, just never had the opportunity to stay at one. Is that your client?"

"Yeah. It's a mess. I don't want to get into the details but you can look it all up on the internet. Bastian Mont-ford is my client, CEO of Montford Holdings. His brother ran the hotels. But his brother is—"

"In jail," she finishes my sentence.

"Did you already look it up?"

"I am in front of my computer. So how is it going? From what I am reading, it looks bad."

"It's a mess. I hired a team since Bastian fired the one that worked here and I have been putting them on cleanup duty while I try to build a new narrative for the hotel."

"Smart. How is your boss?"

"Why do you ask?"

"Well, Sean has worked with him in the past. I heard he isn't the friendliest."

I snort. "I don't think he even knows the meaning of the word friendly, Natalie. He is pompous and arrogant. A tyrant. I mean I guess it's how he built his company the way he did."

"Make sure he doesn't hear you call him a tyrant."

"It wouldn't matter. He knows how I feel about him."

And the motherly sighs are back. "You have to watch your attitude, Cameron. It will bite you in the butt one day."

I don't think my sister has ever sworn a day in her life. "I'll be sure to keep it in check."

"Well that attitude is probably why you got sent off to Paris. No one at the New York office wanted to deal with you."

"Excuse me!"

"Oh Cameron, don't act like you didn't know."

I get up and start pacing the deck. "Natalie, they needed me in that office. I did everything. They just couldn't pay me what I wanted."

"And you had a poor attitude and were overconfident. It came off arrogant."

75

"How do you even know all this?"

She sighs again. "You know I am friends with some of the wives of the executives there."

"Are you fucking kidding me? They got rid of me because they didn't want to deal with my attitude? And the fact I know a lot of shit doesn't mean I am arrogant!"

"I am just letting you know."

I am fuming. I wish I hadn't picked up this call because finding all this out makes me think they really did send me here so I could fail and they could find a way to fire me.

"Just be careful, Cam. I wouldn't want you to lose your job. I know you've worked hard to prove yourself to Mom and Dad. But maybe you should just throw in the towel and come home. Jonathan Williams broke up with his girlfriend. That would be a good match for you."

I wrap my ponytail around my wrist, pulling hard on my hair as to not scream. I am sick of everyone thinking I am worthless. And now it seems Natalie is on the same boat as my parents. "I am not fucking up this job or quitting just so I can come home with my tail between my legs and become a damn socialite."

"Cam, you know it's probably for the best."

I go to scream when I see Bastian standing in the doorway of the terrace, his face stern and his hand tapping that watch he wears that costs more than I care to know.

I pick up the rest of my martini and slam it back, nearly choking on the vodka as it goes down. "I need to go. I'm late for a meeting."

"See these are things you need to—"

I don't even let her finish. I hate when she goes into mom mode. I wish she could be in sister mode all the time. Although, it's something I've rarely ever seen.

I stomp over to where Bastian is standing, ready to grab my bags and go but he isn't moving.

"Drinking in the middle of the day?"

I roll my eyes at him and mutter. "Like you haven't."

He doesn't let me pass. He just stares down at me, his gray eyes studying me.

"Let's go, we're late," I say to him, more defeated than I wish to sound.

I watch his hand go to reach for my arm but he drops it before he touches me. I look up at him again and a look of concern flits across his face. "Are you okay?"

"Peachy," I exhale.

He nods, knowing he won't get much more out of me. He turns into the living room and heads for the door. "Lucas already stopped by and picked up your luggage."

"Okay."

"Our flight leaves in an hour. I'll brief you on everything the board would like to know on the way to the airport so you can prepare yourself on the flight."

I nod as we step out of my room and walk to the bank of elevators. We make our way down to the lobby in an awkward silence. When we get to the SUV, I am surprised that Parker isn't inside. "No Parker?" I ask Bastian as he enters the car.

"No. Parker is working on another project for me. No need for him to go to a stuffy dinner with a bunch of old men that like to talk about their money."

I raise a brow as I look over at him. "Then why have me go?"

I nearly have a heart attack when the corner of his mouth curls up into a smile. I guess you could call it a smile, I am not sure he knows what one is. "They asked for you. And I need someone to entertain them while I get them to agree with what I ask of them. Your attitude is just what I need."

I am not entirely sure what he meant by my attitude earlier. And I am still not sure as I pace the hotel room. We are staying at another Montford but this time I am just in a junior suite, not some crazy extravagant executive suite. This one is more charming and warm. Antique furniture and gold-framed mirrors. Whereas Saint Tropez is black and white, this hotel is soft taupes, enchanting burgundies, and warm bronze.

Bastian said he would be here to pick me up at seven sharp. I glance at the clock and notice it's six fifty-eight. I check my lipstick and then adjust my hair, opting for loose waves instead of my typical ponytail.

I jump when I hear the knock at the door, even though I was expecting it. I smooth my hands over my hips and grab my clutch. I open the door and bite my lip when I see Bastian. He's always in a custom-made suit but he usually has a few buttons open on the top of his shirt. A bit more wild and free, a bit more like he just stepped off a yacht.

But the man in front of me is wearing a navy blue

three-piece suit and never have I seen someone wear a suit as well as him. It sculpts his arms, just enough to show he has muscles. A gray tie is tucked into the vest that makes his eyes look even more silver. His pants are fitted and dear lord, I swear I can see a bulge. His wingtips, mahogany and polished to a shine.

When I look up at him, I realize he doesn't have that impatient scowl on his face he usually does around me. Instead, he is taking me in. My burgundy floor-length dress that hugs me in all the right places. My cleavage present but modest. The slit of the dress showing off just enough leg to tease but not come off as slutty.

His eyes travel over my hips and up to my chest, where I added a hint of shimmery oil to my collarbone next to the thin straps of the dress.

He clears his throat. "You look gorgeous."

"It seems I can clean up nicely," I joke.

"Cameron, you always look presentable."

That awkwardness comes back in the room and I grab my wrap and shut the door behind me. "So where are we eating?"

"Just at a restaurant across the street. It's why I stayed here rather than at my flat."

I look at him as we wait for the elevator. "You have a home here too?"

He nods as the doors to the elevator open. I step inside and nearly jump when he places his hand at the small of my back. I bite hard on my lip to keep from having any verbal reaction.

He removes his hand as quickly as it was there, as if he remembers I work for him and this is strictly platonic.

79

"I have a penthouse over in Knightsbridge. It's stuffy and uninviting so I never really stay there."

I turn to face him. "You don't seem like a man who would keep a place for no reason. Especially one you don't like. I mean, you did make millions from real estate development."

His brow pinches forward and a look of pain crosses his face. He studies me, his eyes fierce as they bore into mine. I think he is about to say something but the doors to the elevator open.

He gestures for me to exit first. We walk across the lobby of the hotel and through the spinning glass doors. He directs me to the left.

"Just down the street? And we are walking?"

He laughs. Well something that sounds similar to a laugh. "It's not far. And we have to cross through a park. I find the walk enjoyable."

"I'm surprised you find anything enjoyable," I say under my breath.

"There are plenty of things I find enjoyable, Ms. Wilder," he mumbles, a darkness about his voice.

"Is this a walk you take often?" I say, going back to the original subject.

He nods. "If I am here for a night and staying at the hotel, yes."

This man baffles me. He doesn't seem like someone who would walk or enjoy nature. He is always working, always has a scowl. Yet as I look up at him, his face is pleasant. His jawline softer in the light of dusk.

He turns and looks at me. "I should have told you since you have heels on."

"I've walked up and down Eighth Avenue so many times in heels, I could probably run a marathon in them."

We turn onto a path that cuts across the park. "Not exactly Central Park," he says as he gestures to the small park. "But Hyde Park is much nicer. I can see it from my flat in Knightsbridge."

"Do you walk there often when you stay there?"

"Yes, but I am not there frequently."

I nod and know at this point not to ask why.

"So Ms. Wilder, for someone who comes from money, lives on the Upper West Side of Manhattan, and doesn't need to work a day in her life, why are you here?"

I stop and look at Bastian. I never told him any of this.

"I do background screenings on all my employees."

"I'm not your employee," I bite as I cross my arms across my chest. His eyes drop to my chest and I drop my arms.

"Close enough. I looked into every publicist that I hired. Don't see yourself as special."

"I don't," I snap as I turn and start walking down the path again.

"I'm sorry. I shouldn't have said it that way."

"Did you just apologize to me?" I ask him as we once again stop along the pathway.

He lifts a brow at me.

"You don't seem like the type to apologize, Mr. Montford."

He smiles at me and I swear my heart skips a beat. "I might surprise you sometimes, Ms. Wilder."

We start walking again for a few minutes in comfortable silence before he asks me another question. "So why is it that you work?" He pauses and holds up his hands. "I'm just curious is all."

I take a minute to answer him because I hate talking about the life my family wishes I lived. "If it was up to my mother I wouldn't."

"I take it you don't care much for what your mother says."

I laugh. "If I did, I wouldn't be here right now. I would be married to a businessman, going to afternoon tea, and having my life strewn across page six. The perfect socialite and complacent wife."

"I don't think being a trophy wife fits you. Besides, your husband would have trouble taming that attitude of yours."

I snort. "It's my best asset."

Bastian makes a noise between a sigh and a cough. "So why not that life?"

"Because I don't want that lifestyle. The designer gowns, the parties, the expectations. I want to be me. I want to be the girl sneaking into a club when she's underage. Not given everything because she grew up with the richest people in Boston. I want to find my own path."

"One that includes screaming Dolly Parton songs?"

"Did you just make a joke, Mr. Montford?" I chuckle as he shrugs with the smallest smirk on his face. "And are you ever gonna let me live that down? And I was singing not screaming."

"My ears still have residual bleeding from that."

I push him lightly with my shoulder and ignore the

spark. Ignore the feeling of this moment. This normal conversation. Where Bastian seems more human than ever. A version of Bastian I could easily get used to. "I've spent my life battling for my own choices. I work hard even though I know I could have easily gotten an executive job with the snap of my fingers. I am sick of the world being handed to me. I want to know what it's really like for people. Not this rose-colored glass surrounding me."

"Out of the gilded cage?"

"That's exactly how my mother makes me feel. How did you know?"

"I know the life you speak of. I know many who would rather have taken your path."

I nod. I want to know more. I can see the look in his eyes as if he is remembering something or someone but I don't want to push him. So instead I just open up a bit more. "My best friend has everything I could ever want. She grew up in a small town. Not that I would ever want to live in a small town but she has her family even through all their ups and downs. They don't set expectations. They don't judge her for the decisions she has made. She married a man she never thought she could have. She sings in damn blues bars in New Orleans. Her life is so freeing. And I want that. I envy that. But every time I try to prove myself, I always find my mother or my sister judging me. They want to know when I will settle down. And I can't. I just can't do it."

We make it through the park and Bastian's hand lands on the small of my back as he directs me to the restaurant just across the street.

He takes a deep breath before we walk inside. "Ms. Wilder, you don't need to do what they say."

I see the sincerity in his face and I have the urge to trace my finger along his jaw. But I don't.

He steps away from me and glances into the windows of the restaurant. A candlelit glow lighting them up.

He clears his throat before looking back at me, the mask back on his face. "They will probably drill you with questions on how you will fix the image of the company. They invested a lot of money into the hotels and they do not want to see billions go to waste, no matter that costs have already been recouped. I will handle anything that comes to the business. You can just," he hesitates as he looks back into the restaurant. "You can charm them."

"Charm them?" I scoff.

"Yes."

I squint my eyes at him. "Are you using me as a distraction Mr. Montford?"

When he looks at me, I almost see a flicker of remorse on his face and I know my answer is spot on. He needs me here for some reason other than what he is leading on.

"Call me Bastian tonight."

My jaw literally hits the floor. But I recover quickly, clearing my throat and blinking a few times. "Fine," I manage to squeak out.

He steps closer to me, a little too close if you ask me, if any eyes are on us. "My father is in there. He's... he isn't very pleasant. He's Mr. Montford tonight."

I nod and let a smirk rise on my face. "Are you going to call me Cameron then?"

"If you wish." With that, he steps away from me and toward the door of the restaurant.

If you wish?

What does that mean? And why did he have to say it in that tone?

He opens the door for me and I miss his hand against the small of my back like in the hotel and on our walk. But I don't miss the sudden change in his mood. I can feel it in the air.

The tension, the anger, the fear.

He speaks to the hostess as I take in the overdecorated and gaudy restaurant. Fixtures of brass and gold hang everywhere showing off wealth but in the most unappealing way. It reminds me of stupid functions and galas I had to attend with my family as I grew up. And that god-awful debutante ball my parents made me be a part of. I try to keep in a laugh as I think about the horrid hot pink dress I wore in rebellion and sneaking off with my best friend to drink on the roof of the building.

"Something funny, Ms. Wilder?" Bastian says to me.

I bite my lip and shake my head. He looks at me curiously and I think he is going to say something when the hostess interrupts to direct us to our table.

I follow the hostess and Bastian to the back of the restaurant, passing tables with expensive bottles of wine and champagne and people with far too much jewelry.

We are led to a back room with a table for twelve. A few men stand around with drinks in their hands. I chance a glance at Bastian and the ever-present scowl on his face grows deeper.

"Can I get you two anything to drink?" the hostess asks.

"Dalmore, twenty-five year."

She nods at him and turns to me and I order my "business meeting drink". "Dry martini."

She walks away and Bastian looks at me. "I took you for a champagne drinker."

I raise a brow at him. "And I took you as someone who orders a two-hundred-dollar glass of scotch. Looks like one of us was right."

The hint of a smile creeps across his face but before he can say anything back, someone shouts his name.

"Bastian!"

We both turn to see an older gentleman make his way to us. He's shorter than me, even without heels on, and his red cheeks and jovial smile makes me instantly like him.

"Mr. Baxter, pleasure to see you. It's been quite some time."

"Well if you hadn't decided to move your offices to Paris years ago, you might actually see me more. London misses you."

"I don't miss London."

"Nonsense. You are just never around to remember its joy."

He laughs. "I think you mean the gloom, Jon."

"It was only ever gloomy over your head."

"It rains here—"

"Enough about the weather. Who is this beautiful woman? Did you finally decide to settle down again?"

Hmm, interesting. Maybe I will learn more about Bastian here.

"This is the woman I hired to repair the image of Montford Hotels." His hand reaches for my arm as he pulls me next to him. "Cameron Wilder, meet Jonathon Baxter. He's on the board of directors for Montford Holdings."

"Pleasure to meet you, Mr. Baxter."

"American? What brings you across the ocean to work for this young man?"

"Just cleaning up his mess," I tease. It's then I realize Bastian is still holding my arm, his grip going tighter at my joke.

"We both know this mess never would have happened if I didn't let Matías take over the hotel group."

Mr. Baxter laughs. "That boy just likes to play too much."

"And with the wrong people," a deep voice says from behind us.

Bastian's grip on my arm tightens suddenly before he drops it quickly, turning around to face the new guest. "Father."

I spin at the mention of his father and am met with a man who wears the same stern look as Bastian but looks nothing like him.

Where Bastian is deep tan skin, dark hair and dark eyes, his father is pale, hints of gray peppering into his dirty blond hair, blue eyes shining in an almost predatory way.

"I see you have finally decided to grace us with your presence for one of our director meetings."

He scoffs. "I hardly call this a meeting. I am sure most of the board will be drunk by the third course and all aspects of business will be forgotten."

His father narrows his eyes at him. "Is that how you think we run the business? Maybe you should be here more often to see that is not how it's done. Instead you gallivant off on your yacht for weeks when there are pressing matters at hand."

A low growl escapes from Bastian. "I wasn't gallivanting. I was handling business. Calming investors who were on the verge of pulling from the expansion."

"By feeding them booze, drugs, and prostitutes?"

Anger flashes across Bastian's face. "You know that is not my business."

"Not anymore," his father says in a cruel voice.

I try to piece together what is going on, curious to what Bastian did before. Did he used to do what his brother did? Use illegal business practices to grow his wealth? I get so lost in the thoughts spinning in my head I almost miss the conversation turning to me.

"And who is this pretty thing?" his father asks Bastian without taking his eyes off me. "You know there are no dates allowed at our business meetings."

Bastian goes to speak but I cut him off. "I'm Cameron Wilder. I am the PR consultant your son hired for Montford Hotels."

"Ahh yes, I remember hearing you would be here. Although I thought you were a man."

I laugh in an attempt to break the tension between

father and son. "Your son thought the same thing when he met me. Let's just say he wasn't very happy. Didn't think a woman could do the job. But he has quickly learned he's wrong."

His father laughs and I relax even though I can feel the anger pulsing off Bastian next to me.

"It's hard for him to trust anyone other than himself. Much less a woman. But times are changing, Ms. Wilder."

"That they are, Mr. Montford."

He takes my hand and I feel Bastian tense beside me. "Please, call me Whitaker."

A server shows up with our drinks and conversation flows freely among the board members until we finally take our seats for dinner.

I sit between Jon and another board member. Bastian and his father both sit at the head of the table. The rest of the guests are board members and a few are heavy investors in the company.

I sip my martini and listen as the men talk business. I know the conversation will come to me soon. But I just sit in silence and listen, taking in any and all information I can. Most of it boring business talk, nothing to teach me more about Bastian or his past.

We are halfway through the third course when Mr. Montford finally turns the attention to me. "So Ms. Wilder, how do you plan on turning Montford Hotels around?"

"Well, it all comes down to the image of the company." I pause because this is obvious to all of them but my next words may not be. "And the branding."

A few of the board members look around but Mr. Montford's eyes hold steady on me. He doesn't say anything, so I continue.

"I've been working hard the last few weeks to erase the bad press that has been all over the media. I hired a team that works twice as hard as anyone else to dig deep and find every news article, video, and commentary that has been said. Meanwhile, I am writing a new narrative for the company. Shifting the brand image with the marketing department."

I spend the next ten minutes speaking to a lot of what we have already done and what we plan to do. I keep silent about the branding I have in my mind since I haven't gone over it with Bastian yet and I definitely keep my mouth shut about the gala.

"You seem to be moving the hotel group in the right direction," Jon says next to me.

"Bastian, what have you seen on the business side?" his father asks.

Bastian starts talking numbers and investors and a bunch of shit I don't know about. I glance back at his father and he seems pleased.

By the time dinner is over, all conversation of business has long ended. Most of the board members have had more than their fair share of drinks and Bastian's mood seems to not have changed.

I excuse myself to use the restroom and smile as Jon tells a joke that has the entire table cracking up.

I do my business and look in the mirror that is just as gaudy as the rest of the restaurant and fix a few pieces of my hair.

I walk back down the hall when I stop suddenly at two voices arguing quietly in a small alcove.

I can barely make out what they are saying. Something about detectives and covering up evidence. I have no idea what it means. I quickly make my way back to the table, not wanting to be caught because I am ninety percent sure it was Bastian's voice I heard.

I sit down and sip my martini and laugh at the jokes of the men around the table, adding to the conversation whenever I can. I feel Mr. Montford's eyes on me and they make me uncomfortable.

Bastian returns to the room followed by one of the men I remember as Benjamin Cole, an investor in Montford Holdings.

I glance at Bastian, but he is staring at his father.

An hour passes before we finally leave the restaurant. The board and investors thoroughly toasted except for a select few. As the night went on Bastian's mood seemed to darken. Which isn't a far stretch from his normal mood but the tiny bit of charismatic personality he had at the beginning of dinner has completely vanished.

We walk back through the park in silence. He keeps a distance from me and whenever I glance at him, I can see his thoughts turning in his head. I can only imagine it has to do with the argument he had with Benjamin Cole and the hushed words with his father.

"Why did you move your offices to Paris?" I ask in order to break the silence between us.

"Personal reasons," he says tersely.

"And those are…" I trail off.

"Personal."

"Come on, Bastian. I am your publicist. It's something I should know."

He steps in front of me, stopping me abruptly. "No, you are Montford Hotels' publicist. And you can go back to calling me Mr. Montford now."

I roll my eyes at him and skirt around him walking briskly. He catches up to me quickly.

"Cameron."

"It's Ms. Wilder," I retort and keep walking.

He growls as he pulls on my arm to turn around, causing me to stumble into his chest. My hands land against the hard muscles, his hand dangerously low on my hip.

"I don't like how you constantly talk back to me."

"And I don't like how you never answer my questions."

He pulls me closer to him. My breathing growing heavier as I watch his eyes flick to my lips. His hand drops lower, skimming over the top of my ass before he sighs and steps back.

"I'm sorry, Ms. Wilder, I will try to be more open to you about things that concern the business."

I study his face and see the sincerity. "Thank you, Mr. Montford."

We turn and continue our walk back to the hotel.

"I'm going for a drink," I tell him as we walk into the lobby.

"We have an early flight back to Saint Tropez, you should get some rest."

I raise a brow at him. "I'll be fine. And after that dinner, I could use a drink."

I watch him as his jaw clenches. I know he wants to forbid me but he also knows he can't control me.

His only answer is a small nod before he walks toward the bank of elevators.

I can feel the smile taking up my whole face as I turn to the lobby bar and make my way to a stool.

I order a dirty martini and relax into my seat.

10

BASTIAN

I watch her from the dark corner of the lobby bar. I scoff at myself, wondering if this is my new favorite hobby.

I am not even sure why I came back to the bar. I meant it when I told her we had an early flight and I don't want to be delayed by her oversleeping. I have an important meeting in the morning in Nice and then need to fly back to Paris.

I made it up to my room and poured a glass of scotch. I barely even took a sip before I headed back down to the bar. I don't know if my intentions were to join her or not. I don't socialize with the staff. But I enjoyed our conversation on the way to the restaurant. And I didn't miss the way I liked the feeling of her body near mine.

I shake the thought as I let my mind filter back to my conversation with Benjamin. He is a newer investor in the hotel group. And the information he gave me tonight did nothing but piss me off. It seems like every time I turn a corner in making this nightmare go away something new develops and pushes me back a few steps.

I know how to kill it. I know how to make it all go away with the click of a button and a few hundred million dollars. But after my older brother, Thiago, passed, I promised myself I wouldn't do it anymore. I would step away from what we did. But I know one foot will always be in that door. I'm chained to my past mistakes, burdens that will never be lifted, wrongs I can never right.

I am a bad man, a dangerous man, and no amount of self-reflection will change that.

Cameron's laughter has my head shifting from the untouched scotch in my hand to her gorgeous face.

A group of young men surround her. I watch them as I grind my teeth.

I don't like how close they are to her.

I don't like the way she is smiling like she has no cares in the world.

I curse myself again for the burn I feel when I look at her, when I touch her.

But when she calls me by my first name, a hunger grows deep in my body, a smoldering need that I fear catching fire.

I take a long sip of my scotch and slam my glass down when one of the men slides his arm around her shoulder.

I try to force myself to ignore it, the beast of jealousy threading through my veins, but when her smile falls from her face I've had enough.

I march over to the bar, pushing the man's arm away from her. "It's time to go," I growl.

She looks at me in pure shock. "Were you babysitting me since your assistant isn't here to do it?"

The man whose arm was around her attempts to step between us. "Is there a problem?"

"No," we both say in unison.

She turns toward the man and apologizes.

I clench my jaw. "Let's go."

"I was having a rather enjoyable time."

"And your job is on the line."

"You can't fire me."

"I can fire your company."

"And where would that leave yours?"

I tighten my fists at my sides as I realize how close we are. Somehow in our argument, she stood from her barstool, the two of us stepping completely into the other's space.

I don't want to answer her question. I don't need to. I know I need her. She has done more than anyone else has. And her conversation at dinner proved it.

I reach around her and grab her clutch off the bar. I grab her arm and haul her away from the men and out of the bar.

"Are you serious right now?" she shrieks at me.

I don't answer and just pull her to the elevators.

"Bastian," she stammers.

The elevator pings and the doors open. I pull her inside, pushing her against the gold walls. "I told you to call me Mr. Montford."

She huffs in my face, her breathing erratic as I lean

97

into her, our chests touching, my eyes darting to her more than kissable lips.

But I know it would be a mistake. To give in to her.

She's desirable, sexy, feisty. The opposite of anything I would want but somehow she has become this parasite of need and I can't get her out of my head.

"I would consider this sexual harassment," she says to me and I immediately step back.

"I apologize, Ms. Wilder."

"You know I can take care of myself. I would have made it back to my room at an early hour without one of those boys."

I step farther away from her and lean against the opposite wall, my arms folding over my chest. "I couldn't care less about them. I just wanted you ready to work tomorrow."

She scoffs. "Okay, *Mr. Montford*," she emphasizes my name. "But it seemed like you were jealous."

I snort. "I was far from jealous."

"Then why did you suddenly appear when one of them touched me."

I shrug. "I didn't notice. I was merely paying attention to the time."

The doors open to our floor and she rolls her eyes as she walks off. But not after I notice the flush in her cheeks and across her chest. I know she wanted me.

"Are you sure it wasn't you who was jealous it wasn't me touching you?"

She stops in the hall and glares at me. "Far from it."

I laugh internally knowing that is far from the truth. "We need to leave by six in the morning."

"Fine," she says shortly.

"I need you to be on time."

"Not a problem."

"I have a meeting in the morning and I cannot—"

She turns to face me just as we reach her door. "I get it. I will be awake and packed." She turns to her door and pulls her key out of her clutch and mutters asshole under her breath.

I spin her around before she can swipe her key card. "Did you just call me an asshole?"

She crosses her arms. "No."

I step closer to her. "Or maybe it was cocky and rude."

She looks up at me curiously.

"Or maybe a fucking prick?"

Her mouth opens slightly.

"Don't worry, Ms. Wilder. There still may come a day when I press you against the glass of my office or fuck you on the deck of my yacht. Besides, you wouldn't mind it, would you?"

She gasps when I say it. And I think she is piecing it all together.

I step away from her, a smirk on my face. "Six a.m."

11

CAM

Fuck. Fuck. Fuckity fuck.

I say it to myself as I kick my heels off and storm the minibar.

He heard every word I said about him that first night on my balcony.

Which could only mean he is really spying on me and has my room bugged or he is in the penthouse above me. The latter much more plausible. Which means he has probably heard me talk a lot of shit.

I am so screwed.

Unless he wants to actually screw me. And there were moments it clearly seemed like he did.

Fuck. I can't think about that either.

I open a mini bottle of vodka from the minibar and slam the thing down.

He was just trying to get under my skin.

And he did.

It's been a week since our dinner in London and I have yet to see Bastian since the flight back to France. And I am not complaining at all. I seem to get a lot more done when he isn't around breathing down my neck. Even his assistant hasn't been around. I don't know if it's because I told him I knew he was babysitting me or if he actually needed Parker for whatever business he had back in Paris.

It's given me time to work with the marketing team to adjust the branding of the company. And they seem to be on board. All but one of them never really liked the old campaigns. Selling sex rather than sexy. But I've seen the comments from the press. I know their opinion on Montford Hotels.

It's sad really. This hotel is beautiful. The one in London was astounding. And the pictures I have seen from the other three properties around Europe and in the Mediterranean, all portray an image of luxury every person would die to stay in. But the campaigns and ads never portrayed the yearning that the general public should have.

And with the expansion set to be announced in just five weeks, we have a lot of work to do quickly. I've been working with Elyse, head of marketing, on deadlines. We both agree the new campaigns should launch two weeks before the announcement. It gives time to pique interest again in Montford Hotels, make the population curious, turn the heads back in our direction, especially the ones that turned away after the raid.

My team works intensely to tease the press on the new campaign while Elyse Morel's team works diligently to book models and photographers for photo shoots.

"Are you sure he will approve of this?" Elyse asks me as we both slump into one of the couches overlooking the sea in the office.

I laugh. "Unlikely."

Her eyes widen as I say it.

"But he tends to disagree with half the shit I say. I just make him agree."

"You make him agree?"

I nod as I pour us each a well-deserved glass of wine after putting in fourteen hours today. "I just repeat myself over and over until he stops saying no."

She looks at me with her mouth agape. "That man scares the shit out of me. His brother was totally different. Laid back, easygoing. Hell, he wasn't here half the time. But I guess that makes it easier to believe all the things that happened."

"Do you really believe Matías did all those things?" I ask curiously.

She looks around the room to make sure we are truly alone since I know we aren't supposed to be talking about what happened. "No I don't."

I lean forward. "What do you think happened?"

She shakes her head as if she is battling within herself if she wants to talk about it. "I really shouldn't be saying anything. Mr. Montford made us sign NDAs after Matías was arrested. If we didn't sign them, we would be fired. And of course, if he finds us gossiping about the situation, he will fire us too."

"I won't say anything."

She sucks her bottom lip into her mouth, then starts talking in a low whisper. "Matías was a party animal. He was doing drugs or drinking, sleeping with different women most of the time. Now don't get me wrong, he was a great boss because he believed in the party lifestyle and we had a lot of freedom here. But he didn't really run the place. I don't even think he wanted to but just felt that he needed to prove his worth to his father and the Montford name.

"Frederick Davenport ran the company. He approved everything, handled all the things Matías let slip. He was who truly felt like the boss around here. He is young, just like Matías. Partied often with Matías. But he was smart, Cameron. Calculated. He knew everything that was going on long before anyone else did. I know that he would have secret meetings at some of the parties. I brushed them off as work, but what if they weren't?"

"Who's Frederick Davenport?" I ask, the name sounding familiar.

"The CFO."

I sip my wine and think about all the things I read about the incident and the arrests. "He wasn't arrested."

Elyse nods her head.

"But Bastian fired him?"

She nods again. "Mr. Mont—Bastian, never trusted him after some personal thing that happened between the two of them. Bastian knew Frederick ran the company more so than his brother, so he fired him. I can only guess on suspicion of involvement."

I nod. "Makes sense."

"Please don't tell anyone I told you these things. I don't want to lose my job. I actually like working here. Even though Bastian is frightening. He seems to take care of his employees and the business well."

I nod as she changes the subject, telling me about her life in the south of France and the small village she grew up in near Bordeaux.

I listen to her as I watch the waves hit the rocky shoreline. But my mind wanders to Bastian and the secrets he and his family are hiding.

I yawn and stretch as I sit down at my desk. I swear I've put in more time this week than the first week I was here but I knew this job wasn't going to be easy. I sip on my iced coffee and rub my temples, ready to battle the next set of stories I need to clear from the press.

I am in the middle of typing an email when my cell rings. I hit the ignore button, as I want to leave at a decent hour tonight. I am exhausted, my feet hurt from running around all day, and I really just want to drink a martini and sit in my bathtub that looks out over the sea.

My phone goes off again and I choose to ignore it. I can only guess it's my mother calling since I sent a not-so-nice response to one of her emails earlier. I practically told her to fuck off when she told me to come home for a charity event and she already had a date lined up for me.

This time my office phone rings and I finally decide to answer it.

"What is this email I got from Mrs. Morel regarding

a marketing plan that you said I would approve?" Bastian growls into the phone.

Ugh, I do not want to deal with you today.

"Ms. Wilder, have you forgotten what I said about firing you?"

Shit, did I say those words out loud.

"Now I suggest you *do* deal with me and start speaking."

Well, that answers that. "Your marketing and social media strategy need to change, Mr. Montford."

"And you think you have the authority to approve it?"

"No. But I told Elyse I would go over it with you. I have just been a little busy covering your brother's ass so I haven't had time to send you an email to find time to discuss it."

"The image of the hotel needs to change, not the entire marketing strategy."

I lean back in my chair and sigh. "It's not a total change of the strategy, really just the message the brand has coming across. I did mention it at the dinner you took me to. The board seemed thrilled with the idea."

"Well, it must not have thrilled me since I don't remember."

I groan into the phone. "Your brand is all wrong. You need to stop selling sex and start selling sexy."

"It's not my brand, it was my brother's."

I hold back the growl I am ready to release because I am seriously too tired to deal with his attitude. "Well since your brother is what should we say? Incapacitated. It's now your brand and I have to say that selling sex is not what's going to sell hotel rooms. There is too much bad press saying Montford Hotels are a place for the rich and famous to bring their prostitutes and one-night stands. The press is calling this place cheap, sexist. If you want to clear the hotel's image, your brother's image…" I pause because I know he will hate my next words. "Your image. You need to adjust the brand."

"My image isn't tarnished, Ms. Wilder."

"Not yet."

He growls into the phone. "Is there something you aren't telling me?"

I think back to the few articles that were brought to my attention today. Articles tearing down Bastian's character, blaming him for his brother's indiscretions, holding his past against him, a past I don't know much about. But I don't want to put that burden on him. I've seen the man behind the mask a few times and I know he keeps it firmly in place for a reason. "Nothing I can't handle."

He sighs into the phone but doesn't say a word.

I go back to the original subject at hand. "Montford Hotels needs to be sexy, not sexist. A dream. A desire. Something any person can try to attain."

"So you are telling me you want it to be affordable luxury?"

I shake my head, even though I know he can't see it. "Don't get me wrong, Mr. Montford, but there is a difference between affordable luxury and over-the-top sexual appeal."

"This is not a cheap hotel brand."

I nearly laugh into the phone at his words. "I am all aware of that, Mr. Montford. I'm not saying that your hotel is cheap but it's coming off as cheap. Sexist. The press is turning the image on you so quickly it's hard to keep up. So turn it back around on them. Make them bite their tongue when they see the brand is not what they think."

He clears his throat and I nearly jump at his next words. "Go on."

"I know that you think when I say affordable luxury you think I'm saying things are cheap but that's not what I mean. I want to appeal to the masses. Make them think that what they're paying for is affordable. It doesn't need to be affordable, but in their mind it is. The experience, the chance to be a part of something luxurious, rich, so nearly attainable they are willing to fork over the money if it's just for a few nights of opulence."

He chuckles into the phone. "I think you should have gone into marketing, Ms. Wilder."

I smile, actually smile, because I know I hooked him. "What would be the fun in that? I much prefer the push and pull of public relations."

"I will send a response to Mrs. Morel."

"And what might that be?"

"I need a more detailed plan."

"Fair enough." I nod as I look out over the pool. The few guests that didn't cancel their reservations after the scandal. I imagine what this place would look like completely booked. An oasis along the Cote d'Azur. "I promise this will work. This will make—"

"Don't make promises you can't keep," Bastian growls into the phone.

He hangs up without another word and I turn back

toward my desk to get to work. My mood even worse after Bastian's back and forth personality changes.

I don't get far when a knock lands on my door. "Come in," I say without looking, assuming it's Elyse after she got the email response from Bastian.

"The man really works you to the bone."

I startle at the sound of a deep voice and am surprised when I see Kilian Bancroft standing in my office. I clear my throat and plaster a smile on my face. "He's not really in charge of me so it's really just my work ethic."

"Strong work ethic is important."

I nod and raise my eyebrow at him. "Can I help you with something?"

I don't miss how his eyes take me in, the way they roam my body like I might be able to help him with something on an entirely different level.

He steps toward my desk and sits in a chair across from me. "I was just looking for the boss man himself. Is he around?"

I lean back in my chair and study the man. The way he owns the room much like Bastian but something about him sends warning bells off in my head. He has a sense of danger about him. "He isn't here."

"Strange. The bastard told me he had a meeting. Said he would be back around now."

I don't know much about the man in front of me. I barely inferred that the two are friends but from the way he referred to him, I am guessing they are much closer than Bastian let on. "The last I heard from his assistant is that they would be back in Saint Tropez tomorrow."

Kilian rubs his thumb and forefinger along his smooth chin. "I see. Huh. Silly me, I must have got the dates wrong."

I look into his green eyes and know he is not a man to mess up dates. Meaning I am sure he is here for another reason. And from the few words I overheard him tell Bastian last time he was here, I can only guess he is here for me.

"Honest mistake," I answer.

"So are you just going to stay here working late into all hours of the evening? It's a beautiful night out. Shame to waste it sitting in an office."

I laugh to myself. I was right about him. He is here for me. "I have a lot to do."

"You look tired."

I guffaw. "For someone who just hinted at finding a way to get me away from this desk it's not smart to start with insults."

A sly grin cuts across his face. "That was not my intention at all, Ms. Wilder. I was merely stating a fact. And you know the cure for looking tired. A night out on the town."

I raise a brow at him. "Is that so?"

He stands up and leans over my desk. "I think you know it is."

I can't help but flirt with the man. He's a natural at it and I am too. I lean forward on my elbows and meet his gaze, my chin resting on my hands. "Mr. Montford will be very unhappy if I don't finish my work."

"I thought you said you didn't work for him."

"Touché."

He grins at me, and I can't help but match his smile. He stands up and offers me his hand. I oblige and walk around the desk, grabbing my bag as I do.

We walk out into the main office area and I notice everyone has left for the day. I never even paid attention to the time. "So Mr. Bancroft, where are you going to take me on such a fine evening?"

His arm slips around my waist. "Please, call me Kilian, Ms. Wilder."

I look up at the sparkle in his eyes knowing good and well this man is trouble. "Then call me Cam, Kilian."

He throws his head back in laughter as he squeezes my hip.

Good thing I like trouble.

"There is no way Bastian pulled a prank like that in secondary school," I shout at Kilian as we enjoy cocktails on a patio at a hole-in-the-wall café in the livelihood of Saint Tropez. Where I thought he would take me to some ritzy-ass place full of bouncers and celebrities, we sit on metal chairs, drinking cheap liquor, and telling stories as we watch revelers walk down the road.

"I shit you not. The lad used to be a total prankster back in the day."

I snort as I think about the story of Bastian lighting a firecracker under one of his teacher's skirts while she was eating outside. I just cannot picture it.

"The bloke was a true ass until he graduated from university. Pretty much the day his dad put him to work he decided to be more serious. Focus on business. I rarely see him come out of his element. Maybe only when he's in... sorry, I shouldn't be talking about him now. Let's go back to the old stories."

I don't push Kilian because I know he's right. The man who works so hard to keep his past hidden. Instead, we talk more about Kilian and Bastian's youth. The two grew up in the rich neighborhoods of London, attended private school together through year thirteen, and then both attended university together. They both come from wealth. Kilian's family started out in the shipping industry in Ireland before moving to England in the early 1900s and expanding the business into investments and eventually hedge funds.

Kilian tells me another story from university about Bastian's inability to convince a girl to go out with him. I want to meet this version of Bastian. The carefree man, one who seemed to smile all the time, one who had fun. Because the version I know, I don't think knows the definition of fun.

As I listen to Kilian, it's not hard to get lost in his green eyes, his devilish smile, his all-consuming charm. He's a ladies' man, no doubt about it.

I sip on my dirty martini and watch revelers as he goes to answer his phone that keeps going off. The warmth of the salt air on my skin brings me a peace I wouldn't have found working in the office all night.

"I hate to cut our night of fun short but I have some business to attend to."

I look at my phone and see it's after ten. "This late?"

He shrugs. "Business calls to me at all hours. It's why I try to take advantage of nights like this when I can."

"I get it. Thank you for pulling me away from work tonight. I would probably still be at it if you didn't distract me."

He smiles at me. "Too bad I couldn't distract you further."

I roll my eyes at him as he makes a lewd gesture. "Gonna have to find someone else for that, Mr. Bancroft."

"Back to Mr. Bancroft?" he asks with a raised brow. "Now that is definitely something I could get used to with other distractions."

I laugh. "Not happening." I pull my phone out to grab an Uber but he pushes my phone down.

"I brought you out here. I'll bring you back to the hotel."

We walk down the street and hop into an SUV. His driver takes us back to the hotel and Kilian follows me out.

"I think I can make it inside just fine."

His hand goes to the small of my back. "I am sure you can, Cam, but since I am also a guest, we may as well walk in together. I'll even show you to your room."

"That's really not nece—"

"I am a gentleman."

I don't miss how he hurries us past the lobby bar, shielding me from whoever is there. I glance up to see him watching the bar and I try to catch a glimpse as to what he is looking at but I can't see around his muscular frame.

When we make it onto the elevator, he frames his arms around me. His nose dropping into my hair and inhaling. "What a night we could have, Ms. Wilder."

I push him off me and he steps backward. "Maybe next time."

"Is that a promise?" he asks as the elevator chimes, we've reached my floor.

"You'll just have to wait and find out."

I watch his jaw clench as the doors shut in his face and I can't help but laugh. I know the man wanted me. Hell, I would want him too. But something about him seemed off. The hint of danger I felt earlier creeping up my spine. Kilian Bancroft is trouble and not the good kind.

12

BASTIAN

I slam my fist against the wall as I exit the elevator to the penthouse.

Fucking Kilian.

Always stepping in where he isn't wanted. The man needs to learn a few lessons.

I had eyes on Cameron. I always do. More for her safety than anything else. And when it got back to me that she was laughing and drinking with Kilian, I just about lost it.

I wanted to rush over to where they were and pull her away from him but I kept my cool.

Of course, when he walked into the hotel tonight and saw me sitting in the bar, I didn't miss how his hand slid lower around her hip, the wink he gave me as he walked to the elevators.

I was ready to follow them both back to her room but clenched my jaw and thought it was best to leave them alone. If she wants to get tangled up in Kilian's web of lies that's on her.

I pour a drink and down it quickly. Just as I pour another, the ding of my elevator goes off. I glance up to see Kilian walking through the foyer adjusting his tie.

I grip my glass tight as he meets me over at the bar, wondering why I gave him access to this hotel suite. "I told you not to sleep with her."

He grins at me and pours himself the most expensive scotch I have here. "You told me not to fuck her. There is a difference."

I snort. "Considering I saw you take her to the elevators no less than ten minutes ago, I am guessing you didn't get very far. Unless you like to lie about your stamina. Five minutes all you need?"

"Feck off, you wanker." He downs his drink and sets his glass down. "She was quick to turn me down." He studies me and I know what he is thinking. "Are you fucking her?"

"No."

"Do you want to be?"

"Why don't you tell me why you are here, Kilian?"

He pours another drink and then saunters over to my couch, flopping on to it. "I'm guessing you do want to be fucking her or else you wouldn't be having her followed. I was quite enjoying our conversation until you decided to blow up my phone with texts telling me not to touch her."

"She is too innocent to get involved with you."

"And what about you?"

I pinch my brows together before sitting across from

Kilian. "Same goes for me. Now, what brings you to Saint Tropez that didn't warrant a phone call?"

He smiles at me. "I just wanted to see your scowling face. I missed it."

I glare at him.

He sighs and drops his hand inside his suit coat, pulling out a thumb drive and tossing it on my coffee table. "More evidence."

I reach for it and spin it between my fingers. "I'm guessing nothing good if you wanted to hand deliver it."

He shakes his head. "Not at all."

"Fuck," I yell at the ceiling.

"It doesn't look good, man. For Matías or you."

I snap my head toward him when he says *you*. "How the hell did my name get pulled into this?"

Kilian swirls his drink in his glass. "We both know your past is not the most honest."

I clench my jaw, thinking of all the mistakes I made, business decisions I thought were leading to fortune, not shame and despair. "Everyone knows I no longer do business with those people."

Kilian nods. "Yes, but you know how people like to dig into the past for any excuse to pull the blame from themselves."

"You still think one person is behind all this?"

"I'm no detective, Bastian. But considering I am not the most respectable businessman when it comes to doing things the right way, I tend to hear a lot of things."

I grip my hair as I run my hands through it. "So you do think one person is behind it. Someone from the hotel group?"

He shrugs. "I've tried to find the source of the information that's being passed around. But not even Tomas can find out who it is."

"I'll look into it."

"Careful, Bastian. You shouldn't go down for someone else's crimes."

"I'm criminal enough. I should have been arrested years ago."

Kilian grins at me, an almost diabolical grin that would give a weak man chills. "But you are smarter than most." He sips his drink. "Like me."

"I'm not like you, Kilian."

"Not anymore."

I stand up and walk to the wall of windows leading out to the balcony. My eyes taking in the black sea. A sea full of secrets, lies, and deceit. A sea that is far too similar to my own life.

"I wish Matías was smarter. He didn't grow up in the business like Thiago and me. I wish he knew not to touch the forbidden fruit like we all did."

I hear Kilian shift behind me. "You got your brother into this mess."

I turn to face him, anger burning through my veins. "By being friends with you? Nice try Kilian, but we both know you provoked him."

"I just gave him names."

"No, you didn't. You gave him a taste of your world."

"He didn't have to bite. And if I recall, you took the same fruit."

I run my hands through my hair. "I was young and wanted money and power."

"Matías wasn't much younger than you when this all started. But you learned the consequences much faster. And were smarter. You played the game right. Unlike Matías."

"You know how he is. He'll bite at anything for women and fame."

"And I gave him a taste. He didn't have to go as far as he did."

I clench my fist as I stare at Kilian, my friend, a man more dangerous than most. "He couldn't get out of it."

"I don't know what to tell you, Bastian. He was either gonna get in deep with me or you."

"He made a deal with the devil before he was able to see it."

"And am I that devil?" Kilian asks with that grin on his face again.

I sigh as I sip my scotch. Knowing good and well neither Kilian nor myself are good men. "I'm not sure if it was me or you."

13

CAM

I send a quick message on my phone as I watch the photo shoot Elyse booked take place at the hotel pool. The woman worked fast to get a move on with the new branding strategy. And I know Bastian is going to be pissed. Elyse asked me early this morning if we should cancel because Bastian hadn't signed off on the detailed plan she sent him last night. But I told her not to worry. I would take the heat for his attitude because I know this is the right path to change the image of the hotel.

I watch the screens as the photographer shoots the beautiful model as she walks out of the pool. The angle is perfect. Lush green gardens surround the edges of the pool as she walks out in a gold one-piece swimsuit with a deep plunge. Sexy and provocative, yet classy. Turquoise waters of the Mediterranean outline the back of the image and I know with a few tweaks to the photo it will look amazing. It will be the campaign this hotel needs.

A flash of white catches my attention from beyond

the shoot and I see Parker walking over, a humorous smile on his face.

"You know he isn't happy."

I lift my sunglasses off my face and push them on top of my head. "I figured as much."

"Did he even know about the photo shoot today?"

I shrug. "He got the email from Elyse. He knew the plan."

"And what am I missing out on?"

"He just hadn't signed off on it yet." I laugh as I say it.

Parker grins at me. "You're bad, Cam."

"What made you come down here if you didn't know what was going on?"

Parker shifts his tablet into his other arm. "The man was dreadful. I had no idea why he was in such an awful mood. I only assumed it had to do with you. Then when the hotel manager relayed the pool closure to me, I knew you had everything to do with it."

I smirk. "You know, he is always saying to work quickly. I worked quickly."

"Isn't this all on the marketing department?"

I glance over at Elyse and the smile on her face as she looks over the images in the monitor. "He knows this was all me. They just planned it."

"I really hope I am around when he blows up on you today. His mood is absolutely foul. It should be entertaining to watch you two bicker."

I wink at him. "I'll make sure to pull you up a chair."

Parker laughs at me before glancing at his tablet. "Do you need assistance with anything today, Cam?"

I nod and make a list of all the things that have been backed up on my desk while trying to get the marketing plan finalized. My team can only work so fast and Parker is a welcome reprieve to it all. I've missed his help while he and Bastian were in Paris the last week.

We head up to the offices and spend the day getting through the list. I'm surprised I haven't heard a peep from Bastian. Every time the phone rings Parker flinches thinking it's him.

A knock on my door has both of us surprised. Kilian stands in the doorway dressed in an all-black custom suit. He looks ready for a funeral.

"Ms. Wilder, I just wanted to stop by and thank you for a wonderful evening last night. We should do it again sometime."

I notice Parker's mouth drop open at the statement before his eyes flick to me.

I smile at Kilian. "It would be my pleasure, Mr. Bancroft."

He smiles at me, the one that I am sure has charmed more than enough panties off young women. "Until next time, *cherie*." He walks away without another word.

"Uh, should I know about something?" Parker asks me.

"No," I say nonchalantly as I turn back to my computer. Let Parker think what he wants since I know he will tell Bastian either way.

"What did you do last night?"

I peer over at him from the side of my computer. "I had dinner and drinks with a friend."

"Is that all?"

I nod and go back to work.

"Does Mr. Montford know?"

"Beats me. But considering Mr. Bancroft was here to see him, I am sure he let the cat out of the bag."

"Mr. Montford won't be happy to know—"

I cut him off. "I am well aware. Why do you think I went out with Kilian to begin with?"

Parker smirks at me. "You really do find every way you can to piss him off. No wonder his mood was so foul this morning. He must have seen the two of you last night."

I look at him curiously. "Last night? I thought you guys didn't get back 'til this morning."

He shakes his head. "We got back around dinnertime yesterday. It was supposed to be earlier but—never mind, it's not important."

I ignore the comment even though the look on Parker's face makes him look guilty for saying too much. "I doubt Mr. Montford saw us. We went into town."

"He planned to meet Kilian in the hotel bar last night."

Everything clicks as he says it. The way I felt eyes on me, Kilian blocking me from view of the bar, the way his hand slipped lower around my waist and gripped me tighter. He knew exactly what he was doing.

"Well, I am sure they had a great time. Let's get back to work. There is a lot to—"

I am cut off by Parker's phone ringing. I watch him as he nods but doesn't say anything and it doesn't take many brain cells to know who he is talking to.

I roll my eyes and go back to the email I was in the middle of typing.

"He wants to see you."

"I'm sure he does," I snort.

"Now."

"Still testy, I'm assuming?"

Parker fights a smile. "Worse."

"He can wait."

Parker shakes his head, laughing. "I wouldn't test him. After ten years together, I know how that man gets. He said 'Send her to my office now. And don't let her push you around. I've had enough of her attitude and her lack of respect for me and everyone else in that office.' Then he hung up."

"Wow. He sounds like PMS is really hitting him. Maybe he needs some Midol and ice cream. I could run to the market quickly and grab some for him."

Parker closes his eyes and his lips form a straight line. "Just go see him. I fear my own job if you test him right now."

I sigh in defeat. "Can you call me a driver?"

"His office isn't in his yacht like he's said. It's upstairs in the penthouse."

"Of course it is," I respond as I stand from my desk. "Do you have a key?"

"Yours works."

"What?" Surprise takes over my face.

"Your key has access to the penthouse. Don't ask me why he requested that."

I huff as I walk out of the office and to the bank of elevators. I hit the button for the one that leads to my floor and the penthouse. When I get on, I am surprised my key does in fact allow me to hit the penthouse button.

I take three deep breaths as the elevator climbs to the top floor. I know myself. And I know how I react. But I need to maintain a professional demeanor. I need to not act out and yell at him.

Demand your worth.

My father's words flit across my brain just as the door opens to the penthouse. If he wants to call me to his damn office for whatever reason, he needs to disagree with me yet again, I don't care. I know my worth. I know this business. And I know I am making the right damn decisions.

I walk across the foyer and am surprised he isn't standing there waiting to fire me. I make my way through the living room. The layout similar to my room. Except this room is dark grays and blacks compared to the white brightness of mine. I walk to the glass doors that lead out to the balcony I now know sits over mine and revel in the view. He's not much higher but the view is even more incredible up here. I go to open the glass when I hear his footsteps crossing the floor behind me.

I don't bother to turn around, just watch the waves crash into the cliff below.

"I told you not to move forward with any plans until I signed off on it."

"You were taking too long," I say sternly. "We needed to—"

"You already had the photo shoot booked before I even got the proposal. I know you didn't book it this morning and then start it hours later."

I shrug, still facing away from him, still looking out into the sea. "That was Elyse, you'd have to ask her."

"Don't make a fool of me, Ms. Wilder," he grits as I feel him approach me. His front very close to my back.

I slowly turn around to face him. Taking in his piercing gray eyes, his square jaw, his dark hair that is loose and falling into his face. He is the most handsome man I have ever laid eyes on. And as we stare at each other this close, I can make out the fine lines around his eyes, the ones he probably got from scowling too much. His dark lashes that flutter as he takes me in. He looks younger when his hair isn't gelled back. Younger and gentler, almost like the man I heard about in the stories from Kilian.

"I would never make a fool of you, Mr. Montford."

He steps closer to me, our chests just inches from each other. "Then why go through with a plan I clearly told you to wait on."

I smirk at him as I say, "Because time is of the essence. And you keep telling me to work quickly."

He growls. "I don't appreciate the attitude, Ms. Wilder. You are on thin ice."

I study his gaze and I decide to poke the bear because I know this more than likely has to do with Kilian and not about the stupid marketing plan.

"Thin ice? Is that because of the marketing plan, Mr. Montford? Or is it because I spent the night with your friend Kilian?" The innuendo I made on purpose to rile him up.

He grips my forearms and presses me back against the glass. "You shouldn't be around him."

"So it is because of him then?" I whisper, my lips very near his and the sudden urge to press mine against his own floods through me.

He lets go of me and steps away. "No."

I bite on my lip as I watch him struggle with emotion. I can't help but be turned on by the way he runs his hand through those longer locks of his hair. The way his eyes flit back and forth between my feet and the ground in front of him. The way his other hand clenches in a fist ever so slightly, I almost miss it.

I don't know what comes over me. I don't know why I say what I say next. Maybe it's the sexual tension I can feel coating the air between us or just my own need for the man in front of me. A man I should have no desire for. A man who checks all the boxes on my list of 'stay the hell away from.' But the pull I feel toward him is intense, unnerving. Yet I can't stop myself. "So it wouldn't bother you if I had dinner with him again."

I'm not even sure what happens next, it happens so quickly. The roar that comes out of him is like an animal claiming its prey. His hands are on me, pushing me forcefully against the glass behind me. His breathing erratic, his chest rising and falling fast and I swear I can feel the rapid beating of his heart through the palms of his hands. "You are not to see him again."

His words staccato. His breath a scream across my lips from the intensity of his words.

I take him in again. The sunlight streaking across his face, turning his eyes malicious. But the deeper I look into them, the more I see. The levels of emotion buried deep but for some reason I can read every single one. His struggle with desire, his need to push me away, an odd sense of protectiveness he has over me. I can see all of them in those eyes. A beautifully fractured man hiding behind lies.

"Bastian." His name crosses my lips in a plea or a question. I'm not even sure. All I know is I feel something between us. Something that should not exist.

But before I can figure out the feelings burning through me his lips crash to mine. Hard and fast. Strong and soft. Like a ship crashing to shore, reckless and unyielding.

A need so intense we both groan at the taste of the other. He tastes of expensive scotch and desire. A taste I want more of. A taste I suddenly *need* more of.

His hands move down my body, rough and needy. He doesn't hesitate, he takes what he needs as they grope my ass, slide up the edge of my skirt, creating chills along my thighs.

I grip his hair as I pull him into me. Needing to taste every inch of him. Wanting every desire that is flooding his mind right now as we savagely kiss against the glass.

But it ends as quickly as it starts.

He pulls away, nearly pushing himself off me. His breaths are heavy, his eyes delirious.

We both stare at each other wondering how that happened. Both curious if it will happen again. Even though it shouldn't.

Silence takes over the space between us sending a chill to the air, razing the all-consuming heat that was just there.

Bastian clears his throat before walking over to the bar and pouring a large glass of scotch.

I run my hands down my clothes, adjusting my skirt and pressing my jacket smooth. I fix my ponytail and walk toward the door. The awkwardness in the space more consuming than the passion that just happened.

When I get to the elevator, Bastian finally speaks. "You can move forward with the marketing plan."

I nod but don't turn around to face him.

"And I'm serious about Kilian."

I take a deep breath but don't acknowledge his words as the doors to the elevator open. I walk in and don't turn around until I hear them close. I slump against the wall, my breathing still erratic. My mind a jumbled mess trying to piece together the last ten minutes.

What the hell just happened?

14

CAM

I smooth my hands through my ponytail once more as I walk out of the elevator. I keep my head up as I walk through the office floor. Telling myself to look normal. Like I did not just share a ravaging kiss with the boss. I feel heat climb up my neck and I will it away.

When I walk through my office door Parker is on his tablet, typing away. I don't say anything as I walk around my desk and sit down, pulling up what I was working on before I went up to see Bastian.

What was I working on?

My mind is a mess. If I was smart or if I had the time, I would take off the rest of the day and enjoy a Friday night and the weekend. But I have things to do and it only feels more obvious if I walk away.

"I take it you weren't fired?"

I jump at Parker's voice. "No."

He lifts a brow at me. "Everything okay?"

I nod. "He wasn't happy but he agreed with the plan."

"That's it?"

"Yep," I answer shortly.

"Huh."

I can tell Parker is confused by my body language. He isn't an idiot and he knows I am acting weird even though I am trying to act normal. His phone buzzes and he turns his attention away from me.

I take a subtle deep breath and pull myself together. I am not acting normal. I head over to the espresso machine in the office and make a cup, returning to my desk, glancing over at Parker who is tapping furiously at his phone. The first sip has me feeling normal again. I start to go through the article I was working on when Parker interrupts me.

"I, uh, need to return to the boss." He clears his throat and pulls at the tie around his neck.

"You alright?" I ask. Parker is usually well put together. Nothing affects him. Even when he is present for the arguments between Bastian and me.

He nods, glancing at his phone before sliding it into his pocket. "I sent you a list of articles, good and bad. You are definitely making progress. I will give you that. Even Mr. Montford seems to think so." He pauses. "Even if he hasn't said it."

"Thank you."

"Now I must get back to the man himself. He seems worse than this morning."

Is that a good or bad thing, I wonder.

"Good luck," I joke.

"If you handled him, I have no doubt I can." He once again gives me a curious look before heading out of the office.

There is no way Bastian told him what happened earlier. He does not seem like a man who would spill a secret like that. Hell, I can barely get any secrets out of him much less a personal detail about him. The most I know is he enjoys being a dick and going for walks through a park in London.

By the time I shut my computer down for the day, the sun is setting. I slide my heels on I kicked off hours ago and grab my purse. I head out to the common room of the office and find it empty. I'm not surprised. It's after seven on a Friday and most of the employees here are young. If I were back home in New York, I most certainly would be in their shoes. Headed out for a night of drinks and dancing. But being here, feeling like I have a job that matters, I am starting to feel older. I don't want to go out anymore. I just want to go to sleep. Maybe it's because this job is exhausting.

I decide to at least head out for dinner. I am tired of the room service here and need something new. I stroll through the town, this part of Saint Tropez quieter, more serene.

I find a quaint Spanish café and pop in to pick up some food to go. As I wait for my order, I head over to the grocer across the street and pick up a few items for the weekend. If all goes to plan, I am taking the weekend off and not leaving my hotel room. Of course, Bastian will probably need me first thing in the morning but a girl can dream.

I grab my food and head back to the hotel. I smile at people as I pass. People here for fun, enjoying themselves, the beaches, and the nightlife. It hits me hard that I've been here a month and haven't really explored the town. Haven't taken the time to travel anywhere and see new things. I'm the same American I was at home, working myself to the bone, except in New York City I still managed to be the Cameron Wilder I've forgotten about. The wild, carefree girl who lived up to her name.

Maybe instead of hiding in my hotel room all weekend, I will go out and explore. Ignore all work emails and calls from Bastian. Live my life how I want to. How I always have.

A smile stretches across my face at my new intentions. I am going to spend my time here how I should be spending it.

I nod at the doorman as I walk into the hotel. He replies with a friendly *bonne soirée* and I smile back as I pass.

I make it just to the hall where the elevators are when I look up and see Bastian in the hotel restaurant speaking with a few men who look like they've had one too many drinks. I watch as he sits down at their table and unbuttons his suit jacket. The movement meticulous, his muscles straining against the sleeves of the jacket. I watch the tic in his jaw as he makes a comment to someone at the table, a tic I have somehow learned as his sign of annoyance with a conversation.

His eyes flick up to mine and I nearly stumble backward when our gazes meet. His eyes darken, a lustfulness in them I know only I am privy to. His tongue darts across his full bottom lip and I clench my thighs together, thinking about the places I would like that tongue to be. The ache unwanted yet I seem to want more.

But just as quickly as our eyes met, his go back to one of the men at the table. I know I didn't imagine it. I know I didn't make up the need that was just felt between us from across a room. But I know it's fleeting. A need that I can't fulfill.

I shake my thought and make my way to the elevator and up to my room. I pour a martini before heading outside on the terrace and listen to the waves crash against the shore. I open the paella I ordered and savor the flavors for a few bites when my phone rings.

I sigh as I stare at it. I left it face down so I have no idea who it is but I would much prefer a night of silence rather than thinking about work.

I grab the device and flip it over, a smile breaking across my face when I see Tacoma's picture on the screen.

"Hey, bitch," I answer with a cackle.

"Hey, slut."

I smile into the phone. "How are you?"

"Ugh, one month back in White Creek and my family is driving me up the wall. I swear to god it's like they haven't seen me in years. Every freaking day there is either a dinner at Easton's or a gathering at the bar and don't get me started on my sister inviting me out to that damn wedding venue to try and get my help."

I crack up. "Don't you work at the bar?"

"Yes! And I am there enough. I don't need to be there more than I am needed. I do have a husband I would like to see every now and then. Of course his cousin is just as bad as my family. He is constantly gettin' him to help with contracting jobs. And if it's not that, then those two idiots are at my bar driving me crazy!"

"Well, you have Laney, don't you?"

"Girlllll, I swear it's like everyone in this town is tryin' to remind me why I left. God, I hate small towns." I snort as she talks. Her Southern accent popping out the more she goes off. "Laney is still datin' the other bartender here. And if I catch them mackin' on each other one more time in that damn bathroom, I'm gonna lose it."

I laugh so loud I am sure my laugh echoes off the sea. "Didn't you have sex there? Like against the bar?"

She huffs. "That was after hours!"

I tsk into the phone. "I don't think you have any room to talk."

"Ugh, whatever Cam, but seriously, why did I agree to live here half the year?"

"Because your insanely sexy husband built your dream house there and you miss your family like crazy and you get to live the best of both worlds by being there half the time." I smile into the phone as I say it because I know Tacoma is happier than she's ever been.

"Why are you always right?"

"Excuse me? Did you just say I was always right?"

"See, I am losing my mind."

I can't help but laugh with my best friend as we catch up on our lives. She and I were two peas in a pod when we lived in New York. Both not making the best decisions but then again that's what twentysomethings do. And she would never say I'm right. Ever. She knew I could get us into more trouble than she could imagine. But the two of us together? I don't know how we both stayed out of jail.

"So has your boss eased up on you?"

"No." I think about Bastian and not the asshole boss who thinks he can get what he wants. But the man who had me clenching my thighs together just from a quick glance not even thirty minutes ago.

"He still got you pressed against a wall?"

"What?" I choke on air as she says it. As if she knew Bastian did in fact have me pressed against a wall earlier, hands groping me as I pulled his body against mine.

"Are you okay, Cam?"

I try to recover but the thoughts of those few minutes Bastian's hands were on me has my mind reeling and my body in a state of need. "Um, what? Yeah... uh I'm fine."

"Shut the fuck up. You fucked him!"

"What!" I shout.

"The Cameron Wilder I know would not be stammering her words unless she did something she shouldn't be doing when it comes to a man. And let me guess interpersonal relationships are a no go there."

I sip my martini and it does nothing to help my stutter. "Well, I mean yes. For both companies but... that has nothing to do... I didn't have sex with Mr. Montford."

"You sure? Did you call him that when he made you come?"

"Oh my god T, stop. I didn't fuck him."

"You better tell me something happened! I am tired of this small-town drama. Give me something juicy."

"You've been back in White Creek for what? A month? I don't think you could already be sick of the small-town drama."

"You're dodging my question."

I groan as I push away from the dining table and move my way over to the couch. I glance up at the balcony above me but I'm greeted with silence. Besides, I saw him at dinner and there is a good chance he is still there.

"I kissed him."

"Shut up."

"Well, he kissed me."

I hear her in the background yelling at her husband to bring her more wine. "Cameron, I've known you for almost ten years now. And I know that if a man that hot kisses you there is no way you didn't kiss him back."

"I already said I did."

I swear I can hear her eyes rolling. "So how did it happen?"

I take a giant sip of my martini. "He called me to his office because he was pissed at me."

"Not surprising."

"Do you want me to tell the story or not, Tacoma?"

"My bad. Please continue."

I pull my knees to my chest as I tell her everything that happened earlier in the day. My heart rate picks up as I detail out the kiss. The intensity of it, the need and lust that ignited my bones.

"So are you going to do it again?"

"T, we shouldn't have even done it in the first place. Off-limits. Besides, you know how I feel about men that come from money."

"True. But that man is money, he doesn't come from it. Not to mention almost any man your mom set you up with did not look like Bastian Montford."

"I don't think many men do." I sigh as I close my eyes and lean my head back against the couch. "He is so intense, Tacoma. But one look from those eyes is enough to make me want to tear my clothes off. The tension has been there for the last month but today we let it take over. Let it take control which in turn made us wild, deviant, unruly. And it ignited something in me, T. It woke up this dormant part of me. And I worry I won't be able to hide it away."

"I don't think that's a bad thing, Cam. You are being yourself again. I feel like it's been years since you let that girl come out. And just because this is a forbidden relationship doesn't necessarily mean it's a bad thing."

"Says the girl who ruined an engagement."

"Ouch, Cameron. You know I didn't ruin an engagement. It was already ruined before I showed up."

"I'm sorry, that was rude of me."

"Apology accepted. I'm happier than I've ever been. But maybe that's what you need to decide. I know you think this is wrong and yeah it probably is but listen to your heart."

"Wow, what happened to you?" I joke.

"I'm going to ignore that. Would you do it again, Cam? Do you want more of him?"

"There is no denying I want more of him. All of

him. But I can't have him. And I am not sure which of those is worse."

I take a deep breath as I open my eyes. And standing on his balcony with his elbows propped on the edge is the man himself. An intensity in his eyes. A look that makes me know he heard every word I said.

15

CAM

I settle onto a beach chair and pull out the latest true crime book I bought. I don't know what it is but reading about murder gives me a sense of peace.

This is what I've been missing. Free time. Maybe it came out because of Bastian. Maybe Tacoma was right and that kiss woke something up in me that I needed. To find myself again.

I've spent the last two years working my ass off at the company, trying so hard to prove to everyone in my life that I could do something, that I was worth something more than just being a piece of arm candy.

I guess it started when Tacoma moved back home, when she fell apart enough that I couldn't even get her back. It must have sent off some sort of chain reaction because I fell into the black hole she was in. I worked my ass off all the time. I barely went out. I even went as far as dating one of those men my mother set me up with. But that didn't work out as he planned. I was too busy. I couldn't attend every function he wanted because I was trying to carve my own path. He wasn't the nicest man when he wasn't happy and it just drove me to work harder, longer. I exhausted myself for two years, working twelve-hour days to prove I was just as good as any of the men in my office. I knew I could have left and went to a different company, one not run by egotistical men who think they run the world and own the women who do the work for them. But me being me, I needed to prove myself there. I needed them to see I was the best.

In the end, I guess it worked out. I finally got my promotion even if it did lead me to another country. But the looks on the faces of the others in the office when they saw me packing is burned in my brain. The smug look that just because I came from money didn't mean I could succeed. No one ever liked me in that office. Thought I just lucked out because of my daddy. Hell, they thought I was fired until Mr. Banks finally announced I was taking a promotion in France.

I breathe in the salty air of the Mediterranean and smile. If they could see me now. See that I am doing exactly what I set out to prove. And dammit, I am going to get Montford Hotels the image they deserve and more business than they had before. Fuck everyone who is waiting for me to fail.

I just need to do it all without Bastian on my brain. It's been two days since that kiss and I swear I can still feel him on my lips, feel his hands owning my body.

I close my book that I am obviously not reading and lay my head back. I need to get the man out of my head. It was a mistake. It can't happen again. No matter how much my body tells me I want him. I know I can't have him. I can't listen to Tacoma's advice. She took the forbidden path and it worked out for her but I can't risk it. I can't risk my job, my reputation, my career on a man that I would never give the time of day to if I met him anywhere else.

He is the exact kind of man my mother would want me to marry. Someone affluent, influential. Someone that doesn't need a woman with brains attached to his arm, just a woman with boobs.

I never understood why my mother never wanted me to try to be my own woman. My sister says it's because I am the youngest but I never saw what that had to do with anything. My parents supported her one hundred percent when she said she wanted to go to law school. Yet after I got the obligatory degree they requested, they expected me to settle down, find a husband, and start popping out kids.

But that has never been me. I'm the wild one. Not domesticated. I don't even understand the whole domestic housewife. I don't think a husband would ever be able to tame me that way. I'd be more feral. Yes, Cameron Wilder, the feral housewife.

Oh god, I think I am losing it.

I pull my sunglasses off my face and toss them into my bag and make my way down the beach to the warm turquoise water. I walk in until I am waist deep then dive under the water, swimming my way out to the calmer current. I float on my back and take in the line of build-ings along the water. I'm in France, the Cote d'Azur, the French Riviera, whatever you want to call it. The epitome of fame and fortune. The idealistic towns that overlook a gorgeous sea. I am here and I did it on my own. Not because of a man or my family's money. I did it. And I am going to prove that I am worth everything.

Screw Bastian.

Screw that kiss.

I am doing this my way.

16

CAM

I haven't heard from Bastian all week and I have to say the office has never been so peaceful.

Maybe he realized what happened a week ago was a mistake too. Or maybe he finally got it through his thick skull I know what I am doing and he is letting me finally have total control.

We've had such a productive week that I let my team go home at one. It's a beautiful weekend and they deserve the few extra hours after all the overtime we've put in. I'm even contemplating leaving when a ping hits my inbox. Then another. Followed by ten more.

My phone starts going off too and I scramble to find out what is going on. I pull open my email and find the alert that could ruin not only Montford Hotels but Montford Holdings too.

SEX, DRUGS, AND SCANDAL: IS THE MONTFORD ESTATE THE NEWEST CRIME FAMILY AND IS BASTIAN MONTFORD THE NEW CRIME LORD?

Was Montford Hotels set up for the crimes that indicted Matías Montford? Or is he truly guilty? From the pictures discovered it seems that maybe he was set up by his brother Bastian Montford. Or are they working together? It's been questioned for years, the doings of Bastian Montford and how he was able to expand the Montford Holdings investment business into the empire he has turned it into today. These pictures of Bastian Montford with known crime lords could be the answer.

I skim through the article, trying to find anything that is blatant enough to put Bastian behind bars.

Murder? Suicide? What the hell is wrong with the press?

And Bastian was married? I filter through the dossier on his company I read and vaguely remember a small mention of his wife. Something at the time I pushed aside because I deemed it insignificant.

"Why do I know none of this?" I ask myself.

"Because he had it buried," Parker says as he walks into my office.

I look up at him. "Is any of it true?"

"Parts of it. His brother died. It was suicide. He was married, his wife left him not long after Thiago's death. It broke him, losing Thiago. He blamed himself."

I nod, a feeling of empathy flooding my body. But then I think back to the other things mentioned in the article. "And the rest?"

Parker shrugs. "Hearsay. Bastian made a lot of enemies as Montford Holdings grew. A lot of people want to see him come crashing down, fail. And they will do anything to make it happen. Even..." He gestures around the room.

"You think someone just wants to take him down and used his brother and this ridiculous scandal to do it."

He nods. "Don't you think it's odd this article came out just as you are getting the company on the right track? Bookings have gone up twenty-five percent in the two days after you teased the new marketing campaign across social media. Someone isn't happy Bastian was able to recover so quickly."

"His brother is still in jail though. I wouldn't call that recovery."

Parker shrugs.

My phone rings and I know without looking it's Bastian. "Kill the story," he growls into the phone.

"I'm already on it," I answer.

"Good." He hangs up without another word.

"We have work to do," I tell Parker.

"That's why I'm here."

"And you better tell your boss I want some damn answers."

Parker stays silent for a moment as if contemplating what to say. "We'll see what he has to say."

I know that's the only answer I am going to get, so I nod and get to work.

It's nearly one in the morning when I finally shut my computer down. I sent Parker home hours ago, knowing that Bastian was probably demanding other things from him.

I think I have managed to shut down the story from every website that posted it but it's the internet and shit doesn't go away.

I rub the heels of my hands into my eyes and stretch my neck. When I look up Bastian is standing in the doorway, two glasses of what looks to be scotch in his hand.

He walks past my desk and stands to look out over the sea.

I get up and realize I look like a mess. My shirt is untucked from my very wrinkled pencil skirt, my shoes are off, and I can feel my hair falling out of my usually tight and secured ponytail.

But I don't care. I just spent twelve hours trying to kill a story that could very much take down Montford Holdings.

I walk over to Bastian and he hands me one of the glasses. "I—"

"Thank you," he whispers.

I turn to look at him but he still looks out over the water. "For what?"

"Not asking questions."

I go to open my mouth but take pause before I say anything too discourteous. "You know as the publicist to your company I should be privy to some of that information."

His brow furrows, one of the few emotions I've seen him make. "I know."

My mouth nearly drops open but I hold my composure. "I'm guessing you have a reason."

"I'm not one to let many people into my world. Even those who I work hand in hand with. Even those closest to me." He takes a long sip of his scotch and I think he isn't going to say anything more but then he speaks quietly, his gaze still fixed on the gentle cadence of the waves against the shoreline. "I despise this place. I hate the wealth, the luxury. The sheer will of these people who flaunt everything they have."

I take a small sip of the scotch, the heady notes of vanilla and smoke coating my tongue, warming my insides. "You are just as wealthy as they are. More wealthy in fact."

"I don't flaunt my wealth. Yes, I like to have nice things. But I don't find the need to show it off. I'm a businessman. I've done well for myself despite growing up with the rich. Those are the perks of being successful."

"If you don't like this place then why did you build a hotel here?"

"I never wanted to."

"Then why did you?"

He sips his scotch and I watch his eyes turn dark, something I've noticed when he doesn't want to talk about something.

"My ex-wife loved Saint Tropez. When my older brother and I decided to start a hotel group, she suggested we start here. It was logical. She knew the world of luxury better than most and we knew to listen to her. She hired the designer. She helped develop the plan for a luxury hotel chain that would surpass all." He closes his eyes. "I listened to her because it was the only time she seemed interested in what I did. She... despite people thinking we had the perfect marriage, we didn't. I was her ticket to wealth beyond what she could imagine. It was the one time I thought maybe our marriage could truly last."

My heart breaks at his words. He hasn't said much but I can infer from the few words he has said that he genuinely did love her. More than she loved him.

He finishes his glass and clears his throat. "I have a call I need to get to."

I raise a brow since it's nearly two in the morning and know he is lying.

"Bastian." I touch his arm without realizing it. His stormy gray eyes look down at my hand and I immediately remove it.

He goes to say something but holds back his words as something shifts in his eyes as he takes me in. His hand goes to my cheek, his touch warm when I always imagined it to be cold.

He blinks like he made a mistake, dropping his hand and walking away. When he reaches the door to the office, he turns back to me. "You've done a good job so far, Ms. Wilder. I expect that integrity to continue."

I watch his back as he walks out of my office and to the elevators.

I don't move for a while. My thoughts churning in my head. My heart beating fast at the words he gave me. He barely let me in. Barely let me know anything. Didn't even touch on the things mentioned in the article but for some reason I feel like I understand him a bit more. Understand the man that keeps himself so guarded he is afraid to let anyone in. Or maybe he doesn't know how.

A man that makes the tiniest crack in my own impenetrable heart.

17

BASTIAN

I said too much.

I barely said a thing.

But I could tell from her touch, the tone of her voice, that she understood me. Saw deeper into me than anyone could from so few words.

I slam my fist into the wall of my bedroom, cursing myself for saying a damn word to her.

I know better than to let anyone in. Let them even a fraction of an inch closer to my secrets. I know what happens when you let someone get too close. Give them too much.

They stab you in the back when it will benefit them the most.

And then they really hit hard when they turn it on your family.

I run my hands through my hair as I think about Thiago. Think about the brother I lost for no reason.

He kept his secrets to himself. Kept me in the dark. And look where that got us.

I grip my hair, pulling on it hard.

I have too much going on right now to let someone in.

Too many things to fix. I can't risk losing everything.

I wake up to my phone ringing and my head pounding from the amount of scotch I drank last night after not being able to get Cameron out of my damn head.

"This is a collect call from La Santé Prison. Press one to accept the charges for this call."

I press one and sigh at the sound of my brother's voice. "Bastian."

"Matías."

"It's good to hear your voice."

I wince. As much as I am happy to hear my brother is still alive, the pain of knowing I can only hear him speak to me from jail pierces my soul.

"Winford told me about the article," he says into the phone, referring to his lawyer.

I rub my palm into my eye. I don't want him dealing with this. "It's been taken care of."

"Bas, I didn't mean for all this to happen."

"No shit, Matías. Do you really think I am so dumb that I think you would want to be in fucking prison?"

He sighs. "I screwed up. I trusted the wrong people."

"I'm well aware," I growl into the phone. "But I don't need to hear another damn apology from you. I'm working on things on my end. Winford is working on every legal way of getting you out that he can. But until then you need to keep your damn mouth shut."

"Wait, you think I had something to do with that article?"

My brother takes bribes far too easy and his lips are loose enough to sink ships. "I find it strange that you were given more freedom in your block just last week and then suddenly an article that could damn us all hits the press."

"How do you know—"

"Damnit, Matías!" I yell. "Do you not think I don't talk to Winford? My lawyer. The one I am handing hundreds of thousands of dollars to in order to try and save your ungrateful ass." I get out of bed and start pacing my bedroom. "You fucked up. You started making deals with the wrong people. You let them take advantage—"

"Those people were your business partners!"

"Former business partners, Matías. Thiago and I told you years ago to stay away from them. But once again you didn't listen to me. And now you're in fucking prison awaiting trial for charges of sex trafficking and money laundering. Don't even get me started on the drug charges. You cast a shadow on the Montford name more so than Thiago or I ever did. And now I am picking up the pieces, trying to recover as many assets as I can so that the entire corporation doesn't fold. Not just the hotel group but everything. And if I can't fix this." I take a deep breath. "If I can't fix this, you won't be the only one in prison."

"Bastian…"

"For once in your life, listen to me. Please. I can't make this go away without it."

I can hear the defeat in his voice. "It's hard here."

"I know."

"The temptation—"

"Act like an adult, Matías. Act like Thiago. We both know he was the better one of us all."

I hang up the phone before I let him speak. It's the same conversation over and over again. Maybe I should have sent him to rehab when I knew his habit started to get bad. But my father intervened. He said it would look bad for the Montford name if Matías went to rehab. He said we finally recovered from our name being dragged through the mud after Thiago's death. He thought Matías was smart enough.

He wasn't.

I walk onto my balcony breathing in the salty air. It's not the same as the home I love. This air feels tarnished by wealth and deceit. This town full of people willing to do anything for fame and fortune.

I close my eyes and hear Cameron's voice. At first I think it's in my head but I open my eyes to see her on her balcony singing along to the music playing from her phone.

I watch as she dances around. Carefree. Wild.

This woman who has no business being dragged into my world.

But for some reason I want her.

One taste wasn't enough.

I need more. I need to feel her body wrapped in

mine. Feel her heat as I pulse into her. Feel her nails scratching my back as I overtake her in the worst ways.

But I know I can't have her.

The one taste I had is all I am allowed.

She is too good for my world.

And I will only destroy her.

18

CAM

After I cooled things off with the last article that went up attacking the Montford family, the press has been strangely quiet. The team's been working around the clock with marketing to get the campaign launched next week. And the timing couldn't be more perfect. Yesterday the gaming commission agreed to let the casino reopen. The only requirements were a new floor manager and a rigorous screening of all employees. HR had already fired the last floor manager and had one waiting in the wings for the reopening approval. They started the employee screenings yesterday and if all goes as planned the casino can reopen in a month.

This will go smoothly with our plans for rebranding. The new marketing campaign is set to launch in two weeks. And if I can get my way on things, we can have a gala the night of the reopening of the casino. The sales team predicts a fifty percent uplift in bookings with the casino reopening. That with the rebrand and the gala, I think the hotel could be one-hundred-percent booked that weekend.

I make a few phone calls for event planners to meet with me. Just as I am hanging up the phone, Parker walks in. His arms folded across his chest as he leans in the doorway, a look of amusement on his face.

"You know he doesn't do galas."

"How do you know I am planning anything?"

He walks into the room and takes a seat across from me. "I heard you say gala."

I shrug. "Well, I am doing this anyway. It's what the company needs. We can call it a launch party."

"He won't be happy."

I raise a brow. "When is he happy?"

Parker snorts and I know he agrees with me. And right now, I know Bastian cannot be happy. He disappeared, well, went on a business trip to Spain. He didn't take Parker with him, so I know he is in a mood. I can only guess it has to do with the article that came out last week. The man seemed broken when he came to my office that night. But like usual, he didn't say anything to give me any sort of insight into his mood.

"I wouldn't be surprised if he fired you."

"Is this what got the others fired?" I ask. I've been here over a month and despite all of Bastian's threats, he still hasn't fired me. But I wonder if this may be my final straw.

Parker hesitates. "One. Yes."

"And the others?"

"One made no progress in a week."

"Well, I am well past that," I say smugly. "And the third?"

"Tried to sleep with him." Parker throws a curious look my way.

I bite back a smart remark. I think that will only make things worse. I have a feeling Parker knows more than he is letting on. That he knows Bastian and I shared a kiss. "Another thing I don't need to worry about."

"I don't think you should do it."

My computer chimes with an email and I look away from Parker to see that another event planner responded to my request. "I'm doing this. Whether he likes it or not. Just don't go telling him until I have a more developed plan."

"It's my job to tell him."

"And it's my job to turn the image of this company around. A launch party will do just that."

"Gala or party, he won't be happy."

I look back up at him. "Well, maybe you should go visit him on vacation and tell him my plans then."

"He isn't on vacation. He's working."

"On an island in Spain!" I shout. "He couldn't handle whatever the hell was going on here so he took a break."

"He has a house there. I assure you he is working."

"Then why aren't you there?"

Parker shifts in his seat. "No one is allowed there. He works in solitude. I don't even think his CFO has been there."

Interesting. "Well, I'm going through with my plans. It's the best thing for this hotel."

"You need to stop pushing his buttons, Cam."

"I'm beginning to think he likes it."

Parker laughs. "So am I and that's why I am worried. Not just for you but for him."

My phone rings and I place my hand on the receiver. "I am doing this, Parker. I don't care what he says."

I smile as I hit send on the email. It might be a bit of an evil smile but either way, I'm smiling.

I almost want to bet with myself how long it will take for him to call. I can already hear the growl in his voice. The thought alone makes me clench my thighs. Not the reaction I wanted to have.

But I wait for nearly four hours with no response.

I sit on my balcony sipping on a martini, staring at my phone, yet he still hasn't responded.

I crack my knuckles to keep myself from picking up the phone and calling him myself.

There is no way he could be fine with my plans for the launch party as I called it in the proposal.

He despises them as much as he despises Saint Tropez.

So why isn't he calling?

By the time I make it into the office the next day, I am tired and slightly hungover. I drank way too many martinis last night, waiting for his call. Then barely slept in anticipation. I don't know why I am so excited to hear from him. Maybe because last time he got mad at me, he kissed me.

And now I feel my chest getting red and my core melting as I daydream about the kiss.

I am startled when I see something drop on my desk in front of me. I look up to see Parker standing there, not amused.

"You sent him a proposal?"

I shrug.

"I had to listen to him go off about you for nearly two hours last night. I thought he was going to fire me for not stopping you from moving forward with it."

"Well, it looks like you still have a job," I respond as I gesture to the tablet that is permanently stuck in his hand.

"And somehow you do too. At least for the next few hours."

"Huh?"

He points to the desk and that's when I see what he dropped on it. A plane ticket to Mallorca. "What's this?" I ask.

"He wants to see you."

"Why the hell would he pay for me to fly out to Mallorca if he is just going to fire me?"

"Hell if I know, Cam. But he insisted I book you a flight to Mallorca as soon as possible. He threatened my job and told me not to ask questions. He also said to pack a bag." He starts to leave but turns around. "You may want to say goodbye to your family because I am not sure if he is going to murder you or not."

I laugh out loud at that. Mostly because I half believe him.

I yawn as I walk up the steps to the gorgeous house sitting on top of a cliff. I had to take two flights to get here. Bastian didn't even have a car waiting for me. Parker's instructions said I needed to grab my own taxi. Maybe Bastian really doesn't let anyone here. Not even his bodyguard.

The driveway doesn't go all the way up to the house, so I am forced to walk up the side of the mountain on brick and cobblestone steps. I am half tempted to open my suitcase I am lugging behind me and take my gym shoes out but I decide to huff up the stairs in my heels. I can only guess he wants to torture me as much as he wants before firing me.

I clear a bend in the winding staircase and nearly stumble backward at the view. The house overlooks the Mediterranean. The water more turquoise than in France. His house is nestled between taller mountains so he has views of land and sea. Breathtaking views. The sun is starting its descent and the sky is filled with rays of pink, orange, and yellow.

I make my way up the last set of steps and nearly collapse as I set my suitcase down. I also happen to notice a service drive off the back side of the house and curse at Bastian for giving me an address at the bottom of the hill.

I make my way to the front door and a shorter woman dressed in black slacks and a black shirt opens the door. "Bienvenido dona guapa." I smile at her as she gestures for me to walk in. "T'emportaré la maleta."

I might know French but I don't know a lick of Spanish. Do they even speak Spanish here? Or is it Catalan?

"La maleta," she says again as she points to my bag. I let it go and she smiles at me. "Ho sento, my English no és bó."

I smile and nod because I have no idea what she is saying. She takes my suitcase and walks away, leaving me standing in the foyer of this grand house confused.

"Ms. Wilder," the voice of a young woman with a strong Spanish accent says from behind me. I turn and find another woman, this one much younger than the other but dressed in the same uniform, walking toward me. "I'm so sorry I wasn't here to greet you. I didn't hear a car on the drive. My mama let me know you were here."

"Uh, my driver let me out at the circular drive near the bottom of the hill. I walked up."

She rolls her eyes and curses in her language. "I wish I had emailed you the directions. Mr. Montford is a pain in the ass sometimes when it comes to letting people be dropped off all the way up here. Says the taxis don't want to drive the winding road. I am so sorry you had to climb all those steps with your bag." She looks down at my feet. "And in those heels."

"It's not a problem. A little exercise never hurt anyone."

She smiles. "I'm Lucia, by the way. My mother whom you met earlier is Marta. Anything you need while you are here, we can assist you with. Now let me bring you outside to the terrace. I believe Mr. Montford is still swimming. You are earlier than he expected."

She walks me through the house. I take it all in. The architecture has an old-world charm, something I never would expect from Bastian. We walk through the kitchen that has a wall of French doors along the entire side that are open to the terrace beyond. A large infinity pool sits on the edge of the cliffside. And the views I saw walking up the steps to the house are even more incredible here. One hundred and eighty-degree views of the mountains and the sea. No other houses in sight. A sense of calm rushes over me immediately.

I turn to thank Lucia but she has already returned to the house.

I walk to the edge of the pool and watch Bastian swim through the water. He hasn't seen me yet, so I focus my eyes on the sea, watching the boats in the water.

I jump when I hear water splash near my feet. I look down to see Bastian climbing out of the pool.

I try to focus my eyes on his but I can't help but look down at the water dripping down his golden olive skin, rivulets lining the outline of his very defined abs.

I go to speak but then he emerges even farther and I realize he is completely nude.

And I cannot tear my eyes away from his dick. It's so large and thick and—

"Ms. Wilder, has no one ever taught you it's rude to stare?"

My eyes snap up to Bastian as he stands in front of me. Water dripping from his wet hair as it frames his handsome face. "I—uh… I was just—"

He laughs as he walks past me. "Dinner is in thirty

minutes. We can discuss your inability to follow rules then."

With that, he walks inside without another word. But I don't miss the sight of his perfect ass just before he wraps a towel around his waist.

I press my hands down the front of the dress I changed into for dinner. My clothes smelled of airplane and sweat. I had just enough time to jump into the shower and rinse off the stench of stale airports.

I walk over to the French doors that lead to a Juliette balcony in my room. The view of the Serra de Tramuntana mountains, a welcome sight. The rocky peaks peppered with greenery and the view of the aquamarine waters just beyond.

I glance at the clock and make my way to the dining room. He isn't here yet so I make myself a martini at the bar cart in the corner. I take a deep breath since I am one-hundred-percent positive Bastian flew me out here to fire me. He probably wanted to see the look on my face but I won't give it to him. I will remain stoic. I will show him I am stronger than he thinks. I'm a fighter, strong-willed, po—

"Ms. Wilder, thank you for joining me for dinner."

I jump at the sound of his voice, nearly spilling my drink. I turn and face him, a sly smile spreading over my face. "Seems to me it would have been much cheaper to ask me to join you for dinner in Saint Tropez. Or is this our thing? Dinners in other countries."

The hint of a smirk hits his face as he approaches me. His hand brushes against my arm as he reaches for his signature scotch at the bar. "Oh Ms. Wilder, I believe we could have much better *things* than dinners in other countries."

His voice is laced with something deep and raw, sending a chill down my spine and an unwanted ache between my thighs.

I go to snap a remark back to him but we are interrupted by Lucia carrying two salads. "Mr. Montford, Ms. Wilder. Emil said your main course will be ready soon. I thought you would already be seated. Ho sento."

"No need to apologize, Lucia. I received a phone call I needed to take. I was late." He gestures to the two place settings on the table. "Please set them down and we will be seated."

I watch his kindness to his staff as the salads are set down and he whispers something to Lucia. She smiles at him and walks away.

He turns to catch me staring at him.

"Please take a seat, Ms. Wilder."

I sit at the longer side of the table since I figure Bastian sits at the head every night. We eat our salads in silence. My thoughts still racing at all the meanings he could have had with that sentence.

Things.

The way he said it. The innuendo coated in his words.

Surely, he didn't fly me here to have sex with me.

I know that can't be true. He has a strict no-fraternization policy.

"A penny for your thoughts?"

"I don't think you have much use for a penny."

He shrugs. "I am sure I could turn it into something worthwhile."

"I'm sure you could."

Lucia walks back in with two more plates, her mother trailing behind her. Marta gathers our salad plates as Lucia sets our dinner in front of us. She quickly moves to grab a bottle of wine from the bar and pour it into the wine glasses on the table.

The food in front of me smells incredible. White fish sits atop a bed of seasoned dark rice. A buttery sauce dripping over the top.

"Fresh-caught fish from the market today," Bastian says to me.

I nod as I take a bite of the delicate fish, the flavors melting into my mouth exquisitely. I sip the cold white wine Lucia poured us and revel in the crispness of the flavor, a perfect complement to the fish.

"So what was on your mind, Ms. Wilder?"

I swallow another bite of fish before I answer. Wanting one more taste of the delicacy before a fight is sure to happen.

"Why did you fly me all the way out here if you are just going to fire me?" I ask as I set my fork down.

"I'm not firing you."

I'm startled with confusion. "So you are going to let me have the party?"

"No," he says sternly before taking another bite of his dinner.

"Then why am I here?" My tone slightly bitter.

"So I can tell you to cancel the damn party you are planning and make sure you actually do it."

"You could have had Parker do that," I bite back.

He slams his hand onto the table, making me jump. "And you wouldn't have listened," he snarls.

"I listen just fine. I just choose to ignore stupid opinions when they don't make sense. This gala will be the biggest thing for the hotel. A launch party at the same time the casino reopens, you can announce the hotel expansion. It's a no-brainer.

"Bookings are already increasing. The new branding tease is enough to entice the wealthy. I don't need the stupid, foolish temper tantrums you are throwing because you don't like going to parties."

"Stop." His voice quiet, stern.

"Is that what it is? You just don't want to go to a party? You don't have to go. It would be better if you made an appearance. But with your attitude maybe it might be better if you didn't—"

"Enough," he growls.

I jump at his anger. I can see it written across his face. The way the vein in his neck is pulsing. The way his eyes beat into mine.

Lucia walks in to refill our wine and he dismisses her, her mother, and the chef for the evening. She gives me a tight smile as she walks out.

I stand abruptly, not wanting to deal with him.

"What are you doing?"

"Leaving."

"Sit down," he roars.

I throw my napkin that was in my hand onto the table and move around my chair. "No."

I head to the doorway when I hear his chair scratch across the ground. "Don't you dare leave."

I turn around, my heart rate picking up as anger floods my veins. I am sick of his alpha behavior, his need to control me. He thinks I can't do my job or that I will mess up somewhere along the way. The man needs to learn that's not how I work. I won't succumb to his orders.

I stand tall as I face him. "Why? So you can tell me how you don't agree with my plan? Don't like what I am doing? Did you forget that I saved your ass last week and got that article taken down from every website I could find? Can you just once believe me when I say I know what I'm doing?"

He stalks up to me and his eyes are feral with need. "No."

"No?" I throw my hands in the air, exasperated by this man. "You are unbelievable. No wonder no one wants to work for you and—"

"Shut up."

"Stop cutting me off!"

He steps closer to me. "I told you to stop talking."

I don't know when I stepped closer to him but our chests are nearly touching. I can smell the heady scent of his fragrance. I can feel the need radiating off him. "Make me," I say in defiance.

His hands are around my waist before I even finish saying the words. "Oh I have no problem making you shut your mouth."

His lips are on mine instantly. My entire body melts at his touch, his kiss. But I won't let him do this again. Won't let him use this as a weapon against me.

I pull away. "You think you can just kiss me to make me shut up?"

A crooked smile curls up on his lips. "I can do whatever I want to you Cameron because I know deep inside you want me just as much as I want you."

"You're wrong," I lie as I try not to think about the way he said my name.

"Am I?" His knuckles brush against my arm.

"Yes."

He steps closer to me, his fingertips trailing down my thigh, leaving fire in their wake. "If I were to slide my hand under your dress, I wouldn't find you wet for me?"

I swallow and hold my pride. "No."

Bastian throws his head back and laughs before gripping the back of my neck, his lips grazing my ear. "You'll show me just how much you want me one of these days. And when you do, you will be begging me to touch you, begging me to feel your wetness, begging me to let you come. And I promise the second you let me fuck you, I'll ruin you for all other men."

He lets go of me abruptly and watches me as I take a step back. Then another. My cheeks are red and my heart is beating fast. Those words ignited something in me but I know if I touch the flame, it will only burn me.

I pull myself together. A smile as sly as his own crosses my face. "We'll see about that, *Bastian*."

I grin from ear to ear as I walk back to my room. The look on his face when I defied him yet again. And I know me calling him Bastian does something to him. I saw the light in his eyes flash then darken at my words.

I take off my dress and slip on an oversized T-shirt. I stare out the window as I lie in bed. The soft breeze fluttering the curtains and making its way over to me trying to clear my mind but his words keep filtering through my head. I would beg for him because I know that every word he spoke was true. If I were to sleep with him no one would compare to him before or after. He *would* ruin me for every man. That is a fact I am sure of.

But maybe it would be worth it.

To feel his lips on mine. To feel his lips on every part of my body.

To submit to the man, I defy more than anyone.

The thoughts leave me aching and wanting.

Cursing my decision to walk out of that room.

My body is telling me I should have stayed just for the purpose of fulfilling a need.

But my head is telling me I made the right decision.

But isn't that why I came here? The memory of his lips on mine. The desperate need we both shared that sparked from our anger.

I am lying to myself if I say I don't want it.

I slide my hand down my body as the ache grows. My fingers sliding through my center that's been wet since that kiss.

Thoughts of Bastian infiltrate my mind and that's the only place I can have him.

19

CAM

I spend most of the next day working. I haven't seen Bastian all day. Lucia let me know he was working in his office and on some days, he doesn't leave until his nightly swim.

I sip on a glass of iced tea as I stare at the pool. Memories of him in the nude causing an unwanted feeling of need.

I close my eyes and curl into the rattan sofa I'm sitting on. My legs are tucked under me as I bask in the warmth of the sun on my skin.

Being in Mallorca is so different than Saint Tropez. At least from this house on the mountain. It's serene, quiet. Almost centering in a way. I can forget about everything else around me and focus on work. I'm not concerned about the unanswered calls to my sister. Or the emails piling up from my mother. I can do what I want to do for myself here. Be my own person. Not the one my family expects of me.

I set my glass down on the table next to me and rest my head against the back of the couch and start to doze off.

"Cameron."

I startle awake at the sound of my name and find Bastian standing in front of me. If I wasn't so tired, I would roll my eyes. But it wasn't until I sat down here that I realized how exhausted I've been from working so hard. And not just over the last month but the last two years.

I go to stand up, but Bastian puts his hand in front of me before sitting next to me. I groan as I move out of the uncomfortable position, I fell asleep in and turn to face him.

His features are soft. Not the man I am used to. He looks more like the man I walked through the park with in London.

"I want to apologize."

I shake my head. "Don't. It only makes it worse."

His hand stretches toward me like he wants to touch me but he pulls it back. "No. I was being irrational. I wasn't thinking straight because of my history with galas. I took it out on you instead of dealing with my own personal issues with them."

"I don't need to do it. I haven't signed any contracts with the planners. I will find a different way—"

He holds up his hand to cut me off. "Sign the contract. I'll figure out how to deal with my own shit."

I raise a brow at him. "Are you telling me to plan the gala?"

"I thought it was a launch party."

A smile breaks across my face. "It is."

He smiles back at me, and I'm once again taken aback at how gorgeous he is when he doesn't have that serious face. He looks younger, less shaken down by the problems of his world. "Just keep me in the loop."

"Are you feeling okay?" I joke.

He shifts in his seat. "Why do you ask?"

"You are actually agreeing with me."

He shakes his head at me. "Cameron, I agree with you more than you think I do."

I blink a few times at his statement as every argument filters through my head and realize he is speaking the truth.

"I don't know if I will attend the gala. As I said before, they aren't my thing but move forward with it. I think it will be good for the hotel and the expansion."

I bite my lip and fight the urge to touch him. But the urge wins as I lay a hand down on his arm. "Why do you hate them so much?"

He sighs and closes his eyes. His own hand resting on my calf, his thumb drawing lazy circles on my skin, and I try not to be affected by it, by his touch, by the urges I feel whenever he is close to me.

"Personal reasons."

"What kind of personal reasons?"

His hand freezes on my leg and he looks at it like he didn't even realize he was touching me. "I need to go into town to meet a friend for dinner. Emil will make you whatever you want for dinner, just let Lucia know."

He stands abruptly and turns to walk away but stops and stands in front of me. "There is something about you, Cameron. Something I can't put my finger on. But you make me want to think differently. Do things differently. Be a better man. Don't lose your touch."

He bends down and presses a chaste kiss to my forehead before taking his leave.

I sit there with my mouth agape completely taken aback by his words.

———

The second Bastian leaves, I get to work on the party. I am days behind in signing contracts and planning. By the time I close my laptop due to eyestrain, I realize the sun has set, and the temperature has dropped.

I throw on a light cardigan and pad my way into the kitchen, looking for something to eat. I find some meats and cheese and decide to make a sandwich. I close the refrigerator door and jump when I see Lucia on the other side.

"I didn't mean to startle you," she says, putting her hands in front of her. "But I hadn't heard from you in hours and then I heard someone in here and thought it may be you. I can have Emil make you something."

I shake my head. "It's late."

She laughs as she grabs the food out of my hand. "This is Spanish culture. We eat late and party even later. Trust me, he will be fine making you something."

I nod toward the food in her hands. "I promise that is more than enough." I look around the kitchen but don't see a wine rack or a bar. "I could use a drink though."

"Of course. I'll bring this to Emil—"

"I don't want to bother him."

She clicks her tongue at me. "I bother him enough. He won't mind. Give me a few minutes."

I wander around the kitchen and through the open arch doorways. The terrace is lit with warm white and soft pink lights, almost like a reflection of the sun when it sets. A cool breeze crests my skin as I walk to the edge of the pool and dip my foot in the water and find it warm.

No wonder Bastian takes late-night swims.

Lucia walks out with a martini glass in her hand.

I meet her halfway.

"I saw you drinking a martini last night. Wasn't sure if you like vodka or gin. But you are American, so I chose vodka."

I laugh. "I'll drink either but I prefer vodka. You didn't need to make me this. I would have made it if you brought the vodka."

"It's my job." She gestures toward the pool. "I know Mr. Montford had you come here last minute. We have extra bathing suits if you need one."

I smile at her. "I would appreciate it actually. The water feels nice."

She looks around then says quietly, "I swim in it when Mr. Montford isn't here."

I laugh out loud and soon she joins me. "I wish I could see the look on his face if he caught you."

She smiles. "I am sure he wouldn't mind. He treats my family so well. He—"

"Mi amor?"

Lucia blushes and heads inside. I follow close behind.

"Ahh, our beautiful guest," the man I am guessing is Emil says in a thick Spanish accent. "A pleasure to meet you finally. I apologize that I have been busy. Please take a seat. I made you a sandwich."

"Thank you. And the pleasure is all mine. That dinner you cooked last night was delicious."

His hand goes to his chest. "Thank you, beautiful. But I have a busy day tomorrow. Enjoy your dinner."

"Is that your husband?" I ask Lucia as I sit down at the massive island where Emil left the sandwich.

She shakes her head. "No. He's, well… umm." She bites her lip and I can't help but laugh.

"Just a friend or do you get the benefits too?"

Her tan cheeks flame with color. "Uh…"

"Please, I won't tell anyone." I nod toward where he left. "He is quite handsome."

She nods. "I've had a crush on him since we were ten. Mi madre's best friends' son."

"So why aren't you two officially dating?" I ask.

She shrugs. "He was always popular. Played fútbol. Had the attention of all the girls. I was just a nerd with my nose in a book."

"He called you his amor."

She looks down at her feet. "He always says that. It doesn't mean anything."

From the look on her face and her inability to make eye contact with me, I know there is so much more there than she is letting on. "What do you like to drink?"

She startles at my question. "Perdón?"

I tap the stool next to me. "Come sit. We are probably the same age. Sounds like it's time for a girls' night."

She looks back out toward the front door like she is worried she may get in trouble.

"Oh come on. Bastian can suck a dick. You already told me you swim in the pool. Have a drink with me. If he gets mad, I'll let him take it out on me." I wink at her and she takes a few seconds before sighing and settling down next to me.

"So what will you have? I'll make it."

She grins from ear to ear. "I'll have what you're having. But make mine with gin."

And that's how I spend the rest of the night. Getting drunk with Lucia. She spills all her secrets of Emil, the boy she's loved for seventeen years but he only uses her for sex. And I let my secrets spill about Bastian.

Where I would normally be worried that I am saying things I shouldn't she lets me know that Bastian wouldn't care. She tells me how this place is his home, where he can be himself. Her grandmother was friends with his grandmother and he has always taken care of her family. But her mother and she never wanted a handout, so they chose to work. They are caretakers of this house. She said she once moved to Paris for a few months to try working for Montford Holdings when he offered her a position, but she missed Mallorca. Missed the hometown feel of Deià.

By the time I drunkenly stumble into my room, I remember I haven't seen Bastian since he left earlier. My drunken head trying to make a mental note to talk to him tomorrow about going back to Saint Tropez. To finish the job I was contracted for.

But as I collapse onto the bed, the cool, salty air floating across my skin, I think maybe a few more nights in this paradise may do me some good.

20

BASTIAN

I jump off the boat that brought me out to Ibiza. I crack my neck as I straighten my jacket and brush my hand through my windblown hair.

Lucas walks behind me as we walk up the steps of the pier and into the bustling town. We walk through crowds of party goers and vacationers, the lights and sounds of the island causing my eye to twitch. I have never liked party towns. They are loud and boisterous. I prefer the serene calm of my home in Deià.

We make our way down a dark cobblestone alley to a small Spanish restaurant. I open the turquoise door and am greeted by the wafting smell of spices and seafood.

"Mr. M," the man by the front door greets me. "Pleasure to have you here. Your guest is in the back dining room. Would you like me to walk you back there?"

I hold up a hand. "No need, Felipe."

He nods at me then looks at Lucas before turning back toward the table of diners he was talking to.

This place is a hidden gem. Not many tourists know of the place. Mostly just locals. And people like me. People who come here to do business but don't want to be seen.

Lucas pushes past me as we walk up to the yellow curtain blocking the hallway to the back dining room. His hand goes to the piece I know he has strapped to his side.

We head down the narrow hall to a black door. He knocks twice, then once and it opens.

"Ahh, Bastian. I am so happy you made it."

I scowl at the man in front of me. He's no better than me. A businessman, a criminal. But where I took the higher road years ago, he dove deeper into the sewers of crime. Using drug lords, guerrillas, and the black market to build his business. A business that tempted my brother too much.

His security guard approaches me, and I let him pat me down. Only security can have weapons in this room. A strange rule Felipe has always enforced.

Weapons aren't needed to destroy a man in this room.

"Charles," I say as I take a seat across the table from him.

"Oh come on Bas, we are old friends. You know I am still Charlie to you and your family."

I stare at him. My face indifferent despite the rage flowing through me as I look at the rotund man in front of me. I met him nearly fifteen years ago. A friend of Kilian's brother. He tempted us both with money and power. And I fell into his trap. Thirsted for the greed that

I already had sitting and waiting on a silver platter for me from my father. But Charles offered me more. Showed me the strength of influence. I was young and naïve. Hungry for the power. My foolish mind thought my father was not maximizing our wealth. I recruited my older brother who fell deeper into the darkness than I did.

We made poor decisions. Bad decisions. We ruined our family.

But I sold my soul to get out.

A price I am still paying for.

And I never thought Matías would learn of this world. He is ten years younger than me. He was just a kid when I fell deep into the world and a kid when I got out of it. But his naiveté was worse than mine. And he was tempted by far greater things than wealth and power. His need for drugs and sex tore him apart. Led him to make terrible choices. Led him to the mess he is in now.

"What do you know?"

Charles grins at me before knocking his knuckles on the table. "Oh Bas. We may be old friends but you know information never comes that easy."

I grit my teeth. "You asked me to come here."

"That I did. But you know there is always a cost for information."

"How much?"

He smiles at me again, a diabolical grin that would scare even the worst criminals. "Hmm, let's see. What do you have that I want?" he asks while tapping his finger against his chin.

"I'm not bartering property or assets with you, Charles. Ten million dollars."

He leans forward on the table, resting his elbows and palms flat across it. The gold and diamonds on his chubby fingers reflecting off the dim lighting in the room. "Twenty million."

"That's a lot of money for information I don't even know will help me."

"That's for the silence, I won't let The Partners know you are back in the game."

I shake my head. "I am not in the game."

He shrugs. "Then twenty million dollars."

My eyes flash to Lucas and he nods at me. "Fine."

Charles leans back in his chair and grabs a file from the table behind him. "Your brother made a deal with Harris."

"Harris?" I ask in surprise. "I thought he was dead."

Charles smirks at me. "To everyone on the outside he is."

I nod at him to continue.

"Matías wasn't making the payments he owed him. So Harris had the hotel raided."

"Payments for what?"

Charles points to the file in front of me. "Why don't you find out for yourself?"

I grab the file and open it, my eyes falling shut at the pictures in front of me. I don't need to see much to understand. I throw the file back on the table and pinch my fingers between my eyes.

"The real question here is how did he meet Harris?" Charles says.

My eyes snap up to him. "It wasn't you?"

He shakes his head. "Bas, despite the downfall we had when you paid your way out, I would never want to cause harm to your family. Not after..." His silence speaks volumes because although it's never been proven or spoken, we both know he had something to do with Thiago's death. "You've paid your dues. You are still paying them. I would never introduce Matías to Harris. But Harris got to him somehow. Went against the agreements that were made when you walked out."

"Kilian," I whisper. My fist clenching under the table. He's made hints about it since the raid. But I never thought he would do this to my brother.

"I don't think it was Mr. Bancroft. He cares about you too much to destroy you."

"Then who—"

I'm cut off by Charles pushing another file in front of me.

"Davenport?" I say in shock. I see Lucas stiffen from the corner of my eye. "He... how was I not informed that he joined The Partners. Our agreement stated—"

"Your agreement stated anyone showing interest in The Partners after you left." Charles' finger lands on the former Montford Hotels CFOs picture. "He was already in it."

"How?"

"Some people pay a lot of money to keep their identities hidden."

"Fuck."

"We can take care of this."

"I am not making another deal."

187

"You can't fix this on your own."

I glare at him. "I can damn well try."

Charles folds his arms over his chest, that smile back on his face. "Davenport is in too deep. You can't fix this. Your brother was an easy target, Bas. Think about it. Why would they do this? What could they possibly want?"

I know the answer is me. I got out. I built my business the way I always should have. They didn't like it. My ties to the criminal world were never severed though. I am still a puppet in their game. I knew they never fully let me go.

"I'll see what they want to do."

I nod. Thoughts churning in my head, looking for some way to get out of this. "We'll be in touch then," I say as I stand from my chair.

"One last thing, Bastian."

I turn to face the man who very well may end my life, just like Thiago's. "That girl you have working for you."

I freeze. "What girl?"

"The pretty one with the blonde hair. The American."

I tense. There is no way she will be dragged into this. "She's my publicist."

"Then you better tell her that should be her only job."

"What do you mean?"

He leans forward, resting his folded hands on the table. "She's been digging. Looking for things in your life. I would suggest you tell her to stop. Unless you want her to end up like Thiago."

It takes everything inside of me not to strangle this man. The one who tore my world apart. Who is still tearing me apart. I won't let him ruin another person. Another family.

"I'll handle her. If she digs. She's fired."

He flattens his mouth, a look of disbelief on his face.

"She won't be an issue," I say with promise in my voice.

"Good."

With that, I storm out of the restaurant. I'm silent as we make our way back to the pier. My insides fuming. My anger over my brother and his stupidity. The fury that I got myself into a mess I know I can never walk away from. I wasn't lying when I said I made a deal with the devil just like Matías did. But I can get him out. My soul is forever indebted to the devil.

My mind flashes with an image of Cameron. The girl who I can't keep out of my head. The one who I knowingly put in danger.

I should have shut the hotel down when Matías started acting differently. But my greed got the best of me. The thoughts of expansion. The wealth and power I could have from it.

Now I won't just ruin my own life but the life of someone who never should have been involved with this in the first place. I thought she could help fix it all. I planned to use her as a pawn to only help my own need for wealth and power. Now I've put another person I care about in danger.

Cameron. My beautiful, wild Cameron.

I take a detour from the pier and walk into the first bar I come across.

"Boss?" Lucas asks me.

I hold my hand up and shake my head. I order a double shot of whiskey and slam it down then order another and then another.

All I can think about is the picture that was sent to me the night before I brought Cam out here. A picture of us together in London. A red "X" across her face.

Now I know where the threats are from.

I slam down another shot. The anger in my veins boiling.

Lucas stands next to me the whole time. Not saying a word. He understands. He gets it. He lost his entire family to The Partners. It's why I hired him. He swore to protect my own family with his life.

I don't know how much I drink. Or how long I stay.

I just remember Lucas holding me up and telling me we will get through it.

I walk through the doors of my home well past ten in the evening. My body exhausted from the day. After waking up with my clothes on, face down in a bed, and hungover, then spending the entire day creating a plan with Lucas to get out of this mess Matías left us in, there is nothing I want more than to crash in my own bed.

I walk into the kitchen to grab a bottle of water when I hear the soft sounds of movement in the pool. I run my hands through my hair as I walk out onto the terrace and see Cam swimming under the night sky. Her blonde hair floating around her as she does a backstroke. I step into the shadows as I watch her. My dick going hard at seeing her. The perfect curve of her body as it floats on top of the water. But her smile is what gets me. The look of peace on her face as she looks at the splattering of stars above her.

I think about what would happen if I lost her. If I let this evil world take away someone so carefree. I curse myself for getting close to her. For touching her. I can't have her. Especially not after last night. Not when I know that I could destroy her.

My phone vibrates in my pocket. I pull it out and see Kilian's name flash across the screen. The man I need to talk to. The one man that could talk his way out of a deal with the devil himself.

21

CAM

I stare at the stars in the sky as I float in the water. I needed this swim. To clear all the thoughts from my head. Another email from my mother telling me I need to come home. She doesn't get it. I am not here on vacation, hell she doesn't even know I am in Mallorca. She doesn't understand I have a job. That I need to prove I can be just as successful as anyone else in the family.

And after the amount of work I put in today, I feel like I am proving myself. Plans are in place. The Montford name is clearing up. And there is a light at the end of the tunnel. I know I succeeded at my job. I know I did the best work I can do. And the launch party in a few weeks will just prove that I was right the whole time.

But I do need to get back to Saint Tropez. My two days here was enough to bring me back to center, direct me on the right path. But there is so much work I need to get done from the office.

I make a note to tell Bastian I am leaving tomorrow. I

booked a ticket that leaves tomorrow night. I am sure he won't be happy to hear I am leaving, mostly because it wasn't his decision. The thought makes me smile. I love pissing him off.

Hopefully, he will be home tomorrow. He didn't come home today, and I didn't even hear a word from him.

The sound of a voice in the kitchen startles me. Lucia let me know she was going home for the evening a few hours ago. It should just be me in this house.

I flip over in the water and swim to the edge of the pool. I just make out the form of Bastian on the phone before he disappears farther into the house.

Now is as good a time as any to tell him I am leaving. I walk out of the pool and grab my towel off a chair. My wet hair drips down my back and onto the floor of the house as I follow the sound of Bastian's voice to his office.

I go to walk in when I hear him say my name in hushed tones to whomever he is speaking to. Something about protection and murder and something else I can't quite make out. I stand in the hallway trying to pick up anything else I can from the conversation but I hear him end the call abruptly, his fist slamming on his desk.

I take a deep breath and walk into his office. His back is facing me as he gazes out the window. "You're home."

He turns around quickly. "Cameron."

"I just wanted to let you know that I booked a flight back to France for tomorrow."

"Why?"

"Because I have work to do."

He crosses his arms over his chest. "You can work from here."

"But I can get more done in the office where my team is."

"I think it's best you stay here."

I raise a brow at him. "Well, I think it's best I go back to the office."

"No."

I throw my hands up in the air causing my towel to slip but I catch it before it falls off. "I don't think you get to decide whether I stay or go, Bastian."

"Unfortunately, I do."

"Are you kidding me?" I yell to the ceiling as I throw my head back. "You want me to get my work done or not? You want me to fix the image of your hotel? Because while it is nice here and all, it's not conducive to the work environment I need."

"We all need to work around things sometimes, Ms. Wilder."

"Absolutely. You can work around the fact that I am leaving."

He uncrosses his arms and runs his hand through his messy dark hair. "You can't leave."

"Not this again," I say as I roll my eyes. "I am leaving, Bastian. You can't make me stay."

He crosses the room and he's standing in front of me within seconds. "That is where you are wrong, Ms. Wilder. I can make you stay."

I look up at him with defiance. "No, you can't."

"You don't have a choice."

"What do you mean, I don't have a choice? I can make my own decisions."

"I know you can. But I am telling you that you cannot leave here."

"Why?" I yell.

"Because I said so."

"You have to be kidding me."

"I'm not."

I want to punch him. I want to hit him for being an ass. Instead, I grit my teeth. "You're an asshole."

"I know."

For some reason those words set me off and I push my hands into his chest. "Stop being so nonchalant." He doesn't say anything as I push at him. My towel falling to the floor. Water dripping everywhere from my wet suit and wet hair.

His hands grip my wrists and his mouth swipes against my ear. "I'm trying to protect you, Ms. Wilder."

"From who?" I whisper as his hands slide up my arms, then over my shoulders, before gliding down my back, leaving a trail of goose bumps.

"Me," he says against my lips before claiming them as his own. My hands go into his hair of their own free will, pulling hard on the dark tresses as his tongue attacks my mouth.

He pushes me backward until my ass hits the bookshelf against the wall. His mouth leaves a trail of kisses down my throat and my chest. He makes his way to my breast and his teeth pull away the red bikini top. His mouth latches on to my nipple and I groan at the sensation. I push my hips into his, needing the friction. I feel his hardness against my hip as I rub against him.

This time I know I won't stop. I can't stop.

His hands glide up my stomach and grope my chest before he rips away the bikini top. His mouth shifts to my other breast as I grind against him mercilessly. My lips trail up his neck to his ear. "We shouldn't be doing this."

He grunts in response. His mouth suddenly on mine, kissing me hard. His own hips pressing into my own so hard I am trapped between him and the bookshelf behind me. A tease of the pain and pleasure I know this man will cause.

"Cameron," he whispers against my ear before taking the lobe between his teeth and pulling on it. "That's part of the fun." His lips suckle on the spot behind my ear that makes my toes curl. "Breaking the rules."

His tongue glides across my neck as his hands slide down my hips, his fingers lightly grazing my skin, teasing me. "I've fought against this. Fought against having you for the last month." He sucks behind my other ear, causing me to shiver with need. "Every time I saw you, spoke with you, argued with you. I wanted you."

His mouth moves back to mine, a punishing kiss that has me pulling his body even harder into my own. He pulls back, sucking on my bottom lip as his gaze meets mine. "I've wanted to fuck you a thousand times. And I am not going to hold myself back anymore."

His hand grips my wet hair, wrapping it around his fist, holding my gaze while the other plays with the bottom of my bikini. "I'm taking you for my own. And every fantasy I ever had of you is going to come true. I wasn't lying when I said I would ruin you for other men. But I am giving you the option. Walk away now or I am going to rip these bottoms off you and lean you over my desk and fuck you until the sun rises."

With those words, he slides one thick finger inside of me. My slickness making it easy. My need apparent as he pulls his hand away slowly before driving it back in quickly.

I know what the right decision is. I know I should walk away. Protect myself from this devastatingly handsome man. But I've never been one to make the right decision.

I open my eyes and find him staring into mine. "Ruin me."

The growl that comes out of his mouth is animalistic as he rips my bottoms off me and tosses them to the floor. He lifts me up and wraps my legs around his waist, the feel of his thick, hard cock beats against my already pulsing core.

My lips find his as he walks us over to his desk, my hands scratching down his shoulders as I become an animal myself, wanton and needy.

He pulls away from me after he sets me down and spreads my legs open on his desk. He stares at me with dark hungry eyes. The silver turning a deep gray as I try to read the indescribable need written across his face. I go to reach for him but he shakes his head.

I watch as he devours me with his eyes. Me completely in the nude, him fully dressed as he watches me. My core pulses with need and I have the urge to touch myself because I need the friction and because I know it will piss him off.

"You are magnificent, Cameron. Perfection. I could keep you spread like this on my desk all day. Like a piece of art. Waiting for me to admire it."

"You could be doing a lot more things than just admiring this," I say as I gesture to my body on display for him.

He smiles at me, the one that makes my insides turn to mush. "Mmm. I could but then I would be giving in to what you want."

"And you don't want me?" I tease. "I can tell by the bulge in your pants that you are dying to have me."

"Am I?" he asks as he steps closer to me. He unbuttons his pants, pushing them down just enough to pull out his stiff cock. He grabs my hand and places it over him. "Or are you dying to have me? I can tell by your breath, your touch, that you want nothing more than for me to push myself inside of you. Take you with everything I have until you are screaming my name so loud people on the boats in the harbor will hear you."

I swallow at his words as I pump him. I am dripping for this man. And he has barely touched me.

He steps back and kicks off his pants while he takes off his shirt. "I may want you, Cam. But I am not dying to have you just yet."

I blink at his words. He's almost naked in front of me. What is he waiting for?

"I'm dying to taste you."

He drops to his knees instantly and his mouth is on me before I can even catch my breath. His full lips sucking my clit so hard into his mouth I have to bite down on my lip to hold in my need to scream in pleasure.

His hands push my knees farther apart as he devours me. His tongue sliding into my center while his thumb pushes down on my clit. I grip the edges of the desk as he brings me so close to falling over the edge but he pulls away at the last second.

He looks up at me, a diabolical grin on his face, as I see myself on his lips. "Did you want more?"

I gasp for breath and nod.

"I didn't hear you."

I swallow with need. "Yes," I say on a breath.

"Good."

But instead of his mouth on me, he stands abruptly, pulling me off the desk and flipping me around. Within seconds he has my chest pressed into the hard wood of his desk. He leans over me and I feel his dick press into my back. His hands take mine and he moves them to the edge of the desk.

"You are going to need to hold on," he whispers into my ear.

Before I can even respond, he slams into me. His thick cock almost painful as he takes me hard. His hands grip my hips as he pulls out and presses back in. He shifts my body so my clit rubs against the edge of the desk and within seconds I am screaming his name.

He doesn't hold back after I come. He releases the beast within him, fucking me with a punishing rhythm. I can feel his fingers leaving bruises on my hips as he unleashes his need on me. He leans over me, causing him to go even deeper. One of his hands leaves my hips and glides up my back before wrapping my hair back around his fist. He pulls so my head turns to the side so I can see his face.

"This is better than any fantasy I have ever had of you, Cam. The way your body responds to me, sucks me in. I don't think I will ever get enough of you."

I whimper against the desk as my body starts to tingle with release again. Synapses firing through every limb as I feel my orgasm reach its peak. Bastian must feel it too because he shifts his hips, lifting mine up so my toes barely touch the floor as he drives into me. His hand wraps around my front and presses into my clit and it sets me off.

"Bastian!" I scream so loud I am convinced everyone in this town heard me.

He bites down on my shoulder as I feel him pulse within me. My name a whisper on his lips as he sits seated inside of me.

We stay like that for minutes, maybe hours. When he finally lifts off my body and pulls out of me, I get a chill from the loss of his heat.

I don't move. I don't think I can.

But I hear him moving around. Hear the clinking of his belt and the unmistakable sound of a zipper as he gets dressed.

I close my eyes. My hands still wrapped around the edge of the desk. I don't want to face him. Don't want to have that feeling where I was used and left to fend for myself.

That thing inside of me I thought he awoke wasn't just the unrestrained woman. Maybe he awoke that part deeper inside of me. The one that wants the steamy, reckless sex but with the coddling after.

The need to feel wanted.

I hear his footsteps leave the room without so much as a word toward me. I bite back the tears I am too embarrassed to shed. I slowly unhook my hands from the desk, stiff and rigid from being in the position for so long. I swallow and take a deep breath.

I'm ready to push myself off the desk when his footsteps return. I turn my head and open my eyes to see him walking toward me with the shirt I wear to bed.

His large, soft hands glide up my back and back down again. I nearly jump when I feel the wet towel I dropped on the floor slide between my legs. He hoists me up and turns me around so I am sitting on his desk again but in a much less compromising position.

"Are you okay?"

I look up at him and blink, surprised he has such a calming demeanor to him. "Uh, yeah."

He looks me over then rubs his fingers over my hip bones. I look down to find them marred and red. "You might have some bruises."

I don't know what it is about his behavior but I throw my head back and laugh.

"What's so funny?" he asks as he stands in front of me.

I shake my head. "You… it's just unexpected."

"You look crazy."

I laugh even harder. "Aftereffect of the orgasms."

I look up at him and the cheesiest smile breaks across my face when he gives me that smile that I love.

He rubs his thumb and forefinger along his chin, the handsome smile on his face causing the corner of his eyes to crinkle. "Then maybe we should do that more often."

I throw my arms around his neck and kiss him. I don't have any other thought than that. But this isn't like one of those kisses we shared before. This one is soft, playful.

He pulls away from me and grabs my shirt he set on the desk, pulling it over my head as I slide my arms through it.

"You sure you're okay?"

I nod and jump off the desk.

He presses a swift kiss to my forehead. "I need to get some work done. Someone distracted me."

I smile at him as I pick up my swimsuit off the ground.

I don't think about how he never answered my questions earlier or why he says he needs to protect me from himself.

Instead I walk out of his office, sated, content, carefree.

I walk into my room and fall asleep within minutes. A flush to my cheeks and the biggest smile on my face.

22

CAM

I should have known that when I woke up the next day, it would be like nothing ever happened the night before.

I know Bastian. I know the type of man he is and how those men work.

Lucky for me, I didn't have my hopes up.

I knew this morning would be different.

I figured he would pretend nothing happened the night before despite the bruises on my hips.

But I never expected him to be so cold.

I got up early and answered some emails before heading into the living area of the house. I expected more bickering with Bastian, considering one of those emails this morning was from the airline saying my flight was canceled, and I knew it was him that did it.

But when I walked into the kitchen where Marta was serving breakfast, he completely ignored me. His face buried in his laptop. That scowl that is always on his face prevalent.

I went to walk away, and he slid a piece of paper over to me. I laughed in disbelief when I saw it was a prescription for the morning-after pill. It pissed me off. He didn't even have the audacity to ask me if we were safe. I crumpled up the paper and threw it at him, telling him I was on the pill.

I stormed out of the kitchen and took my coffee and my computer outside.

It wasn't until after lunch that I even talked to anyone. Lucia came out and asked if I wanted to go into town since she knew I'd been cooped up in the house for three days. I agreed even though I had a lot of work to get done. I think she may have also heard from her mother what Bastian did this morning.

Now I am sitting on a pier, drinking cava, and laughing with three of Lucia's friends. It's hard to keep up because only one of them is as fluent in English as she is but I am enjoying myself, nonetheless, forgetting about the morning with Bastian.

"Have you been to the shops?" one of them asks me.

"No. I've been working the whole time I've been here."

Lucia squeals. "Oh my gosh, we have to go shopping. There are some amazing shops here. And from the looks of your work clothes, I know you will love them. Dresses to die for."

"I never say no to shopping." I giggle.

So we spend the rest of the afternoon shopping and

laughing. I'm reminded of my days in New York with Tacoma. The fun we had. The trouble we got into.

I can imagine the trouble we would get into here if she was single. We would be able to write stories about it.

By the time we get back to the house, I feel relaxed and happy. Glad I spent the day doing something other than working.

But when I walk into my room I find Bastian, scowling more than usual. He's also dressed in a pair of gray slacks and a white button-down with the top few buttons open and the sleeves rolled up on his thick forearms. I bite my lip to keep from drooling. I might still be a bit tipsy from the cava we drank.

"Where have you been?" he growls.

I toss my shopping bags on the bed and kick my sandals off. "Out."

I swear I can see smoke coming from his ears at my answer. I snort as I picture the visual in my head and walk to the connected bathroom.

He stops me by grabbing my bicep and pulling me into him. "I told you not to leave."

I look into his eyes and see the storm brewing in them. "I didn't leave. I went to lunch and went shopping. And now I am going to shower." I pull away from him and walk into the bathroom. Not at all surprised when he follows me.

"Make it quick. We are leaving in thirty minutes."

I spin around. "What?"

"I have a dinner to go to."

I purse my lips at him. "Sounds great. Have fun."

I go to turn back around but he grips my hips. "You are coming with."

"Are you asking me?"

"No."

"Well, I would rather stay in."

He pulls me closer to him, and I can smell his cologne. The crispness of juniper and the muskiness of pine. "It's not an option. You need to come with me."

I fake a yawn. "I'm tired."

His hand wraps into my ponytail, tugging my hair back so I am forced to look into his eyes. "You shouldn't have left today without telling me. I'm not leaving you here alone tonight."

The seriousness in his gaze sobers me up. Has me thinking about those words he said last night about protecting me. "Why?"

"Can you just please do as I ask?"

I sigh. I've learned that when he ignores my questions, I better not push him. Although if I did, I know where it would lead and I am completely fine with that outcome as well. But the look in his eyes makes me submit. "Fine."

He lets me go and walks out of my room without another word.

This should be fun.

The ride into Palma is quiet.

I was surprised when I saw Lucas at the house holding the door open of the black SUV. Parker made it sound like no one came here besides Bastian. But I should have known his bodyguard would always be around.

The quiet drive let me take in the sights. When I arrived here the setting sun made it hard to see the mountain drive but since the sun has yet to set, I can enjoy the serenity of Mallorca. At least until we get into Palma. The noise and lights reminding me a bit of Saint Tropez. I am surprised Bastian likes it here.

"This reminds me of Saint Tropez," I say to him.

He runs his hand through his slicked-back hair, the shorter sides in need of a trim. "In a way. It's why I spend my time in the mountains."

"You like the peace. Kind of like the park in London."

He looks over at me, almost in surprise that I remembered something so insignificant.

He doesn't say anything. Just clears his throat and looks out the window.

Ten minutes later we pull up to a hotel I can only guess has a Michelin star restaurant inside. The building looks simple enough. White sandstone and an oversized double wooden door. The outside of the building accented with colored lights. Simple yet mysterious. Unlike the screaming wealth of Montford.

"Who are we meeting?" I ask since I want to play the part right.

"A few investors. A few friends."

I study him and his nonchalant tone trying to figure out what exactly this dinner is about. From what Parker told me and from the hints from Bastian, I know

Mallorca is his safe space. The place he goes to get away. Yet here he is doing business. Maybe it's different since we aren't in Deià but something still feels off.

Lucas opens the door and I grab his hand as he helps me exit the car.

I feel Bastian behind me but he makes no move to touch me, claim me, like last night never happened.

I got lucky that the bite marks and bruises he left along my neck and collarbone faded during the day or else the dress I have on would have revealed far too much.

I bought it today. A simple white silk dress with an asymmetrical hem perfect for a beach. The deep V of the front gives a bit of a tease but the neck wraps around my throat pulling off sophistication. The second I saw it, I knew I had to have it. I didn't think I would wear it so soon but I found it fitting for the night. Enough to tease Bastian. A trick I like to play on his insistence I come with him despite my objection.

I paired the dress with a strappy pair of heels I was grateful I brought with me. A nude heel with a rhinestone ankle strap. It plays well with the diamond bracelet and diamond drop necklace hanging between my cleavage.

As I walk across the cobblestone street a young man opens the large wooden doors and greets us just before we walk in. Bastian passes me, leading the way through the open courtyard filled with lush foliage and greenery.

We reach a small podium and the woman smiles at him as she takes him in. I get this unwanted rage of jealousy wanting to claim Bastian as my own. But after today I am not sure he even remembers last night.

He talks to the waitress in Catalan, leaning his elbows onto the podium. I have no idea what they are saying and can only pick up a few words here and there. A flirtatious grin hits his face but I can tell by his eyes it's a ruse. She laughs with him, and I fight the urge to wrap my arm around his waist.

Instead he stands up and she walks away. He starts to follow her but looks at me first. He reaches out his hand but I refuse to take it and pass him.

The waitress winds us through doors into an enclosed restaurant. I look at the guests and the plates of food in front of them and can tell this place is definitely for the upper echelon of society. She leads us through another door to a secluded outdoor patio. Only a few tables are out here, divided by lattice walls, plants, and mini waterfalls to block out noise.

We must be the first to arrive since the table set for seven is empty. Bastian's hand lands on the small of my back when I stop at the threshold of the secluded dining area. The hostess walks away and Bastian leans into my ear. "Just like before."

I shrug him off me and take a seat near the end of the table. A man walks up to him and I hear Bastian mumble off a drink order before he takes the seat beside me.

"What's wrong?"

I shake my head. "Nothing."

"You've been acting strange."

I slouch into my chair as unladylike as can be. "I'm

tired. I spent the day in the sun and would have preferred to crawl into bed instead of play the part of socialite."

"You know I would never make you play that part."

I see the sincerity in his gaze. The understanding that he remembers our conversation in London as much as I do. "Yet here we are."

He grabs the back of my neck. His soft touch sending chills down my spine. "I wouldn't have brought you here if it wasn't important."

I turn to face him. "What could be so important, Bastian? This is a meeting with people who have nothing to do with me or my job."

His thumb rubs against the sensitive spot behind my ear. "Cam," he sighs. I am slightly taken aback at his use of my name. He's only ever called me Cam once. And that was last night. "I need to make sure you are safe."

My body freezes at those words. Because I am starting to wonder if everything I have found about him is true. If the rumors lead to truths I shouldn't involve myself in. "Safe from what?"

He sighs. His eyes drop to his feet as his grip tightens on my neck. "There are things, I should have—"

"Bastian! So surprised to hear you are in Mallorca!" a man cuts him off.

Bastian's arm drops from me quickly. His demeanor changing in a flash. He introduces me to an old friend of his that grew up here but now lives in Madrid. More people show up including one of his investors Benjamin Cole who shoots me a strange look as I sit at a table full of men.

Maybe I do need protection from him but is it too

late for that? Has he already drawn me into a world I can't get out of?

I treat this dinner like the last. Acting the part. The crazy, loud New Yorker, even letting my Boston accent slip a few times. No signs that anything has transpired between Bastian and me.

And he does the same until a man walks up to the table causing Bastian to stiffen. A man I have never seen before. An older man with dark eyes, rotund and short. A thick British accent. I assume he is just an old acquaintance of Bastian's father, Whitaker. But with the way Bastian's hand goes to my knee under the table and grips it hard, I know that's not the case.

Even as I casually glance over at Benjamin, I see the ghost in his eyes. I glance back to the man who has yet to introduce himself and hold back the shiver of fear I can feel tingling in my spine.

"Why don't you join us for a drink later, Bastian? Catch up on old times," he asks him then nods toward me. "Bring your publicist."

Bastian stiffens and drops his hand from my knee. "I would love to, Charles, but we both need to work early."

"Pity," Charles answers. "I would love to get to know her better."

I fight the urge to glance at Bastian but know it will give something away, although I am not sure what.

When Charles leaves, I look over at Bastian but his face is stoic. He throws back the rest of the scotch in his glass and Benjamin leans over to tell him something. Bastian only nods and soon enough it's like Charles never showed up.

An hour later we are back in the car, Bastian as silent as he was on the way over.

Whatever transpired tonight, I choose not to ask. I can tell by the tick in his jaw and the emptiness in his eyes he doesn't want to talk.

Lucas starts to head back toward the mountains but I notice he turns and heads south rather than north. I go to ask what we are doing but Bastian seems unfazed. So I continue to sit and not ask questions. I am sure he knows the questions will come soon enough.

Lucas stops us in front of a nightclub. Bastian jumping out before I can even ask what's going on. I climb out after him and follow him toward the doorman. At least fifty people are waiting to get in but just a few words and we are being led past the velvet ropes and into the dark club. The music's beat low and loud thumping through my body.

I follow Bastian as he guides us through the crowd and up to a staircase I realize is for VIPs. I climb the steps, watching the crowd below me as I climb. The pulse of the club making me yearn for a few more drinks so I can get lost in the beat of the music.

We walk into a private section surrounded by red velvet curtains pulled back so we can see the crowd below. Only one other man sits in the room and I recognize Benjamin Cole in a heartbeat. He nods to me and I smile back.

Bastian orders us drinks the second the waitress shows up. Benjamin starts talking about business and I listen until I realize how boring the conversation is. Lucas walks into the room and stands in the corner by the door with his arms crossed.

I keep my eyes on the crowd, watching people below us. Flashbacks of my nights in New York City with Tacoma make me smile. I haven't been to a club in a while, work taking up too much of my time. But Tacoma and I sure did know how to party.

By the time I am finished with my second martini, I am bored out of my mind. Bastian and Benjamin are still talking business. One of my favorite songs comes on and I feel the urge to dance. I lean over and let Bastian know I am going downstairs. He eyes me curiously but nods. He nods toward Lucas and I know I am going to have that lug of a man following me. After the cautious eye Bastian had on me tonight, there is no way he would let me wander around a club.

I make my way down the stairs and slide into the crowd of people dancing to the music. Some are drunk and others are on drugs. I let the feeling of the booze I drank flow through me as I sway my hips and get lost in the music.

After a few songs, I make my way to the bar to order another martini. I look around and see Lucas standing nearby against a wall, his eyes on me. I turn back to face the bar, rolling my eyes in the process. I have no idea what Bastian's deal is but I am ready to walk out of here and see how he likes not knowing where I am. The thought sends a wave of goose bumps over my skin because I know how it will make him feel. And I'm not going to disagree to another fight.

"Can I buy you a drink?" someone asks me with an

English lilt.

I turn to my right to see a young blond guy standing next to me. He looks to be around my age. He's handsome with strong features and blinding blue eyes. His tan skin slightly pink across the bridge of his nose, probably from too much sun.

"Sure," I answer, giving him my award-winning flirtatious smile. Okay, it hasn't won any awards but still.

The bartender walks up to us and we both order.

"On vacation?" the stranger asks me.

I shake my head. "I wish. I'm here for work."

"You work at nightclubs?"

I laugh. "No. I am merely here to let loose a bit tonight."

"I like letting loose," he answers. I watch as his hand reaches for my arm I have propped on the bar but the bartender returns and he drops his hand.

"I'm Martin."

"Cam." I take a sip of my drink. "You on vacation?"

He nods. "My mate is getting married in a few weeks. Came out here for his stag."

"Fun."

"So what do you do for work, Cam?"

"PR."

"Sounds about as exciting as my bank job."

I laugh. "Depends on the client."

The music changes and I can't help but move my hips to the beat. "Well, I'm gonna get back out there."

"Care to dance with me?" he asks.

My eyes dart over to Lucas but I can't see him in the crowd anymore. "Sure."

We make our way out to the dance floor and we dance together for a few songs. The music's tempo changes again, slowing down slightly which causes Martin to wrap his arms around me. I glance up toward the VIP area but can't see Bastian. I know he will be pissed if he sees me dancing with another man. He seems to have put his claim on me last night. At least I think he did. He's so hot and cold it's hard to tell.

After a few minutes and no sign of Lucas or Bastian, I relax a little more and scoot closer to Martin. His hands start to grope my body and I try to pull away but he pulls me closer to him. I can smell the alcohol on his breath as he gets even closer. His head drops to my neck, his nose trailing down to my clavicle and I swear he is smelling me. I stiffen at his touch as his hands grab my ass, pulling me into his hips.

I try to push off him again but he won't move.

I start to panic when the smell of citrus and pine floods my senses. The familiar arms of Bastian wrap around me from behind, pulling me away from Martin.

"What the fuck, man?" Martin says when Bastian pulls me away.

"You need to keep your hands off her." I can hear the ice in Bastian's voice.

"She was the one touching me."

Bastian is silent and I know he is just glaring at Martin.

"Whatever, man. Take your little slut. I'll find another one."

Those words set Bastian off. I can feel it in the way his grip loosens on me and the growl comes out of his

217

throat. I spin around, wrapping my arms around his neck before he can punch the asshole in his face. "Don't."

"He deserves it."

I shake my head. "Ignore him. He's just drunk." I use my hand to direct Bastian's gaze back toward mine. "Dance with me."

Bastian nods his head at someone and I can only assume Lucas was with him and is now taking care of Martin. I glance to my left and sure enough see Lucas dragging the guy away. His body relaxes as his arms wrap low around my hips. His body sways with mine to the beat of the music and it surprises me. So much so that I start laughing.

"What's so funny?" his husky voice says into my ear as he pulls me into him.

"You know how to dance."

"I wouldn't call this dancing."

"What would you call it?"

He doesn't say anything as his lips land on my neck. His hands slide down to my ass, pulling me into his hips, grinding his own into mine. "Foreplay."

His lips are on mine and I wish we weren't on this dance floor. This is not the man who ignored me all day. This is a different man. This man reminds me more of the man I spent time with, walking through a park in London. Or the man who devoured me last night.

I wish we were back in his office or maybe his bed with my hands tied down as he worships my body. The languid movement of his tongue creates a slow burn throughout my body, the feeling spreading from my core to the tips of my fingers and toes.

He finally pulls apart from me, his lips swollen and red from my own. I brush my hand over his mouth, wiping away the lipstick staining his lips.

His eyes look behind me and something flashes through his eyes I've never seen before. I try to turn around to see what he's looking at but his lips trail down my neck and up to my other ear. "Put your arms around me. Keep your face buried in my neck."

"Why?"

"Just do it."

His voice is hoarse, demanding. Back to the businessman in the boardroom.

One quick glance at his stormy eyes and I see the empty look he had at dinner when that man interrupted. I do as he asks, my head in his neck. It doesn't take me long to realize he has us moving out of the crowd. My mouth leaving small kisses along his neck every time he squeezes my hip. I get the game we're playing. Whatever or whoever he is trying to hide me from.

The click of a door and the humid air hits my back as Bastian guides us through a back exit of the building. I turn as I hear the wheels of a car in the alleyway, Lucas behind the wheel.

Bastian opens the door and pushes me inside. Lucas slams on the gas as he takes us flying out of the alley. I throw my seat belt on and turn toward the man next to me.

"What the hell was that about?"

Bastian looks at me but doesn't say anything. He turns back toward the front of the car and pulls his phone out of his jacket, texting someone intensely.

I glance into the rearview mirror and see Lucas' eyes on me. I give him a questioning look but he shakes his head and I know I won't be getting any answers.

The drive home is as silent as the drive into Palma. By the time we pull up to the front door, I am ready to get out of this car.

Bastian gets out without a word and slams the door behind him. I scramble out of the car and chase after him.

He walks quickly through the house, making his way to his office.

"Bastian!" I yell.

He ignores me. And I grunt as I walk as fast as I can in my heels.

"Bastian," I say again as I catch up to him, grabbing his arm, pulling him to face me.

"Not now, Cameron."

I fold my arms over my chest. "Not now what? You are hiding shit from me and I deserve to know."

He groans as he turns to face me. "Did you ever think I am hiding things from you for a reason? What makes you think you deserve to know anything about me?"

I want to slap him. Hit him. Do something to knock some sense into him. What happened to the man telling me dancing at a club was foreplay. Foreplay that I for sure thought would lead to getting more of what he gave me last night.

"I guess I don't." I give up.

I turn around and head down the hall toward my room. Annoyed and frustrated that he won't talk to me and I'm stuck in this damn house for some reason he isn't telling me.

"Cameron." I hear his voice just as I reach my bedroom door.

I close my eyes and take a deep breath before turning to face him. "What, Bastian? I know you aren't going to tell me shit."

"I need you to stop digging."

"Excuse me?" I ask, surprised.

"I know you have been digging into my past."

I go to speak but have trouble forming a sentence. Because I honestly have been digging into him. Looking for anything that could get him out of whatever the hell mess his life is in. Don't ask me why. But for some reason I feel this need to protect him just as much as he says he is protecting me.

"I'm a dangerous man, Cameron," he sighs.

"Aren't all rich, powerful men dangerous?" I ask, not denying the fact I've been looking into him.

"Some more so than others."

"What are you trying to protect me from, Bastian?"

His eyes flash with desire when I say his first name. And I know I am not getting any answers from him.

He pushes me against the wall outside my bedroom door. His hands grabbing my wrists and holding them above my head.

"I already told you, it's me I am protecting you from."

I grind my center against the leg he shoved between my own. "This doesn't seem like the best way to protect me. And I really don't see that being a true—"

His mouth is on mine before I can even finish the sentence. His tongue rough and hard against my own.

I pull away from him. "You can't shut me up with your mouth."

He grinds his hips into mine. And a shudder runs down my body.

"Why do you always argue with me?"

This time I bite into his lip. Out of frustration, anger, lust. Who knows which one? "Foreplay," I tease.

This time he lifts me up, wrapping my legs around his waist and I know the foreplay is over. His thick length presses into me and I can't help but grind against him.

He walks us into my room and tosses me onto the bed before shrugging out of his jacket and peeling off his shirt.

I scoot up the bed as I try to take off my dress.

"Leave it," he commands. "You've been teasing me in that thing all night. And I want it on as I fuck you."

I smile at him as I hike the dress up my body and spread my legs.

I let go of all inhibitions as I let him take advantage of me. I wasn't lying when I said our arguments are foreplay. I've never been so turned on by an argument as I am with him.

I let him take over my pleasure as he fucks the anger and the questions out of me.

And when he leaves my room after properly satisfying us both, I have a hard time falling asleep. He used sex to get me to stop asking questions. I'm not sure if he will ever tell me his secrets.

23

CAM

I've spent the last three days working. Bastian has been cordial to me as we both work from the comfort of his home in Deià. I have so many questions I want to ask him about this house. Why he lives here, why it's so special to him but I never ask.

Instead I work through the day and let him use my body at night. I know it's not smart. But I can't help it. Bastian knows what he's doing. Knows how to work me into a frenzy and then satisfy me like I've never been satisfied before.

It's become a normalcy. We work all day, barely talking. Have dinner, with few words. Then he ravishes me either in my bed or somewhere in the house. Last night it was the pool as we watched the sunset. Or at least as much of the sunset as I could watch when my eyes weren't closed from the throes of pleasure he put me in.

We each then go to our own rooms and don't speak a word of it the next day. It's kind of my ideal situation in all the ways I could want. Too bad he is my client and I could lose my job over this.

I'm sitting at the kitchen island working, enjoying the warm salty breeze of the sea floating in through the open French doors when I get another email from my mother. Another email asking me to come home to go to another gala and to meet another man. I groan in frustration over the email and slam my laptop shut.

"Bad day?"

I jump at the sound of Bastian's voice. I look over at him as he pours a cup of coffee and shake my head.

"I thought you were gonna chuck that thing out the window."

"If I didn't need it to work, I probably would."

To my surprise, he sits on the stool next to me. "Another bad press article?"

"No. Everything has been quiet since that last one."

"Good." He sips his coffee and watches me. His hair is wild on his head, not slicked back like usual. A few pieces of it falling over his stormy gray eyes. That's when I also notice he isn't in a suit but dark jeans and a white T-shirt. His hand lands on my thigh. "What's wrong then?"

I look down at his hand. "Personal things."

"Ahh. Well, maybe you should get out of the house."

I look up at him. "I thought you were keeping eyes on me."

He grins. "I am. But you've been working every day since you got here. So have I. But I also find time to relax when I come here. And I have yet to do that. Besides, I can keep my eyes on you if you are with me."

"What did you have in mind?"

"Have you been to Mallorca before?"

I shake my head.

"Well, so many people come here for the beaches and Palma. But they don't know of the small towns along the coastline that are hidden gems."

"So you want to show me Mallorca?"

He nods and the look on his face is something I haven't seen before. Giddiness, almost like a child who is getting what he wants.

"Okay."

He flashes the most vibrant smile at me before crushing his lips to mine.

This is not the Bastian I know.

The man drives like a maniac in his sports car as we wind down the mountain road. I swear he is going to kill us. Every time he takes a sharp turn, I grip on to my seat and the door. He just laughs as I freak out.

When we get into Deià, I breathe a sigh of relief. "You drive like a madman?"

"I know those roads like the back of my hand. I was perfectly safe."

I roll my eyes at that. Not even having the energy to argue with him. He pulls up to a small café and we both get out. He tells me to sit at one of the tables outside while he goes into order.

I watch the people walk by and appreciate this small town even more. When I was shopping the other day, I

fell in love with the cobblestone streets and brick build-
ings. Maybe small towns aren't as bad as I thought.

Bastian comes out with two coffees and takes a seat
next to me.

"Why Deià?" I ask him.

"I grew up here."

"Really?"

He nods. "When I wasn't in London, I was here. My
grandparents lived just down the road, they owned a
bakery. My grandmother made some of the best food
I've ever had. I loved it here as a kid more so than
London but my father wanted me in all the best private
schools to get the best education so I only was able to
come here during the summers."

"It's a beautiful town. Peaceful."

"I wish I could come here more but it's hard to find
the time when I am running a business."

"How did your parents meet?" I ask.

"My mother always hated this small town. She never
appreciated the beauty of its serenity. She went to college
in London and met my father."

A waitress brings out two breakfast sandwiches and
places them in front of us. Bastian thanks her and then
bites into his sandwich.

"Where is your mom now?"

"After she divorced my dad, she moved to Paris. She
always loved it. Part of the reason I moved my offices
there. Much like her, I preferred it over the dirty streets
of London. When my brother and I expanded the business, I decided to be closer to Mom. So he ran the
London office with my father and I ran the Paris office."

"Do you come here a lot? Your house is beautiful, peaceful. I would want to spend all my time there."

A sad look crosses his face. "I wish I could be here more. But after my older brother died, I work more than I ever have. It's hard for me to get away."

I don't ask him more about Thiago. From previous conversations, I know his death was hard on him.

I finish up the last bite of my sandwich and Bastian stands up. "Shall we start our adventure?"

I grab the hand he is holding out to me. "When you say it that way, it makes me scared. Is it going to involve more of your crazy driving?"

He chuckles as he opens the car door for me. "You'll have to find out."

We end up driving to a marina. "What are we doing here?"

"Seeing the island."

"On a boat?"

He gives me a curious look. "Yes."

"I thought you were just going to drive us around."

"I could, but this is more fun. Besides, the views are better and my friend let me borrow his sailboat."

Oh dear god I am not getting on a boat. I would rather take his erratic driving. "I'll take your word for it. Let's just drive."

He must see my face pale. "Are you afraid of the water?"

"What? No! I love the water."

He parks the car and turns to face me. "But not boats?"

I stare off into the marina to avoid his eye contact.

It's beautiful out here. The mix of sailboats and speedboats sitting in the blue water recessed between the mountains. Bastian grabs my hand, and I turn to look at him. "Fine. Yes. I hate boats." I sigh and then start to ramble. "How does a piece of wood float on water and not sink? It's a disaster waiting to happen. Look at the Titanic that thing went down with thousands of people on it! And don't get me started on—"

"You know they've been around for centuries."

"And do you know how many boats have sunk?"

He throws his head back in laughter. "Cam, it's perfectly safe."

"It could sink!"

"You get on planes."

"Don't argue with me over the difference in the risk of boats and planes."

A goofy grin takes up his whole face. "We're getting on the boat."

"Have fun. I'll be right here."

He shakes his head at me then gets out of the car. He grabs our overnight bags he insisted I pack then heads out to the pier.

I watch him as he walks out to the end of the quay. I lose sight of him between the boats. He can't think I was actually going to follow him. After a few minutes, I grab my phone and check emails. I might as well spend my time being productive.

I'm in the middle of replying to someone back at the office when my door opens.

"Let's go."

I look up at Bastian. "I'm not going."

He shakes his head and leans into the car, plucking my phone out of my hand and unbuckling my seat belt.

"What are you doing?"

He doesn't say a word then suddenly grabs me out of the seat and flings me over his shoulder.

"Bastian, put me down right now."

I feel his throaty chuckle vibrate through him as he carries me to the pier. I hit his back and struggle to break free but he's too strong.

He finally sets me down when we get to the boat. I figure I can run off but the bastard set me on the boat and quickly stepped into my space so I can't get off.

"You're a bastard."

"And you don't listen."

I purse my lips and clench my hands. "I do not—"

"You seem perfectly fine."

"We're tied to a dock!"

He smiles at me and damnit, that smile makes me want to give in to him. "So it's not the boat. It's being on the water."

"Well, that's where boats sink," I stammer.

He chuckles as he walks me backward until my knees hit a bench, forcing me to sit. That's when I notice two other people on the boat. One gathering the ropes tied to the dock, the other at the helm.

I feel the boat start to move and I have every intention of jumping off due to my stupid irrational fear but Bastian has me held against him. I grab his hand in hopes it will calm me down.

As we pull away from the pier and through the waterway leading to the sea, I start to hyperventilate. I grip his hand tighter. The open water is expansive. Beautiful but deadly. I close my eyes as I start to get dizzy. Then I feel Bastian's lips on mine. His mouth slowly coaxing mine open. His tongue moving into my mouth. I kiss him back, the fear gripping my body slowly melting away as his hands replace that fear. My hands travel up his chest, around his shoulders, and into his hair as he pulls me onto his lap so I am straddling him.

He holds me tight against him. I'm so surprised by his kiss I don't notice the wind pick up. So surprised he is showing me affection in the presence of others.

He pulls away from me. His hands gently caressing my back.

I look around and see we are out on the open water. I think I want to panic but the urge is gone.

Bastian's thumbs rub circles on my hip bones as he stares at me. "You okay?"

I nod as I look into those gray eyes that are almost silver as the reflection of blue water hits them. I study the man I am sitting on. He isn't the man I am used to. This one seems carefree, young, like he has retreated back to his youth while being around his childhood home. The crease between his eyes is less prominent. His lips look fuller with the slight smile crossing them. His skin glowing against the heat of the sun. And his hair, one of my favorite things about him, sits wild against his head, some in his eyes, some blowing in the wind as we sail along the coastline.

"Why are you looking at me like that?" he asks on a whisper.

I brush his hair out of his eyes and smile at him. "You're beautiful when you're like this."

"Like what?"

"Carefree. Like nothing in the world matters when you're here, on this boat. All your problems disappear and you look like the man you should be."

His grip tightens on me, pulling me closer into him. His lips are at my chin as I look down at him as he talks. "You do this to me, Cameron. You make me feel this way."

I shake my head. "I think I piss you off more than anything, Bastian."

He chuckles. "Oh, you do that too. But being out here with you makes me want to be the man I should have grown up to be."

My hands slide from his hair and cup his face. "And what kind of man is that?"

"A good man. A respectable man."

I brush my lips against his. "You are a respectable man."

"I told you I'm dangerous."

"Sometimes danger can be fun."

"Not with me. With me, it's reckless."

I shake my head against his lips and kiss him deeply. I want him to see the man I see when I look at him. His arm slides up my back, holding the back of my head in place as he pulls away from me a few inches.

"I should never have brought you into my world, Cam."

I rub my thumb along his cheekbone. "It's too late now."

He sighs, a defeated noise as he rests his forehead against my chest. "I know."

The way he says it has me thinking about the other night. The fact that he keeps telling me that he needs to protect me. I still have no idea from what but his words make me think it's from more than just him.

But I won't let that ruin our day. Hell, I am actually on a boat. In the water. I should be rejoicing over that.

I slide off his lap and stand up. My legs shaky as I get used to the wake of the water. I walk over to the railing and take in the Mallorcan coastline. The beauty of the mountains along the sea. The immaculate houses peppered into the rocks. The blue of the water. The way it crashes hard into the shoreline.

Peace. That's what it feels like out here.

I feel Bastian's hand on my back before he stands next to me. "It's beautiful out here, isn't it?"

I nod.

"See what you were missing out on this whole time?" he teases.

I elbow him in the stomach and he throws his head back in laughter. He wraps his arms around me and rests his head on my shoulder as I take in the views.

"Why are you so scared of the water? You don't mind the pool."

I bite my lip. I really hate this story. I shake my head because I don't want to tell him and feel dumb. Because it really is stupid and I should have gotten over it by now.

His lips find my neck and he whispers into my ear for me to tell him.

I grip the rail of the boat and sigh. "The ocean, the

sea, it's endless. The depths of its soul dark, unknown." I can't help but think how much that reminds me of Bastian.

I flutter my lips as I let out a deep-seated breath. "I've been scared of deep water since I was a kid." He kisses the spot behind my ear and I continue. "I had a friend who almost drowned when their sailboat capsized."

His arms tighten around me. "That's horrible."

"The family survived. My friend perfectly fine but it affected me in a way that's always haunted me when it comes to boats."

He presses his lips to my forehead. "So were you scared of the water ever since then?"

I nod. "My parents have money. A lot of their friends have boats. And every time I went to step on one, I couldn't do it. I just kept thinking I would drown."

"Then I guess you are over your fear now."

I shrug. "Maybe. This definitely helped." I sigh and bite my lip, not sure if I should say what's on my mind. I spin in his arms to face him and say it, anyway. "You make me feel safe, Bastian."

His arms tighten around me, but his silence is deafening. He thinks I need to be protected from him, yet I've never felt safer around anyone before.

The boat slows down and Bastian tears his gaze from me and changes the subject. "We just got to one of my favorite places."

I spin around and find us reaching a cove. Giant sandstone rocks jut out of the water, encircling an area of bright turquoise waters. A few other boats sit in the cove and a small beach shows a few sunbathers.

"Put your swimsuit on."

I look up at Bastian, fear creeping into my vision. "Are you making me jump off this boat?"

"I wasn't going to. But after that story. Yes, I am making you change your mind about the water."

"Why?"

He pulls me into him. "Because if you ever end up on my yacht one day you are going to want to get over your fear."

I blink at his words. The sideways promise of a future for us. I thought we were just having fun. I figured when we got back to Saint Tropez, we would pretend this tryst never happened. But the sincerity in his eyes has me questioning everything. I just nod as he grabs my hand and shows me to the small bedroom below deck so I can change.

When I emerge out of the cabin, I find Bastian talking to one of the deckhands quickly in Spanish. I think he is directing him where to anchor the sailboat but the deckhand seems to be disagreeing. I laugh as I watch him. He really needs to be in charge of everything.

Maybe that's why I like him so much. I like to challenge him. I like the banter between us when I push his boundaries. And I push them a lot. Everyone knows I do. And I am sure I will continue to do it today.

But this poor deckhand is not going to win against him. He eventually throws his hands up in the air and walks over to the captain. The captain nods and steers the boat farther into the alcove. A smug look on Bastian's face.

"Do you ever listen to what anyone has to say?" I ask him as I approach.

"No," he says grumpily.

"Well it looks like you got your way."

"I had to compromise."

I rest my hand on his forearm and smile up at him. "You compromised? I didn't even know you knew what that word meant. Do I need to explain it to you because I am not sure—"

He pulls me into him so roughly it shuts me up. His hands grip my ass hard. "I'll show you later that I don't know the meaning of compromise when I have you begging for me to touch you, taste you, fuck you. When I leave you alone, tied up in my bed because I have much more important things to take care of than your needs."

A chill covers my body as his words turn me on. "Too bad I know that if you have me tied up in your bed, you won't be able to keep your hands off me."

His fingers slide down my ass, dangerously close to the heat between my thighs. "You don't know how good I am at self-control, Cameron. But I am willing to show you."

His lips hover over mine and just when I think he is going to kiss me and stop teasing me with his fingers that are dangerously close to sliding under my bottoms, he pulls away.

"Capità," he yells as he walks away from me.

Asshole.

I sit on a bench along the railing of the boat as we slide into the alcove. I've watched Bastian for the last five minutes as he talks to the captain and ignores me. He thinks I don't know the game he's playing but I do. He wants me needy and squirming for him. He wants to shock me by telling me he wants to tie me up. Well, he doesn't know I've done it before. And I like it. I like the restraint. Someone forcing their control over me. But he doesn't need to know that. He doesn't need to know I look forward to him doing those exact things he said to me.

When the anchor is down, he finally walks back over to me.

"You ready for this?"

I grab his hand he is holding out for me. "No."

He smirks at me and I want to kiss it off his face. God, who is this girl? When have I ever wanted to do that to someone?

I follow him to the bow of the boat. He steps to an area where the rail ends and clearly looks like it was made as a jumping platform. He looks me over as I pull off the cover-up I had on and he grins at me in approval.

I step up next to him and my stomach drops as I look down at the water. It's not super deep. The clear turquoise water making the bottom nearly visible but all I can think about is drowning.

"Jump," he tells me.

I shake my head. "You go first."

"If I go first, you won't jump in."

"You don't know that," I mumble.

"You are clenching your fist so hard it's turning white."

I flex my hands. I wasn't even aware of what I was doing.

"Do I need to throw you in?"

I glare at him. "Maybe I'll throw you in, you turd."

He throws his head back in laughter. "Babe, I don't think you have the strength."

I know I don't have the strength but it was a fun thought. "Don't call me babe."

He leans over to me and whispers in my ear. "Fly, mi cielito."

I look at him curiously, wondering what that word means. Or the fact he told me to fly and I can only wonder if he is talking about that gilded cage I told him I felt stuck in. But I don't let myself think about it for too long. I plug my nose, close my eyes, and jump.

I start to panic but then the rush of the warm water around me feels freeing as I climb to the surface. I breathe deeply as I break through, treading water as I look up at the boat and Bastian's pearly smile taking up his face.

He dives in. His movements fluid and smooth, like he was made for the water. Like he is at home in the water.

I swim out to meet him as he surfaces. All my fears completely gone as I soak up the warm summer rays.

"You look like you belong here."

"In the water?" he asks as he pushes his wet hair out of his face.

I nod.

He lifts the left side of his mouth into a smirk. "Why do you think I bought a yacht?"

I splash water at him and flip onto my back, floating in this magical place. I understand why it's his favorite. Despite the people here, it's quiet and serene. The rocks cutting off all noises from the boats sailing up and down the coastline. The water warm enough it feels like bathwater. I wonder what it would be like here at night floating on the water and looking at the stars.

As if Bastian can read my thoughts, he swims up next to me. "You should see this place at night."

"It seems so far away from any towns. I bet it's so dark." I turn my head and look over at him.

"It's not too far from Sa Calobra, but far enough the mountains block out the lights. You can see so many stars in the sky. Not as many as being in the middle of the Med on a yacht but enough to feel like you are in your own world." Bastian has the childlike look on his face again.

"Did you come here often as a child?"

"My best friend as a kid had an uncle who worked out here at the park. So whenever we got someone to drive us here, we always came."

I sink back into the water, keeping just my head above the water. "I can't imagine growing up here. I was so used to Boston. To a city I thought was so loud but in hindsight was nowhere near as loud as New York. I was excited when we could go out to the suburbs and explore the lakes. Or head to the beaches along the cape."

Bastian swims around me. "That was most of my childhood too. I wish I could have gone to school here, spent all my youth here and only went to university in England but my old-fashioned British father would have none of that."

"I'm sure your mother didn't care much either since you said she always wanted to get out of here."

238

He nods. "Yeah, the only people that wanted me to grow up here were my grandparents."

"At least you can be here now."

He swims up to me. "And I have you with me."

"Because you won't let me leave."

"Such a tragedy." He winks at me, and I can't help but roll my eyes.

"Come, let me show you something."

I follow him as he swims between two narrow rocks. A canopy of trees crosses the rocks above, blocking the sunlight. When we emerge between the gap we are in a smaller cove. I see a cave off to the right and nothing but blue sky above us.

Bastian turns around abruptly and I swim right into his hard body. "Are we supposed to be back here?"

He shrugs. "It's never been cordoned off. But the park rangers recommend not coming back here. The tide can make the waters rough in here. And you have to hide out in the cave until they retreat. But it's low tide now so we're fine."

"I like it. It feels like our own little oasis."

He grins at me, the one that sends a bolt of electricity to my core. "Precisely."

"Did you bring me back here to take advantage of me?" I tease.

"Perhaps." He smiles at me and presses me back against the rocks, making me gasp.

"Well, you can't tie me up here."

He shakes his head. "Don't be so sure about that."

Our lips collide and he has his hand in my bottoms so fast I don't have time to shift my legs. He spreads my center, thrusting two fingers inside me. I moan loudly into his mouth.

He pushes me harder against the rocks. "You need to be quiet or someone might hear on the other side of the grotto."

I nod as he works his fingers in me, his thumb rubbing my clit every so often. I grip his biceps as he brings me close to the edge. He leans forward and uses his teeth to pull my bikini top down. His mouth latching on to my nipple and sucking hard.

I groan and he pulls away, tsking at me for making noise. "Do I need to stop? Or are you going to stay quiet?"

I just nod and he gives me a devilish grin before his mouth is back on my breast. I bite hard on my lip as he presses firmly into my clit causing my entire body to spasm.

His lips make their way up my chest and my throat. "Now it's not so hard to be quiet, is it?"

I shake my head just as his mouth adheres to mine. His hands caress my bottom and my thighs as he pulls us closer to the mouth of the cave. A few vines dangle down from the trees, tickling the top of my head and my back.

I run my hands down Bastian's abs and he growls into my ear as I slip my hands into his swim shorts.

"What are you doing, dirty girl?"

I look him in the eye, his thirst for me prevalent. "I need you," I beg.

"I don't know if you'll be able to keep quiet though."

"There is only one way to find out."

He bites down on my lip at the same time he presses

himself against my core and I can barely hang on to the moan.

He pulls back and smiles at me as he glances up at the vines. His devious smile making my legs clench. Before I know it, he unties my bottoms and uses his hips to hold me against the rock. He pulls my arms off him and wraps my wrists in the bottom of my bikini. He then pushes my arms above my head and ties the vines above me through the bindings on my wrists.

He lets go of me, pushing away from the rock, swimming backward and staring at his handiwork. I am surprised the vines are strong enough to hold my weight. But as I move my wrists they don't give.

"And you said I couldn't tie you up here?" He grins at me.

"I never should have underestimated you."

He swims back to me, cupping my jaw. "No, baby, you shouldn't."

His hands go back to my hips and he thrusts viciously into me. My back rubbing against the limestone. I meet his hips thrust for thrust and succumb to the power he has over me. I start to pant as he hits that spot inside of me that makes me go blind. I struggle to stay quiet but with every rotation and thrust of his hips, my whimpers grow louder.

He pulls out of me completely and I ache for him to fill me again. His fingers trace up the side of my body, leaving a line of fire on my skin the water can't put out. "You are not good at following instructions."

"Well, when you do that thing with your hips, it's hard for me to not scream at the top of my lungs."

I watch as his tongue licks across his full bottom lip. "Mmm. I need you on my yacht then."

He swims close enough to me that I am able to wrap my legs back around his hips. His mouth presses against mine in a soft kiss that surprises me. So much so that I don't feel him untying the top of my bikini. His hands squeeze my breasts and his hips push against my own just as he pulls away from my mouth and shoves my bikini top into my mouth.

"Now where was I?" he asks just as his hands grip my ass hard and he plunges back into me.

My eyes bug out of my head at the force and this time I don't care about the noises I make because they are all muffled through his makeshift gag. And I don't fight against it. I let him ravage me, destroy me, dominate me. I love every second of it. An orgasm hits me out of nowhere and I crumple in his hands. My arms still taught in the vines but my lower half has turned to Jell-O.

Bastian pounds into me as he licks my clavicle, kisses up my neck, sucks on my ear. I want to touch him, pull him even deeper into me but I'm bound. He must feel my need though because he lifts one of my legs higher up and onto his shoulder so are bodies are tighter against each other. With every powerful thrust into me, he rubs against my clit. My whole body is electrified from the tips of my tied fingers to the ends of my toes. I don't think I can survive another orgasm but it comes anyway. My muffled screams floating away on the breeze in the grotto.

I feel Bastian explode inside me. His grip on my waist and my ribcage intense as he empties himself into me.

His mouth leaves a trail of hot kisses up my throat. He pulls the gag out of my mouth and presses his tongue into my own. This time he lets me groan as loud as I want as I feel residual pulses of him inside of me.

He smiles against my mouth and I can't keep the smile off my own face.

What we just did was taboo, erotic, reckless.

And I would do it all over again.

"Merda," he mumbles against my lips.

"Mmm," is all I can say.

We both startle when we hear kids laughing, getting louder. Bastian peers around the edge of the rock and sighs. "We got company."

His hands reach for the vines and he unties me. He slips my bottoms on me as I adjust my top and retie the strings.

I go to swim away from him but he surprises me with a kiss so intense my knees would buckle if I wasn't swimming in the water.

His hand brushes down my throat. "We should do that again sometime."

I giggle at his words. This girl who was just bound and gagged, giggled at the words saying we should do it again.

He lets out a laugh as he pulls me with him, swimming backward to the opening of the grotto. We both wave at the kids who have no idea what we just did against the rocks near the cave entrance and then swim back into the cove.

24

CAM

W e both lie out on the boat as the captain sails us out to Port de Pollença. Bastian said it was one of his favorite places to visit when he was a teenager. He and Kilian went out there a lot when they needed a break from school. He said it was a tourist town but much quieter than Palma and the waters even more blue than the marina in Deià.

By the time we dock at the marina, I am starving. Bastian laughs as my stomach growls. I change back into the romper I wore onto the boat and brush out my hair that is mostly air-dried. Instead of putting it back up into my classic high ponytail, I opt to leave it down. It floats in waves down my back from the salty sea.

One of the deckhands helps me off the boat and onto the pier. I take a seat on the edge of the dock and slide my wedges onto my feet as Bastian paces a few feet from me on his phone.

I wait for him to finish his call and look at the small

port city before us. The white stone buildings with terracotta roofs dotting the coastline. People shouting along the beaches. The marina filled with speedboats, sailboats, and yachts. Just from looking around, I can see why Bastian loved this place as a young twenty-year-old. It screams wealth but not in a way like Saint Tropez.

"Sorry about that. Parker needed something." He looks agitated from the call but I don't think much of it.

"Do I need to take your phone away from you?" I tease him.

That seems to shake him from his thoughts. "No, babe, I promise I won't answer it again." He winks at me. Once again, this is a Bastian I could get used to.

"I told you to stop calling me that."

He doesn't say anything. He just grabs my hand and we walk into the city. We stop at a small café and order sandwiches and drink iced tea. He tells me more about his time here with Kilian and I can just imagine the two of them as players, partying and sleeping with every willing girl.

I tell him of my partying days with Tacoma in the city. They weren't that long ago, not as long ago as his. But I like reminiscing. I miss my friend and I hope once I am done working for Montford Hotels, I can take a week off and see her in White Creek.

"You look beautiful, by the way, Cam. You should wear your hair down more often."

I purse my lips at him. "It's a pain to take care of. I like it up, gives me the power suit vibe."

He shrugs. "I am just saying I like it down."

"Well, maybe if you are lucky, I will wear it down for the gala."

He smiles at me. "I don't know, you might want the power suit look for that since you will be running the show."

"Oh, hell no. I am not running that thing. Honestly, I hate them. Half the reason I was in a mood this morning was because my mother wanted me to fly home next month for one that she is throwing. I mean, I get it, they raise money, they are usually for a good cause but they reek of money and power and the need for everyone to show off. Tell me you have much more fun in a club tossing back shots than shaking hands and people pleasing."

He chuckles. "I don't even know the last time I went to a club and took shots. If I am at one, it's to discuss business without being overheard. And I hardly drink. But I know what you mean. That's why I hate galas too. So tell me, why are you so insistent on one for the hotel?"

I sigh and lean back into my chair. "Because it will cause the biggest shift in appearance for the business. Rather than a night of raunchy entertainment and despicable gambling. It will be a night of positive energy and benefit a good charity. And I'm calling it a launch party."

"Parker told me about your choice of charity. I was worried at first about your plans to donate to the trafficking organization but I think it's smart."

"Out of all the accusations that fell on Montford Hotels and your brother, I think that was the most absurd. The most far-fetched. I did a lot of research, Bastian. I investigated his past, into your past. Nothing ever led me to believe that human trafficking was going on behind closed doors. The drugs and illegal gambling, even the prostitution, absolutely. But trafficking seems out of character for you."

"But not Matías?" Bastian cuts in, his voice cold.

"If you let me finish, I would have said no to him too. Your brother liked to party but from how he treated the woman at the hotel I could never see him selling them. He cared too much, protected them."

"How did you find all this out?"

I raise a brow at him, wondering why he even cares. "I asked some of the employees, some of his friends. It's not hard to find information on the internet."

He flags down the waitress and hands her his black card before folding his arms over his chest. "You need to stop digging into the past, Cam."

"It was part of my job to fix your damn business," I argue.

He pinches his brow with his fingers. "I need you to stop looking. Forget about the past. You've turned up enough shit."

"What do you think I am going to find?"

The waitress comes back with the bill and his card and I can tell by the look on his face the conversation is over.

Now I am just annoyed and frustrated. I step away from the table and onto the boardwalk of the beach without waiting for Bastian. I am tired of his secrets and his attitude. What happened to the man from an hour ago that was holding my hand and calling me babe? Not that I want to be called babe.

"Cameron."

I ignore Bastian calling for me and turn down a path that looks to lead past the market and onto the main road. I have no idea where I am going or what I am going to do. Bastian never gave me back my phone, and I sure as hell don't want to get on the boat.

I see a bar a few buildings down and start to head that direction. A martini always clears my head. Well, makes it foggier but it tends to clear my anger and frustrations.

I think I lose Bastian as I run across the street, dodging traffic, but an arm pulls me into an alley. If I couldn't smell his signature scent on him, I would scream. Instead, I fold my arms over my chest and turn my head to the side. I don't want to listen to his shit.

"Cam, I'm sorry."

"I am so tired of you and your... wait, did you just apologize to me."

He nods as he steps closer to me. "I did. I know I push your buttons a lot. Just like you do to me. But I really worry about what you will find." He sighs and steps into my space. "I can't tell you."

I groan in frustration.

"But I will."

I look up into his eyes and he looks just as surprised as me that he said it. "Okay." It's all I can say. Because I can tell by looking at him, I shouldn't ask for more. I know he will tell me his secrets when he is ready.

"Where were you running off to?"

I step out of the alley and Bastian's hand finds mine again. I look down at it, still surprised when it happens.

"Cam," he whispers into my ear as he cups my jaw. He presses the softest kiss across my lips.

I look up at him and my heart aches. What the hell is going on with us? With me? Why does he have me feeling all sorts of ways?

I shake the thoughts and look toward the way I was headed. "I have no idea. The bar. The beach. I don't know."

"Well you have a terrible sense of direction if you were looking for the beach since you ran from it."

I roll my eyes at him. "Asshole."

He presses his lips to mine. "Did you get a dress for the gala... I mean, your launch party yet?"

I shake my head. "No, I was hoping to get one in Paris. I thought I might find something good there. Modern and edgy yet classic and elegant."

"You should get one here," he says to me as he pulls on my arm, leading us in a different direction.

"Why?"

"So you'll always remember Mallorca."

I stop in my tracks, nearly tripping over a loose piece of cobblestone as I do. I don't know why that hit me so hard. I love it here. I feel like I am in a whole new world. And the thought hadn't crossed my mind that in a few days, at some point, I have to go back to reality. Back to the real world. Back to a world where I don't hold hands with Bastian or kiss him or dance with him.

"You okay?"

I blink a few times and then start walking again. "Yeah, fine. Why are you so interested in this gala suddenly? I mean, you haven't said a word to me about it since last week when you finally gave me the go-ahead."

He shrugs. "I guess I just want to know what you are planning. Be prepared for it."

"So does that mean you will go?"

"I am not quite sure yet."

"Are you ever going to tell me why you don't like them?"

He is quiet for a few moments as he leads us down a street filled with shops. A bunch with beachwear, some with trinkets and wares, and others with dresses. "Maybe one day," he finally says as he stops us in front of a shop with glamorous dresses. It looks expensive and I can only imagine this is where the celebrities and the wealthy shop.

He holds the door open for me and I enter the shop and am immediately greeted by a stunning Spanish woman with long dark hair and gorgeous olive skin. Her cheek bones are prominent and her lips full like Bastian's. She is elegant as she walks toward me in a romper like my own and four-inch heels.

"Well look who has finally decided to visit me!" she exclaims.

I turn to look at Bastian, a grin on his face. "Hello, Yvette."

She gives him a big hug, turns to me then looks back at Bastian. "You didn't tell me you were dating anyone."

"He's not," I say at the same time Bastian says, "I'm not."

She looks between the two of us a few times and then

I realize I never introduced myself. "I'm Cam. Bastian, I mean, Mr. Montford is my client."

She eyes me suspiciously. "Mmhmm. Sure. Well, you can call him Bastian in here. I won't tell anyone. My cousin is something else. Always demanding people call him Mr. Montford." She rolls her eyes. "So pretentious."

She pulls me toward a sitting area and takes my bag from me, setting it on a table as she pushes me onto a couch. "Well, as I am sure he didn't tell you from the look on his face, I'm Yvette, but you can call me Yve. Now, what can I help you find? Dresses, business wear, formal wear, maybe some lingerie?" she asks as she raises her eyebrows at Bastian.

He clears his throat. "Maybe I shouldn't have brought you here."

"Oh, don't be a dick, Bas."

"Formal wear," I answer. "I am throwing a gala slash launch party for Montford Hotels."

She looks over at Bastian and then back to me. Pointing at him, she says, "And he's going?"

"Find something that will look good on her," Bastian cuts in.

"Well, it's not like I am going to put her in anything bad," she mumbles as she walks away.

I look over at Bastian who still looks slightly flustered after that phone call he took on the dock. I'm not one-hundred-percent convinced it was Parker from his clipped response. His phone rings. I'm surprised with how little it has today. It's usually always ringing or notifying him of an email or text.

"I thought you said you weren't taking any more calls," I say as he goes to answer it.

He stares at me, almost like he forgot he said it. He looks quickly at his phone then back at me. "You're right." He slips his phone back into his pocket and takes a seat next to me.

"Sorry, Bastian. I mean, if you have business to take care of, I shouldn't be interrupting you. Although you did take my phone away and I do have business I need to tend to."

"It can wait."

I raise a brow at him. "Yours or mine?"

His hand drops to my thigh and squeezes. "Both."

I go to speak but Yvette comes back into the sitting area. "Okay, I grabbed you a handful of dresses. I really think the rose gold dress will look the best on you."

I stand up off the couch and walk into the dressing room where I see about ten dresses lining the walls.

I turn around and see Bastian still sitting on the couch, watching me. "Are you going to just sit there?"

He nods.

"You know he is bossy as hell. He isn't going to let you have a say in the dress you pick. When I was picking a place for my shop, he pretty much told me he would find me one. Such a brute."

I laugh as she closes the dressing curtain behind me but not before I see the scowl on Bastian's face.

I try on a handful of dresses, each one of them Bastian shrugs when he sees me. I can see Yve fuming every time he looks nonchalant about a dress and I know she is pissed at him but I think he is doing it on purpose.

I finally grab the rose gold dress that she first suggested. It's the most beautiful one. The second I saw it I knew it would be the one but I wanted to see the others first just to prove my point. I slide the dress up my body and Yve helps me with the zipper in the back. She pins the straps so the dress sits tightly against me.

I turn and look in the mirror as I slide my hands over my hips. The light pink silky fabric forms to my body. Rose gold sequins play off in a pattern over my chest and hips giving the illusion of a perfect hourglass shape. The dress is fitted to my knees where a slit comes up the front just a few inches off the center. The bottom flares out into a mermaid train. The sweetheart neckline accentuates my breasts but isn't overly sexual. Classic, elegant, and sexy. The exact look I was going for.

Yve smiles at me as I look at her in the mirror. "I knew this was the one."

"So did I. Before I even put it on."

"Bas is going to have a heart attack."

I shrug. "He's just my client. It doesn't matter."

She purses her lips at me and raises her brow so high I think it's going to hit her hairline. "Right." She steps back and looks at me again. "Well maybe you should go show *your client* this dress."

She pulls back the purple silk curtain of the dressing room and I step out. Unlike the other dresses where Bastian looked as indifferent as he usually does, I notice the difference right away. The way his eyes darken, the lust taking over. The way he clenches his fist when I know he is holding himself back. And the shift he makes in his chair tells me he would very much enjoy taking this dress off me.

"Just a client?" Yve laughs as she notices Bastian's reaction.

I blush at her words because it's obvious he is more than that.

Bastian clears his throat. "This one."

I smirk at him. "Are you sure, Mr. Grumpy?"

He gives me a look that would probably scare the shit out of most people but to me that look has an entirely different meaning.

Yve claps her hands together. "Yay! I knew he would love it. I have the perfect shoes to go with it too. We will need to get the straps hemmed so the dress fits this way but other than that it was made for your body."

I smile at Yve then look back over at Bastian. The look he is giving me is making a thousand butterflies hit my stomach. I turn back to Yve as she babbles about something else to me. I follow her to a wall of shoes when I hear a phone ringing.

I look over at Bastian and his brow is crinkled as he looks at the screen. "You can take it. It's fine."

He doesn't say anything, just nods at me before standing up and heading out the door.

"He is a brute sometimes," Yve says after he walks out.

"I've gotten used to it."

She snickers. "I'm sure you have."

I shake my head at her and laugh. "There is nothing going on between us."

"Oh really?" she asks as she folds her slender arms

over her petite body. "But you can call him Bastian instead of Mr. Montford?"

"It just slips sometimes."

"And he wants to see you try on dresses for a gala when he hates them?"

"Like you said, he is overbearing."

She throws her hands in the air before throwing them onto her hips with sass. "Dios mio! He brought you to Mallorca, Cam. Stop denying the fact that there is something going on. He doesn't bring anyone here. He's never brought a girlfriend, an assistant, a business partner, hell he only brought his ex-wife here once. So stop denying it!"

I let out a big sigh and collapse onto the chair across from the shoe wall. "There wasn't anything going on when I came here."

"He probably wanted you though."

I nod. "He did. At least I think. Honestly, the two of us were like oil and vinegar when we first met. He hated my ideas and the way I did things."

"And I am guessing you just kept doing it."

"Of course. I'm not the type of woman that will just cower in a corner if someone disagrees with me."

She smiles. "I could tell."

"So he flew me out here because he was pissed about this damn party I am planning. I wouldn't let him tell me no and I kept going against him. Then when he made me come here, I thought it was surely to fire me. But then things got... heated."

"Mmm. I love me a good enemies to lovers story," she giggles.

I shake my head at her. "I didn't mean for this to happen."

"I'm sure he didn't either. But you can't deny chemistry. And I felt it sizzling off you two the moment you walked into my shop."

I look out the window but don't see him. "He's different here. He's not the hardened man who is always brooding and demanding like he is in Saint Tropez."

Yve takes a seat in the chair next to me. "Bastian isn't a bad man. Sure he's made some really shitty decisions in his life. But he's not the man he portrays himself to be. Hell, he paid for me to go to college when my parents couldn't afford it and then he bought me this shop. He has a heart of gold. He just doesn't show it to most people."

I want to be shocked over what Yve told me he did for her but from the stories he's told me that sounds exactly like the man hidden behind his iron gates. "I wish I could see this side of him more. But I know it won't last."

"Why not?"

I look over at her. "Whatever is going on between us can only be while we are here. We can't do this back in France. I'll lose my job. It goes against both our company policies. It's a mistake."

"Does it feel like a mistake?" she asks me.

I want to say yes but deep down I know it isn't. I am battling these feelings for this man who is nothing like the man I first met. A man who sees through my walls, who tells me to break free. A man who I could fall in love with if he let me.

"You feel it here," she says as she presses her palm to her chest. "Your mind wants to tell you that whatever is happening isn't real. That it's wrong. But in your heart, you know what's true. What's real. Take heed of the advice from your brain but listen to your heart." She points toward the front of the shop. "That man out there never listens to his heart and he has lost so many things because of it. He knows that too. He knows about the mistakes he made. He knows if he had taken a different path how much different his life would be.

"But I also see the way he looks at you, Cam. I have never seen him look at anyone the way he looks at you. Maybe you were what he needed. You challenge him. You stand up to him. No one ever stands up to Bastian Montford. And I always thought that the person who finally stood up to him would break his walls down. I'm just happy it's a woman. That it's for love. Not for business."

I bite my lip as I think about her words. My heart is racing. Is she right? She knows him better than I do. Could this thing we have going on actually be real? Could it amount to something more? But our reality won't let us have it. There are too many things fighting against us. Our jobs, his walls, my own guarded heart. He is the exact opposite of what I told myself I would ever have. With Bastian I would be the housewife, the woman on his arm, not the woman in charge. My mother would probably be elated over it. But is this the life I want? If we could somehow make this work?

What am I even thinking? We've spent a week fucking each other. We barely talked about anything up until today. Yes, we had our moments before anything got physical between us but that's all those were. Moments. Meaningless interactions.

Bastian and I can't be together. It's not what either of us wants. But that flutter in my chest is telling me something different. And Yve's words about my heart being right knocks the air out of me. Is this what I want?

"Okay, let's stop thinking deep thoughts and think more about shoes."

Her comment breaks up my thoughts and makes me smile. We spend the next twenty minutes picking out shoes and looking at a few fun cocktail dresses. I try on a couple of them and they truly are gorgeous.

"You have amazing taste, Yve. Do you buy all the designs that are in the shop?"

She gives me a shy smile. "Yes. But some are my own."

"What?" I say wide-eyed.

"I went to fashion school. I design dresses. It's kind of my thing."

"The rose gold one?"

She nods. "Yep, that was all me."

"You have a real talent, Yve."

She laughs. "That's what Bastian always said and why he bought me this shop." She looks around as if she is in awe of her own life. "I'm young. I'm still perfecting things. But one day you might see this boutique mixed in with all the designers on those high end streets through New York, Paris, and London. At least that's the dream."

"I believe in you."

She blushes. "Thank you. That means a lot. I've had

a lot of success so far, no thanks to my cousin. I'm excited to see where life takes me. It can only go up from here."

"You have the most infectious positivity."

"When you learn to appreciate the little things, it's not hard."

I think about her comment and bury it deep in my soul. Words I need to learn to live by.

I grab the midnight blue dress Yve insisted I buy. I don't know what Bastian's plans are for tonight but at least I have something to wear if he wants to go to a nice dinner.

Yve rings me out and says that Bastian paid for whatever I needed. I tried to let her at least let me purchase the blue dress but she said her cousin had enough money to buy the damn island, he can buy me a three-hundred-dollar dress.

I hug her before I leave and walk out of the shop with a smile on my face. Sometimes shopping is all you need to put you in a better mood.

I don't see Bastian as I walk out of the shop. I look down and across the street but he is nowhere to be found. I am about to turn left when I hear his muffled voice to my right.

There is a small alleyway I didn't see before. I take a few steps toward it but stop when I hear him talking.

"We both know Matías wasn't smart enough to do this... Yes, I know I'm an asshole... I'm not worried about the money."

He shifts and I flatten myself to the side of the building so he can't see me. I can hear him pacing on the broken street, his loafers scuffling the rocks.

"Just get it done. If it costs more, I will pay more." He practically growls into the phone. "She stays out of this."

Is he talking about me?

"I told you she won't look into things anymore… No, she isn't for sale."

Isn't for sale?

"I'm risking everything for this. Everything I worked hard to erase. I won't ask again. Get it done or you won't get your money."

The sound of his footsteps approaching has me quickly stepping back toward the store.

"Cameron."

I wonder if he knows I overheard him.

"I was just coming back in to see if you got everything taken care of."

"Yep. All done. Shoes and all."

He smiles at me and grabs the bags from my hand. "Great. Let's get to the hotel."

I guess he didn't know I was eavesdropping. I let out a sigh of relief as we make our way back down the cobblestone walkways.

The hotel isn't very far from what he told me but it's enough time for me to overthink everything. Is Bastian involved in trafficking? Why would he say I'm not for sale? Is he really behind this entire scandal and put the blame on his brother? He did say something about how Matías wasn't smart enough. And what is he risking?

But then I think back to what his cousin told me. About the man that's hiding behind the mask. And I know he can't be behind this. He has a heart hiding behind those walls. He would never get involved in something so terrible, would he? I need to find out what he is protecting me from. Maybe then I'll get some answers.

When we get to the hotel, Bastian hangs my dresses in the closet and heads for the shower. I find a bottle of champagne chilling in the sitting room, so I pour myself a glass and head out to the balcony overlooking the marina. The sun beats onto the terrace as I sip on my champagne my thoughts all over the place.

I think about what Yvette told me. The man she knows Bastian to be versus the man I know. But I see the parts she talked about shining through. Like the walk we had through the park in London. Or the moment we shared after that article hit that could have destroyed him. And all the moments of today. Every single one of them memorable. Something I will always cherish. The way he helped me get over my fear of the water. The sex in the cove. Our conversation as we spent the afternoon on the stern of the boat sunbathing.

Bastian Montford is a mystery. He says he is dangerous, yet he is always around protecting me. From himself and whatever else he is hiding. He is a lover and a fighter. He is rough around the edges yet can be as gentle as the calm seas. He is a conundrum. A man who works hard to cover his scars and his heart. Yet I want nothing more than to break through them. Touch them, feel them, heal them.

I want to be with him despite all my qualms about rich men.

Because unlike every other man my mother forced on me, Bastian won't take my voice away. He won't let me sit on the sidelines or in the gilded cage waiting to be let out. I know he is the man who would unleash me from my chains, let me shout from the mountains, let me be a warrior.

I just don't know if it would ever work for us. Or if he would want the same thing.

"Cameron."

I look over and see him sitting across from me in a pair of lounge pants. His feet and chest bare. His hair towel dried and hanging in his face. He looks the most handsome like this, with his walls gone.

"What's on your mind? You've been quiet since we left Yvette's store."

I rotate the champagne flute in my hand as I look at him. I don't know how to ask him. How to say the words I've been thinking for the last hour. I have so many questions, so many things I want to know. What's really going on? Are we in danger? Has he been lying to me?

But the hardest question for me to ask, how does he feel about me? Is this real?

I swallow down the rest of the champagne in my glass. Using the alcohol to combat my nerves.

"Cam." His voice is soft. A whisper on the wind.

"What are you protecting me from, Bastian?"

He sighs and looks out across the water. "I told you. I'm protecting you from—"

"Cut the bullshit."

He looks over at me, surprise etching his features.

"It's not you. I know you would never do anything to harm me. That's not the kind of man you are." I clench my fist around the stem of the champagne glass so hard I think it may break. "So tell me, Bastian. Please."

A look of regret crosses his features and then a look of defeat. He reaches across the table between us and grabs the champagne flute from my hand and sets it down. "I'm not a good man, Cam."

"You've told me that countless times but that doesn't tell me shit," I huff.

He bows his head and sighs deeply before getting up and kneeling in front of me. He cups my jaw and searches my eyes. I get lost in the beauty of his face. His slightly crooked nose, the line between those mysterious eyes I've come to love, his full lips. He brushes his thumb over my own lips and I watch as the defeat darkens his eyes.

"I really do want to protect you, Cam. You do some- thing to me. Awaken something in me. Ever since that day I met you on the pier by my yacht. Your attitude, your strength..." He pauses as his hand slides down my throat to my chest. "Your heart."

He closes his eyes and I slide forward on the chair, needing to be closer to him because I am afraid whatever he is going to tell me is going to destroy us before we can ever even be an us.

"I never wanted to put you in this position. I never wanted to make you a target, a pawn. But I couldn't keep myself away from you. I couldn't let myself just look at you from afar. I made the mistake of touching you, feeling you. I know what every part of your body tastes like and feels like. I'm addicted to it. And now I am afraid I have gone too far. But yet here I am still unable to let you go."

"Do you really think it was a mistake to touch me, Bas?"

He pulls my face to his. "Fuck no. Every touch between us makes me feel more alive. It makes me feel more like the man I should be than the one I became. If I had the choice I would do the same thing over again a hundred times, Cameron." He rests his forehead against mine. "And I'm a selfish bastard because every time it would put you in danger."

That word again. Danger.

I should feel apprehensive over it. Maybe scared. But his other words have more power. The words that tell me he would choose me over and over again.

"What are you talking about, Bastian?"

He sighs and stands up, pulling me with him. His face is in my neck as he wraps his arms around me. "I didn't want to pull you into this. Into a world I've been trying so hard to get out of. But I should have known they would use you. I've put you right back in the cage I said you could be free of."

"Bas," I whisper against his neck.

He doesn't say anything, just pulls me into the room, shutting the balcony door behind us. He sits on the corner of the bed and pulls me into him, gripping the backs of my thighs.

I look down at him, pushing the longer pieces of his hair out of his face and then resting my arms on his shoulders.

"Do you promise you won't run away from me?"

"I don't think I could."

Those words do something to him. He pulls my face down, searing a kiss across my lips. I open up to him as he pulls me onto his lap. "Why are you perfect?"

I laugh against his lips. "I'm far from perfect, Bastian."

"Call me Bas. I like it when you call me Bas."

"Bas," I whisper and his lips pull me in again. His hands hold me to him like he never wants to let me go.

When he finally pulls away, I know I am finally getting the truth I've been asking for the last six weeks. And for some reason, despite all his warnings, I'm not scared. Because he brings me a sense of safety when I am wrapped in his arms.

"When I was in university with Kilian, I was introduced to a world no one should know about. The criminal underworld, drug dealers, traffickers, weapons dealers. I was young and naïve. Kilian and I both were. We didn't know any better.

"There is a group of businessmen that oversee a lot of the black market. They keep things hidden, they make business transactions look legit. They promise they can make you wealthier than you could ever imagine but they don't tell you the price that comes with it. Neither of us thought much of it. His family has been involved with them for years. One taste was all I needed. Before I knew it, I was deeply involved with them. I never sold drugs or humans or weapons, but I aided in the sales, used Montford Holdings as a backer. It caused the business' insane growth.

"I became addicted to the money and the power.

Thiago had just taken over for our father. I convinced Thiago that this was the right choice. We both fell down the rabbit hole, getting more and more involved with the group. I was still so young. Younger than you are now. I didn't see how it was wrong. Our father knew we were up to something, knew that the business couldn't grow on its own at the rate it was growing. It never had in the fifty years it had been around. But the group knew how to cover things up, keep people on the outside in the dark. Hell, they've never been investigated. I can only assume there are government members that I just don't know about.

"Two years before Thiago died, he knew we were too deeply involved. Our younger brother was getting ready to graduate from university. We knew he would want to work for the family business. Thiago was overprotective of Matías. He didn't want him involved. Thiago and I argued all the time. He wanted to pull out, I wanted to stay in. I knew we couldn't get out though. I knew that if he tried something bad would happen to one of us.

"They threatened us for years. Thiago kept trying to remove us. And he was finally able to. We paid a lot of money to them and they promised we would no longer be a part of the group. I didn't have a good feeling about it. I was worried the entire company would collapse. That our father would disown us. But that's not what happened. They let us go freely. And six months after that, Thiago was murdered. Of course they made it look like a suicide. But I never believed it. He was happy. His wife was pregnant.

"That was the price we paid to get out of the group.

But somehow Matías found a way to be dragged back in. I thought Kilian had something to do with it. But he denies it. Maybe my brother found a way in through me a long time ago and I never knew. But they had something to do with the raid. With him going to prison. And now I am being dragged back into that world. To protect you."

I blink at his words. His story insane yet I believe it. I can understand why I never found anything when I looked into his past after that article came out. But I don't get what this has to do with me. "Why me?"

He sighs and pulls me tighter into him. "They know who you are. They've seen us working together. Honestly, they thought you were my girlfriend before they were told otherwise. But it was too late. They are trying to make me an offer for me to save my brother. Once I knew they were involved, I contacted them. They are willing to make it all go away but they want you."

"The phone call in the alley?" I ask as fear creeps over me.

He nods. "I wondered if you'd heard. You've been acting strangely ever since then." His hands slide up my back and hold my head in place, so I look at him. "You need to know I would never sell a human. I would never sell you to the highest bidder to save my brother. But I need to protect you. I need you under my watch at all times. It's why I brought you here. From the first threat on your life I needed to keep you safe."

"It had nothing to do with the gala?"

A smirk crosses his face so quickly if I were to blink, I would miss it. "That too."

I smile and brush my hands through his hair. I remain calm despite the things he is telling me. "What kind of threats did they make?"

He presses his lips to my shoulder. "They never said anything clearly. They never do. They told me to tell you to stop digging. That I needed to keep my eyes on you. I wasn't sure what it meant. But all I could think about was Thiago and I couldn't let that happen to you too."

"You didn't kill your brother."

"I know that. But I am to blame for his death."

"So you brought me here to make sure nothing happened to me?" He nods. "Is that why you were so mad when I went out shopping that day."

"I didn't know you left. When I couldn't find you in the house, I was worried something happened. I was worried you were kidnapped right under my nose. Then Marta told me you went out with her daughter. I got overly worried. You could easily have been taken to teach me a lesson or as a payment to a debt I owe them."

"I'm sorry, Bastian. I didn't know."

"Because I didn't tell you. I still shouldn't have told you. But you are too damn stubborn to listen to me."

That makes me smile. "Did you think this would happen?"

"What?"

I look down between us, my fingers grasping the ones he has on my thigh. "This. Us."

He lets go of my hand and lifts my chin so our eyes meet. "No. I wanted it. I've wanted you since the moment you talked back to me. But I knew you were off-limits. Something I could never have. I restrained myself around you all the time. Do you want to know how many times I wanted to fuck you in your office or call you up to my penthouse? One time I almost knocked on your door. The night I kissed you. I was hard all day. I wanted nothing more than to fuck you every way I could. I was angry with you because after you left, I couldn't concentrate on shit and all I thought about was sliding into you. Fucking you against a wall, on the terrace, in your shower. I was yearning for you in a way I never yearned for anyone before.

"So to answer your question. I fantasized about a million ways I could make you mine at my home in Deià. But I never intended to act on any one of those urges. Until I saw you in that damn swimsuit, dripping water all over my office floor."

"Do you regret it?" I ask.

He flips me over onto my back and balances over me. "I would only regret it if I ended up hurting you."

"I would take the hurt if it meant I got to keep you, Bas."

He growls and then claims my mouth, then my body.

I don't care about anything he told me. I am not worried about my safety around him.

Maybe he is dangerous.

But with him, I've never felt safer.

25

CAM

B astian insisted on taking me to one of his favorite places for dinner. But he told me we had to wait until the sun set.

We spent a few hours in bed, worshiping each other's bodies. We didn't think about the truths he finally revealed, didn't ponder on what could happen with us being together. We just let ourselves live in the moment. Listening to our hearts and not our heads.

"With everything you told me, I am surprised Lucas isn't with us."

Bastian looks at me as he buttons up his dress shirt. "He's around."

"He wasn't on the boat."

"He drove here. If I need him, he'll show up."

"Okay."

I slip on a pair of strappy sandals that are dressy enough to go with the midnight blue dress I bought earlier. Bastian said we have a twenty-minute walk and I did not want to be in my wedges and was grateful I brought these with me. I adjust the straps on my dress. It's a deep V dotted with a ton of crystals along the bodice and straps that crisscross in an intricate pattern across my back, reminding me of stars in the sky. The bottom flares out and hits mid-thigh.

"You ready?" I ask him, my voice quiet.

He walks over to me and I am enveloped in his smell. A seduction of the senses, I almost don't want to leave.

He presses a chaste kiss to my lips. "Let's go."

We walk through the labyrinth of streets until the noise from the marina and nightlife quiet down. I expected him to take me to one of the fancy restaurants along the coastline but he takes me deeper into the cobblestone streets. It's a maze of alleyways and one-way streets but eventually we end up in front of a simple wooden door with a sign on it that says "A Les Estrelles."

He reaches for the door handle and pulls me inside. I am surprised to find a set of stairs in front of me. I look over at him and he whispers into my ear. "It means 'to the stars.' Come on, you'll see."

He has me go first as we climb the winding brick staircase. Lanterns with real candles hang along the turret wall every few steps to give us enough light to see in the dark. We climb at least four floors until we meet another wooden door just like the one downstairs. I go to open it but he pulls me back into him until my back hits his chest.

He pushes my hair to the side, the hair I wore down for him. "Did I tell you how beautiful you look tonight?" he whispers in my ear.

I shake my head.

"You look just like the night sky in this dress. It's fitting."

I don't know what he means by that until he lets me go and opens the door in front of me. We are on top of a roof, far enough from the nightlife that there is barely any light up here. Before I can look around, he pulls me against him and turns my head to the sky. The lack of light pollution shows a thousand tiny stars sparkling in the sky.

"Your dress matches the sky."

"Did Yve know you would bring me here?"

He kisses me behind my ear. "Of course she would dress you like this."

I go to kiss him but we are interrupted by a man in a suit. "Mr. Montford, so happy to have you back. Let me show you to your table."

Bastian takes my hand as we walk past a handful of tables along the roof. Only candlelight is used to light the tables, giving just enough light to see but not enough light to block out the stars.

We walk up a small set of stairs to a separate area of the roof and are directed to a secluded table with no one else around. The table backs up to a corner of the building completely cutting us off from everyone and any ambient light from the town.

"How did you get this table?" I ask after the man leaves.

"I may know the owner."

I go to ask him who it is but a server comes over to us with a martini and a glass of scotch.

"For you and your guest, Mr. Montford."

After he walks away, I ask, "How did he know our drinks?"

Bastian smiles at me. "They know things here."

I go to kick him under the table but he grabs my hand. "I've always loved looking at the stars. Ever since I was a boy, laying on my uncle's boat in the middle of the night. They made me feel like I had a thousand different paths I could take. I've looked at them ever since then. Yet they always seem brighter here. Like they are directing me to take a certain path. In London, I always felt lost when I looked at them. But never here.

"I stumbled upon this building once while my uncle was doing business. I got in a lot of trouble when the owners called the police for me trespassing." I laugh at his story, picturing a little wild-haired Bastian running around the street of Pollença. "When I was old enough, I bought the building. I spent a lot of time up here staring at the stars, looking for answers. Especially after my brother died. After my divorce. I always went back to London or Paris with a fresh mind.

"I wanted to share that experience with others. I wanted them to find their way through the stars. So I opened this restaurant. *A Les Estrelles*, to the stars. Since that is always what I found behind that door."

I stare at Bastian, completely dumbfounded. This man is more beautiful than I ever could have imagined. His soul has so many stories. His worth so great. Yet he hides behind a monster, never letting anyone see the real him.

"Why are you crying?"

I didn't even realize tears were streaming down my face. He wipes them away. "You are a beautiful man, Bastian. I don't care how dangerous you say you are or how coldhearted you act to others." I place my hand over his heart. "You are a beautiful man in here. And I feel lucky to have met this version of you."

He leans in and kisses me. A slow, seductive kiss I feel all the way to my toes.

I don't know how long we kiss for. The sun could be rising for all I know because that kiss fortified my heart. I know that from here on out, the only man that will ever own my heart is Bastian Luciano Montford.

When he finally pulls away, our server comes to our table with our first course. Like he was waiting for us to share that moment.

We spend the rest of dinner conversing easily. The food and wine served with each course is delicious. Bastian sure picked one hell of a chef to run this place.

"Dance with me?" Bastian asks after we share a dessert.

I smile at him and take his hand as he leads me to the area next to our table. The soft Spanish music from the speakers is lovely as he spins me around under the stars. I feel like we are in our own world, separated from everything we are dealing with. Just Bastian and me under a Mallorcan sky.

His mouth is by my ear whispering what I can only think are sweet nothings to me in Catalan as we dance. I feel so damn lucky I found this man. He is everything I promised myself I would never take yet with him, it's different.

One of his hands slide down my back, cupping my ass as he peppers kisses along my throat. "Mi cielito."

I pull back and gaze into his eyes. "You called me that earlier. What does it mean?"

He presses his lips to my forehead, my nose, my cheek then whispers in my ear. "It means my little sky. Because just like the stars showed me the right path to take, so have you, Cam. And you deserve to be free to fly like a bird without a cage. You weren't meant for that. You were meant to fly free."

This time it's me who smashes my lips to his as he says words that mean more to me than I could ever express. This man understands me. Gets me. And I think I may be falling for him.

When I pull away from him, he spins me around to the beat of the music. I land with my back against his chest with his arms wrapped around me and look up to the sky thanking the stars for showing me the path that led to him.

26

BASTIAN

I'm quiet as we walk back to the hotel. My hand is firmly wrapped in Cameron's and for the first time in a long time maybe my entire life, I feel whole.

I asked the stars when I was a boy to lead me in the direction of success, wealth, power. And they did. But then I questioned them when I fell into a deal with the devil, when I joined The Partners, when I sold my soul to gain that power I desired so much as a child.

But looking at the stars tonight, with the most beautiful woman I've ever laid eyes on wrapped in my arms, I realized the stars had me on the right path the entire time. Because I think she was what they were leading me to.

Wealth and power have nothing over this feeling burning inside of me. Just like the stars fall, I feel my own heart falling for the woman next to me. This woman who takes me for who I am. Who pushed me so many times when we first met. But I wouldn't want her any other way. She's strong, independent, wild.

When we get near the marina, she goes to turn in the direction of the hotel but the water is calling to me like the stars in the sky.

"Let's go look at the stars."

She follows my line of sight and squeezes my hand tighter. I got her to feel fine in the water earlier but that was during the day. And the sea at night seems much darker and deadlier.

I lean into her ear, pulling her platinum waves back. "I've got you, mi cielito. I'll always have you."

Goose bumps spread over her skin and I know my words affect her in more ways than one.

I pull out my phone and send a text to the captain. He let me know earlier he would sleep on the boat overnight while the deckhands stayed on the mainland.

I originally had every intention of sleeping on my friend's boat tonight but after Cameron's story, I thought it best we stay at a hotel. She can learn the safety of a boat on my yacht.

I want her there. Hell, I want her everywhere. By my side for as long as she will. But I know it's a rough road ahead of us. Too many forces that will keep us apart. But I will fight like hell to make her mine forever.

I thought I would be scared of those words. But I'm not. After I lost Thiago and my wife left me, I thought I would never love again. Never let anyone in. My ex-wife destroyed me when she left but for some reason the spit-fire clinging to my arm has changed me. She put a kink in my armor. And I know in time she will tear my walls down completely.

When we make it to the boat, she kicks her sandals off and steps onto the boat willingly.

"You're a sailor now, huh? No need to freak out from the water."

She laughs, that wild, carefree laugh that used to keep me up at night when I heard it from my terrace at the hotel. "Let's not get ahead of ourselves, Mr. Montford, we are still tied to the dock."

I pick up my own shoes and follow her onto the boat. When she turns around to walk to the helm, I wrap my arms around her waist, picking her up just slightly off the ground. "If you are going to start calling me Mr. Montford again, I suggest you do it in private."

She wiggles her ass against my hips and I know she can feel my length getting harder. I let her go and smack her ass. "I'm not afraid to punish you."

She spins around and throws her arms around my neck. She starts speaking in the weakest British accent I've ever heard. "Why Mr. Montford, are you threatening me with doing the dirty?"

I pull her into me, one hand sliding underneath her skirt, my fingers teasing the edge of her panty line. "It's not a threat, sweet cheeks."

She bites my earlobe harder than I expect her to. "Good."

Fuck, I wish we just went back to the hotel.

The captain clears his throat from behind us and lets us know to sit down. He turns the engine on so we don't need to worry about the sails. He is only taking us a few kilometers out. Just beyond the north tip of the bay where the water is relatively calm but no lights from the island can be seen.

Cam is calm as we sail out to the spot I told the captain to go to. She is a much different person than the one from this morning. It's crazy to think how much has changed between us in just a day.

When I flew her out here a week ago, it was truly to protect her. The first threat came in late at night and I had a ticket for her the next morning. I couldn't risk losing her. Losing someone I had no right to. But I couldn't let her be a pawn in this game. If her company sent a different publicist then we wouldn't be here. I never would have met her.

I look up to the stars, sending a silent prayer yet again for leading me on the path to her.

The sound of the engine cutting off means we've arrived at the perfect spot to gaze at the stars. I pull a blanket out of the bench seat and lay it out on the bow of the boat. I kneel down and Cam follows suit, lying next to me as we look up at the sky.

"It's so magnificent, the stars," she says. "When we were in Saint Tropez, I was mesmerized by them. I would sit on the terrace or in that bathtub that lets you see them so clearly. They were nothing like this but compared to New York or Boston it sure was something. I don't even think I've seen stars like this until now."

"You should see them when you are in the middle of the sea. You can see the galaxy."

"I would love to see that someday. If I don't chicken out from the size of your boat."

I chuckle as I trace circles on her bare thighs with my fingers. "You didn't chicken out from—"

"Please don't cut in with a dick joke. We were having such a nice night."

I grab her hand and bring it to my lips, kissing it softly. "I was going to say you didn't chicken out from hanging out with me today."

She turns and looks at me, and I meet her stare. "No you weren't."

I smile at her. The smile I used to have all the time as a kid but slowly faded away throughout the years. Through everything I endured.

"Why do you hate galas so much?" her voice is quiet as she asks me.

I sigh. My lips press to her shoulder. "I was at a gala when Thiago died."

She turns to me, propping her elbow up to rest her head on. Her hand reaches for my own and she squeezes. "Bas…"

I close my eyes and relive the moment. The phone call I received. The memory of my scotch glass slipping from my hand, crashing to the floor, the glass shattering everywhere.

"We were both supposed to be at the gala. But he said he had a meeting. I could tell from his tone of voice who he was meeting with. I was pissed. We got out of their clutches and he was jumping right back in." I pause, thinking about that night. "I still don't know what happened. They made it look like suicide. I know he was murdered. And I can't stop blaming myself for not forcing myself to join him. If I was there then maybe he wouldn't have been killed."

Cameron squeezes my hand. "You don't know that. You could have both been killed."

I nod. I know that was a strong possibility. I roll onto my back, pinching my fingers between my brow. "His wife hates me. To this day she won't talk to me. Won't let me see my nephews. She only talks to Matías. I have my people check up on her. She's surviving somehow. She moved back to Scotland after his death. She has a good family to support her."

"Maybe you should try to talk to her again. It's been, what, five years?"

I nod. "She won't."

Cameron reaches over and brushes my hair out of my face. "What happened with your own wife?"

I clench my fists at the thought of her. My jaw tensing as I think of her promiscuity with Matías, Frederick Davenport, and whoever else she spread her legs for when she was in Saint Tropez.

"Bas…"

"She didn't love me. She cheated. She lied. And she had no empathy when I was broken over Thiago's death. She left me while I was in mourning."

Cameron gasps next to me. She tugs on my hand, pulling me to face her. I get lost in her blue eyes, her soft features. This woman who is doing things to my heart. A woman who is forcing me to let her in.

"She wasn't worth your time then. And she sounds like a total bitch. It was best she left."

I smile at her words as I feel her energy beating off her from the anger she feels toward my ex.

"Besides, if you were still with her, we wouldn't be here. And I like being here. With you."

She turns back to the sky but I keep my head toward her as she gazes at the stars. I can't keep my eyes off her. She is my star now, my little sky full of stars.

When we make it back to the hotel, I can't keep my hands off her. I didn't miss how she wore her hair down for me. And it drove me crazy all night.

When we finally make it to the door of our room, I barely have it shut before she is jumping on me. I catch her ass as her lips latch to mine, sucking them into her own. I let her control me this one time.

Her hands go to the buttons of my shirt, ripping it open and caressing my chest, her nails digging into my skin. I run my fingers between her thighs and find her wet for me just like I knew she would be. When she tries to grind against me, I stop her.

I walk her to the bed and ease her down gently. "Don't move," I tell her as I take my shirt off, slip out of my shoes, and unbuckle my pants.

She listens to me. Her body is sprawled across the bed, her breathing erratic, her heart beating hard, causing her breasts to slide out of the top of her dress.

Once I am fully naked, I crawl over her body. I kiss her lips softly, showing her how I feel rather than just taking. Then I slowly kiss down her body, starting at her clavicle, then down her arm, over her clothed stomach, then to her center. When I know she wants more, I move my lips down her thighs until I reach her ankles.

I slip both of her sandals off then rub her feet, releasing all the stress from the day. She moans as I do it, teeth biting her bottom lip as the tension flows out of her body. When I finish her feet, I move up her legs, running my hands up and down them, changing the pressure as I go. My tongue and lips follow, licking, sucking, caressing every inch of her.

When I make it to her hips, I find the zipper on the side of her dress and slowly slide it down. I push her dress up and over her hips, revealing the black lace panties I knew were hiding underneath. I press a kiss to both her hip bones then move my way up her stomach, giving the top half of her body the same treatment I gave the bottom half.

As I move up, I push her dress higher and higher. When her tits bounce free, I suck each one into my mouth, biting lightly as she squirms beneath me. She tries to thrust her hips into mine. "Stay still," I whisper as I pop her left nipple out of my mouth.

I pull her dress over her head as I make it to her lips. She's greedy as she kisses me and I don't blame her. I've spent my time worshiping every inch of her body. My cock is so hard it's painful and I want nothing more than to tie her down and show her how much I need her body.

But this time is different. This time I don't want to take advantage of her. I want to worship her. Make love to her. Let her see that I am falling just as hard as she is.

"Bas," she moans as I press a kiss to her clavicle. "Please."

I move back onto my knees, my hands resting on her hips. "Please what, mi cielito?"

She moans at the nickname. "I need you."

"What do you need?"

"You."

I click my tongue as I slide my thumbs under the top of her lace underwear. "Where do you need me?"

She groans as I lightly wipe my thumb over her clit with the whisper of a touch as I pull her panties around her thighs.

"I don't care. I'm soaking. You're teasing me."

I chuckle as I pull the lace the rest of the way down her legs. "Baby, I'm not teasing you."

"Yes, you are."

I throw the black lace behind me and spread her thighs, watching her desire drip out of her pink lips. "Mmm. This isn't teasing," I say as I use a featherlight touch to swipe between her legs.

"Yes, it is. Please, Bas."

The sound of my childhood nickname on her tongue sends me over the edge. I push her legs farther apart then lean over her, my dick touching the tip of her wetness, making it throb even more than it already is. I plunge into her all the way to the hilt.

She screams my name and I swallow her screams with my mouth as I kiss her deeply. She wraps her legs around my hips and her arms around my neck as she meets me thrust for thrust. Her warmth wraps around my dick as I slow down and speed up, changing the rhythm over and over but I never let go of her. Never overpower her. My hands move from her hips to her arms, never letting go of this woman who has my heart in a choke hold.

There is a shift in the air and I feel her pouring her soul into me like this, all we both will ever need. Just the two of us, in our own world, away from it all.

I feel her ready to climax and I want us to do it together. Because this time we are different. We may not say the words but we both know what this is. My hands slide to her throat, gripping it softly as she starts to let go.

She explodes around me just as I find my own release. She sucks me in, milking everything out that is inside of me. When I finish, I collapse my head into her chest. Her heart beating as fast as mine.

"Bastian." Her voice is barely audible.

"I know," I whisper. "I know."

I pull out of her, already missing her heat. I go to the bathroom and clean up, warming a wet towel as I do it.

When I walk back into the bedroom, Cam is a sight to see. Her blonde hair wild and free over the pillow. Red marks on her hips and arms and throat where my hands were.

But what nearly brings me to my knees is the smile on her face. The way her eyes meet mine, like she can see through me, see all my darkest secrets. The difference with her over everyone else, she still wants me even with my darkness.

I wipe the towel between her legs and toss it on the ground behind me. I scoop her up, bringing her back to my chest, our bodies completely flush against each other.

"Bas."

I press a kiss to the back of her neck and pull her even closer to me.

"Bas... I... I don't know what we are doing but I can't get rid of these feelings inside of me."

"I know, mi cielito, I know."

Neither of us say the words. I am not sure either of us know how. But right here in this moment, this woman has shattered the walls encompassing my heart.

I've fallen for her. Hard.

And it may be the one thing that destroys us both.

27

CAM

The warm salty breeze on my skin feels good as we sail back to Deià.

Last night was incredible. In fact, this whole trip has been. I'm so tied up in Bastian I almost forgot we aren't even supposed to be anything. The boat slows down and soon makes its way to a different cove than before. Bastian told me if we made good time we could go swimming again.

I think he was simply happy to see me so eager to jump off a boat. After last time I don't know why I waited so long to go back in the water. It's amazing out here. I could live here.

I strip off the oversized T-shirt I had on as a cover-up and head over to the edge of the boat to jump off but before I can get to the ledge, Bastian has his hands on me.

"Where did you get this?" he growls.

I laugh as he takes me in. Yve had a few swimsuits at

her shop and I had to buy them. This is a turquoise one-piece that reminds me of the crystal clear water we jumped into yesterday. It's one shoulder and the middle is completely cut out, revealing my tan skin. It's a thong style. Much more Instagrammer-worthy than practical but I knew it would give Bastian a heart attack.

"At Yve's."

"You shouldn't be seen in public in this."

"Why not?"

"It's not appropriate."

I scoff. "Yes it is. I just think you don't want anyone else looking at me."

He glares at me. "That's not it at all."

I pat him on the cheek. "Okay, you brute. But there is literally no one here to see me."

"There are two deckhands."

"Ah-ha. So it is that you don't want anyone to see me." I pull out of his grip and turn to jump into the water but he pulls me back into him.

"Fine. I don't want anyone looking at you. You're mine and I am the only one that gets to see you naked."

I bristle at that even though I am swooning inside. "I'm not naked."

He groans and pulls me back into him. "No, you aren't. But my handprint is painted across your ass from this morning and I would prefer if no one saw that but me."

I throw my head back in laughter and jump into the water. He really is a brute.

We make it home in time to shower and change before we are back on the winding roads of Mallorca to head to dinner at his aunt and uncle's house. They live just outside the adorable village of Soller. We wind up a curvy road and come to a modest house.

"What's your uncle do?"

"Imports and exports."

I look over at Bastian. That kind of answer is what I would expect with what he told me yesterday. "That's vague. Don't tell me he is involved with—"

Bastian's smile cuts me off. He grabs my hand and squeezes as he parks the car. "I'm kidding. He works at the university."

I put my hand to my chest. "Did you just tell a joke? I think I might have a heart attack."

He responds by grabbing my neck and pulling me into a kiss. "You'll pay for that later."

"Sounds terrifying." I wink and open the car door.

He quickly gets out and grabs my hand as I stand. He shuts the door behind me and then presses his body into mine. He pushes my hair behind my ear as he cups my face. "You okay with this?"

"Meeting the Spanish side of your family?"

He nods.

I put my hands on his chest. "It's weird, if I'm being honest. I don't know what we are, Bas. I don't know where we stand. When we leave this island, we have to go back to what we were. You are my client and I am your publicist." I sigh as I look up at the house. "I guess I don't know what to think."

"If we didn't go to Yve's shop then none of this

would have happened," he said as he smiled. "She talks a lot."

"I noticed."

"She told her brother who then told her sister who told her dad then he told his wife. Typical of this family but I love them for it."

I watch him as he glances at the house. "It's the family life you didn't have."

His gaze meets mine. "Yes. And I get to have that when I am here."

"It's why you love this island so much."

He nods.

"Did you come here with your brothers like this?"

"Not really. Thiago came more often than Matías ever does. But Thiago had a family. I think he battled with his own mind on whether he wanted the family life we grew up with or this ideal one our cousins had. I guess I feel the same."

"You know the grass is always greener on the other side, Bas. Just because this looks ideal doesn't mean it is. I'm sure they struggle as much as every other family does."

"I know. But it's nice to think about."

I shut down the thoughts that cross through my mind immediately. The ones where Bastian and I live here happily ever after with our own kids running around, playing on the beach and in the sea. It's not something we could have.

"Hey," he says, pressing a kiss to my forehead. "I didn't mean for you to get lost in your thoughts either."

"I know you didn't. It's just—"

"Are you two just going to make out even though you aren't dating or actually come inside?" Yve shouts from the front door.

Bastian chuckles against my forehead and I feel the vibrations through my entire body. "Busted."

Bastian and I are both slightly tipsy when we get home. But his aunt gave us a bottle of her sangria to take with us. We laugh as we walk into the kitchen and pour another glass.

"Do you know what sounds fun right now?" I ask Bastian, who is watching me with predatory eyes.

"Punishing you for making fun of me earlier."

I giggle. "You know that wouldn't be a punishment."

"I think I am going to have to find ways to punish you that actually work as punishment."

I shrug. "I don't think you'll be able to."

He shakes his head at me and sips his sangria. I open the doors to the terrace and walk out, taking in the view of the sea and the mountains. I feel Bastian behind me as I lean against the rail. "It's so beautiful here. I can't get enough of it."

"It is."

I look over at him and see him staring at me. I know he was talking about me. My mind flutters back to the thoughts of how this will all end soon and I can't have him looking at me like that. Because it will just make this harder.

I step back from him and set my glass down on a

table. I pull my dress over my head and slide my panties down my legs.

"What are you doing?" he asks, desire growing in his eyes.

"Having fun." I turn around and walk down the steps into the pool, swimming out to the infinity edge so I can take in the view.

The soft splashes of water behind me lets me know he has joined me in the pool. I turn around just as he swims up behind me.

"This is your idea of fun?"

"You don't think skinny dipping is fun?"

"Maybe when I was fifteen."

I trace my nail across his chest. "You liked it the other night when we were in here."

His hands land on the ledge behind me but he keeps his body away from me. "Neither of us were naked when we got in the water. Completely different."

I shrug and try to pull him against me but he keeps his distance. He then pushes off the wall and swims backward away from me.

"What are you doing?" I ask.

"Having fun." He smirks at me.

I swim after him but he plays keep away from me. I pout playfully and then swim toward the steps to walk out of the pool. I turn around to see him watching me. I think he is going to come after me but he doesn't.

I pick a towel up and wrap it around me and head into the house. When I am halfway down the hall to my room, I hear Bastian's voice.

"Where are you going?"

I turn around to find him completely naked and wet in the hall. "To bed."

"Wrong bed."

"What?" I ask.

He doesn't say anything, just walks toward me, scoops me up and spins us around, carrying me to his room.

He sets me down when we get into his bedroom. I've never been in here. Hell, the only time we actually shared a bed was last night at the hotel. We always slept in separate rooms. Yes, he might have fucked the hell out of me in my own room but he always went back to his.

I take in the décor. Where I expected dark tones and smoky accents, his room is bright. Tasteful artwork of the island is on the walls. A set of French doors lead out to a huge balcony that I remember seeing from the outside of the house. It overlooks the bay.

He walks up to me and pulls my towel off. Then lifts me up and carries me over to the bed. He's gentle, soft, and slow. This isn't like the other times at the house. This is more like last night when I swear he was making love to me.

We spend time worshiping each other's bodies and when we come together, I swear I feel every part of my walls shatter in my heart. This man owns me. My heart, my soul. He owns every inch of my body. And I know that I am in love with him. But I can't tell him because this fairy tale will be over soon.

I wake up sweating and kick the sheets off my body. Bastian is wrapped around me and he groans as I move the covers off us. The doors to the balcony are still open and the breeze from the water floats into the room. It's barely sunrise, the sky a muted blue with small hints of orange shooting across the top of the sky.

Bastian shifts behind me, and I can feel his very hard dick pushing into my back.

"I like this," he mutters into my shoulder.

I smile because I like it too. I like waking up to him wrapped around me.

He presses kisses down my spine before flipping me onto my back and hovering over me. "Good morning, mi cielito."

His hair is wild, falling into his face as he looks down at me. I swear the look in his eyes is love. Maybe I just want it to be because my heart is beating a million beats a second as I stare into the eyes of the man I no doubt am in love with.

"'Morning," I whisper.

I spread my legs apart as his mouth meets my own. I moan into him as he slides into me. Every thrust making me fall more in love with this enigmatic man.

"I want to spend all day like this," I say to him as he pulls me into him when we finish. Our chests are pressed against each other and I can feel his heart beat against mine.

"Mmm." He nuzzles his face into my neck. "That would be ideal."

His lips press under my ear but he stops suddenly

from the vibrations of his phone going off on the nightstand.

He groans into my neck. "Too early."

"Ignore it."

I think he is going to but when the ringing stops and then starts again immediately he releases me from his hold and rolls over. I watch him as he looks at the screen, a deep crease forming between his eyes. He sighs and answers the phone. I can't hear anything on the other end but I can feel the tension in his shoulders like it's in my own.

He gets out of bed and walks across the room. My eyes glue to his perfect naked form. How is this man so perfect? It's like he was molded by gods.

He leaves the room just as he starts to argue with whoever is on the other end of the line.

I slide out of bed and find one of his T-shirts on the bench at the end of the bed. Our clothes are still out by the pool. I slip on the shirt and head outside to the balcony. I hate that my mind automatically goes to the fantasy life I wish we could have. I don't understand it. My entire life I was against this. I didn't want a relationship. I wanted freedom. Yes, one day I would get married, maybe pop out a few kids but that would be after I found success. After I made a name for myself.

Now I wonder if I was lying to myself the whole time. Too scared to allow myself to become attached to someone. When all my choices would become our choices. I wouldn't have my independence but instead be locked back in that cage my parents put me in.

I chew on my lip. My mind flustered. My head a mess.

Before I can fall deeper into the rabbit hole of my mind, Bastian comes storming back into the room.

"Cameron. Pack your bags. We need to leave."

I spin around and look at him as he hurriedly moves about his room. He starts putting on a suit and I know it's back to business as usual for him.

He looks up at me as I stand in the doorway of the balcony. "Quickly. You have ten minutes."

The man I was falling for is gone. And the harsh, powerful Bastian Montford is back.

I swallow down the emotions flooding through me. I nod at him and hurry out of the room.

Lucas has the SUV ready and our bags already in it by the time I finish getting ready.

"We're late," Bastian says with a harsh tone.

I look at him as I crawl into the back seat where he is already sitting. "Calm down. You gave me ten minutes to get packed and resemble some sort of normalcy. You left my hair in a knot last night. It took time for me to brush it out."

"I don't need excuses, Ms. Wilder."

Great. Now we are back to last names.

We drive to the airport and get on Bastian's company jet. The flight to Saint Tropez is short. I watch Bastian on the flight. His eyes are lifeless. His mouth in a firm line as he stares at his phone. I tried to make conversation with him once and he shut me down.

Whatever that phone call was put him in a mood. He had that mood a few times when we were in Mallorca and he still found a way to touch me, acknowledge me. It gave me a sense of security, that we were okay even before we were anything more.

But he hasn't touched me once since he got that phone call. Not even a graze of his fingers along my thigh. It's as if the last week never even happened.

When we land in the south of France, Lucas walks me off the plane but Bastian remains seated.

"What's going on?" I ask him when we step onto the tarmac.

Lucas looks up at the plane as a flight attendant carries my luggage down the stairs. "You know I can't tell you, Ms. Wilder."

I look up at a window as if I could see Bastian through it. "Something happened. He's a completely different person."

Lucas folds his arms over his chest. "No, Ms. Wilder, he is the man I have always known."

I give Lucas a look of disbelief as a car pulls up beside us.

He looks back up to the plane then back at me. "The man you saw is a rare glimpse into who Mr. Montford could be. I wouldn't expect to see it again, Ms. Wilder."

He walks up to the SUV and holds the door open for me. I crawl in because I know I have no other choice. As we pull away from the plane, a tear falls down my face.

I'm not sad over the dismissal from Bastian.

I am sad over the words Lucas told me.

I don't think Bastian will ever let his demons go and will forever feel indebted to the world.

28

CAM

It's been three days since I got off that plane. I haven't heard a word from Bastian. Not a call or text, not even an email.

Parker has been with me the whole time and he has only said that he had business to attend to. I can tell by the look on Parker's face that he is just as worried about Bastian as I am. Parker is usually with him when he is in Paris.

My team has been working diligently while I was in Mallorca. The gala is just over a week away and everything is falling into place. The media has taken a liking to Montford Hotels again. All the bad news is behind us as we continue to push the new branding. Bookings are up eighty percent. The casino is staffed and ready to open. Everything is going as planned.

But my heart is somewhere else.

I head up to my room after another long day and

pour myself a martini. I drink it quickly and make another. I know I should eat something but I am just not in the mood. I sent a text to Bastian a few hours ago but it's still radio silence. I just want to wash away the memories of him. Of that stupid fantasy I had where we lived happily ever after.

This isn't me.

I am not some lovesick fool.

I scroll through my phone and call Tacoma but it goes to voice mail. I just need to talk to someone. I think about calling my sister but she is far too rational for my thoughts right now. I need someone to tell me to chase after him. Because that's what I want to do. I want someone to tell me it's what I should do. And I know Tacoma would.

I finish my third martini and the effects of alcohol have my mind spinning. I lie down on the sofa on the terrace and look up at the sky. But the stars are just another reminder of the man who has a stranglehold on my heart. I close my eyes to keep from seeing them but it's like they are imprinted in my brain.

The sound of glass breaking startles me awake. I must have fallen asleep with my martini glass in my hand. But when I open my eyes, I see it on the coffee table. I must have dreamed the sound but muffled noises above me have me shifting my gaze upward.

A faint blue glow comes from the balcony above me. At first I think it's moonlight but then my foggy brain realizes it has to be a phone.

Is Bastian home?

I listen for more sounds but can't hear anything. Maybe I really was dreaming. But me being an idiot and desperate for any word from the man, I drunkenly decide to head up to his room. I know my key will get me into his penthouse.

I stumble inside and find the black key card on the entry table. I open my door and make my way down the hall to the elevator. Before I let my drunken self second-guess what I am doing, I swipe it in front of the access panel and hit the P for the penthouse.

The elevator door opens and it's pitch black inside. Maybe the glass breaking came from below me, not above me.

I tiptoe through his penthouse, peeking behind the closed curtains to the balcony but there is no one out there.

I make my way down the hall, looking for his room. I swear I can smell him, his warm masculine scent. But it must be my imagination because he isn't here.

A sadness washes over me as I wrap my arms around my body. What is wrong with me? It's like I am chasing a ghost.

Lucas was right. The man I saw a glimpse of doesn't really exist. Last week was the dream and now I am in reality. A reality where I am creeping inside someone's house. I am losing my mind.

I sigh deeply and crawl into his bed. Just wanting to smell him on his sheets, wanting to relive our last happy memory. When we both wanted to wake up next to each other every morning.

I don't mean to fall asleep. I just wanted to feel him near me even if it was just in my mind.

I wake up to a dream. His arms sliding around me, his lips on the back of my neck. His whispered confessions of love in Spanish as he holds me tightly to him. I drift back asleep. This dream bringing me peace.

I startle awake as a ray of sunlight beams across my face.

Shit, I forgot to set an alarm.

I look over to the nightstand for my phone but it's not there. That's when I notice the dark tones of the room, not the bright whites of my own.

Oh my god.

The memories hit me of my drunk ass sneaking around Bastian's penthouse last night. The sadness I felt when I realized he wasn't here. The memory of the dream I had where he was wrapping me in his arms.

I roll over, hoping to smell the remnants of his cologne on the sheets. Needing one last memory before I drag myself back to the reality where he doesn't care about me anymore.

As I stretch my arm across the bed, I find the sheets warm.

I shoot up wondering if he is here. I say his name but there is no response.

Maybe that was my own body heat I felt on the bed.

I walk out of the penthouse, everything looking the exact same as it did when I broke in. I scan my key card over the elevator panel and slowly descend back to my own room.

As I walk barefoot down the hall to my door, I force my heart to put the walls back up protecting it once again.

Two days before the gala, Bastian returns to the office. His mood as pleasant as it was the day I met him.

Parker is following him around the office as he snaps and barks at every department. I don't want to deal with him so I quickly shut my office door so I can work on the final arrangements for the press at the launch party.

I'm halfway through an email when the door bangs open.

"Didn't I say no closed doors?" His voice as cold as my heart.

I look up at him and then back at my computer screen.

"Ms. Wilder, you know I expect an answer when I ask a question."

I don't say anything and just continue to write the email I was in the middle of.

I jump when I hear him slam the door. "What the hell?"

He storms over to me. "I asked you a question."

I look over at the door, then up to him. "Well, it seems you wanted the door shut anyway." I see the fury in his eyes and for some unknown reason I can't help but poke the bear. "You were being loud and obnoxious out there. I have no idea why you thought it was necessary to yell at all those people trying to get your business back on track. I need quiet while I work. Like it was before you came storming into the office."

Rage simmers in his eyes but I don't miss the lust that sits behind that rage. I shift in my seat, clenching my thighs together. I can't think about that.

He doesn't say anything, so I go back to my email.

He doesn't like my defiance. I knew he wouldn't.

He hits the button on my desk that fogs the glass so no one can see into the office then slams my laptop shut.

"Bastian, what the hell? I am trying—"

He pulls me out of my chair so quickly I stumble into him.

His lips are on mine instantly. I try to pull away from him but he pushes me against the windows facing the cliff.

He lifts me up by my ass forcing my legs around his hips. His kisses are heated, brutal, intense. I try to not kiss him back. I try to push him away but my stupid heart is getting in the way.

I grind against him as he pushes my skirt up my thighs. His thumb slips under my thong and into my wet heat. I moan as he slides it up and over my clit.

"That's it, baby," he murmurs against my lips as I get closer and closer to orgasm.

His lips slide across my neck and he sucks on my earlobe. "Mi cielito."

The words make me freeze.

"Cameron?" he asks as I manage to push him away.

He sets me down and I adjust my skirt. "You should go."

He steps into my space, cupping my face with his large hands. "What's wrong?"

I close my eyes, not wanting to look into his. I'm on the verge of tears. And I don't want him to know. Don't want him to see the power he has over me.

He pulls me into him, wrapping his arms around me in a tight embrace.

"You need to leave, Bastian." He doesn't say anything and just holds me tighter. "Please," I beg.

He must hear the strain in my voice because he finally steps away from me.

"I have work to do," I say to him as I sit back down at my desk.

I glance over at him and see the defeat on his features. "I'll let you get back to it."

He walks out of my office without another word, shutting the door behind him to my surprise.

I break down in tears after that. I am so confused. The man that forced himself on me was not the man from Mallorca. It was the man I shared that first kiss with. The one who used me for his own sexual needs. And I may like that man at times, but that is not the man I needed at this moment. Not the man I wanted to see after not hearing anything from him in over a week.

When I dry my tears, I let my team know I am not feeling well and head up to my room. I should work with the party planner to get the final details for the gala finished. I should be sending out the last of the press invitations. I should be checking with the hotel manager to make sure everything is set including all security measures.

But I don't.

I crawl into bed and sleep until the next morning.

29

CAM

I yawn as I walk into my hotel suite. It's just after nine at night and I am exhausted. I had to catch up on all the work I didn't get done yesterday. But everything is now set and ready for the launch party tomorrow.

I slip my suit jacket off and throw it across the kitchen island. I walk toward the bar cart in my room and make a martini. I am in desperate need of something strong after a fourteen-hour day.

Bastian and Parker were around the office all day but he kept his distance. I don't know if he heard something in my voice yesterday or if he just didn't care anymore. But it's not like I didn't catch him looking at me, staring at me when he thought I didn't notice.

If I wasn't so petty, I might have talked to him. Acted like everything was normal. But I couldn't do it. Because I knew if I tried to talk to him, I would just fall apart. So I spent as much time running errands around the hotel as I could. Anything to avoid him.

I look out the floor-to-ceiling windows and watch the rain fall on the terrace. I open the doors to let the smell of the rain overtake my mind. A chill hits my skin from the cool air flowing in. I move over to the couch and pull a blanket over my shoulders. I rest my head against the back and sip my scotch.

After tomorrow's launch party, I only have a week left here and then I return to Paris. Back to HSD and on to a new client. Maybe they will be in Paris and I can find a flat to rent rather than the tiny closet the company had for me.

My eyes start to close when I hear a knock at my door. I pick up my phone, making sure I didn't miss any important calls from my team. But no notifications are on my screen. I hear the soft knock again and get up, the blanket falling off my shoulders.

I look through the peephole and see Bastian on the other side. I sigh and lean my forehead against the door. My heart rate picks up at the thought of him here. But my mind is telling me to ignore him. To move on with my life.

Too bad I've become an idiot over the last few weeks and only listen to my heart now.

I open the door and Bastian looks distraught. The wrinkles around his eyes more prominent, dark bags below them. The sleeves of his shirt are rolled up and his hair is disheveled.

"What are you doing here?" I ask, blocking the doorway, not ready to let him in.

"I'm apologizing."

"For what?"

"Everything," he releases on a deep breath.

I raise a brow at him. "I don't know what you mean by that but after yesterday I don't want to see you."

"I was upset, Cameron."

"That doesn't give you any right to use me as your whipping post." He steps toward me but I hold my ground, putting my hands up in front of me. "You treated me like I meant nothing. Like I was nothing."

His hand reaches for my face but I push it away. "Mi cielito."

"No Bastian. You can't call me that."

He manages to push me a step back, his body taking up the doorframe. "Let me in, Cameron."

I shake my head.

"Please."

"Just leave. It's too hard to be around you."

He reaches for me again and this time I slap him across the face. "I told you to go," I cry out.

This time he does step back, a look of hurt on his face. I don't miss the opportunity to shut the door.

I wipe the tears from under my eyes and walk back to the couch. I pick up my martini off the coffee table and swallow the glass down.

Why am I like this? Why am I letting him affect me so much? This isn't me. Damnit. Maybe I should go out. Dance the night away at a club. Let some random man ravage my body, erase all the memories of Bastian.

But I know that won't work. One night of debauchery won't heal the wounds inside of me. Bastian buried himself in my heart so deep there is no hope that I will ever be able to love again.

I'm standing in the living room, sad and confused with tears leaking from my eyes when I hear the click of my door.

I should have known he would just barge in here.

"Bastian, please leave me alone."

His arms are on me, spinning me around so I am forced to face him. "Can't you see, Cameron, I can't leave you alone. I tried. Last week I forced myself to shut down my feelings. I was cold to you. Detached. I ignored you the entire way here because I knew if I looked at you, if I touched you, I would be done for. And that phone call, that moment in time, I knew if I kept you in my world that I would shatter you. I would destroy you. My past is back to haunt me Cam and I can't have you be a part of it."

I stare at his chest while he speaks, my arms wrapped around the cold silk of my tank. "I thought I was in danger. And you left me alone like it didn't matter. Like I didn't matter." I fight to keep the tears at bay even though he already knows I've been crying.

"I've had eyes on you the whole time, Cameron."

"Then why come back here? If you are so dangerous, if you are just trying to protect me, then why come back? It's obvious someone else could do the job."

He grips my chin, forcing me to look at him. "Because despite every fucking urge inside of me to let you go, I can't. I shouldn't be here. I shouldn't feel like this. Enthralled. Mesmerized. But I do. Those stars led me to you for some reason. Maybe I am a fool, a bastard, a tyrant, for being here, risking not just my own life but yours too. And I know we shouldn't be doing this but for some reason I can't let you go, Cam. You captivate me."

I gasp at his words. A million emotions running through me. Love, anger, fear. I shouldn't want to risk my life to be with him but I can't help the way my heart beats. "You scare me."

"You scare me too. I'm scared of the way you make me feel. The way it feels like nothing else in this world matters but you. And I needed this night with you, Cam. I need you in my arms, even if it's just for one more night."

I shouldn't agree with him. I shouldn't let him have me. He is telling me one more night like there won't be any more after this.

Instead of telling him to go, I press my lips to his. He kisses me back with such ferocity my knees give out. He picks me up and carries me into my bedroom. His lips trailing down my skin with so much tenderness, tears continue to fall from my eyes.

His lips move up to my cheeks, kissing away my tears. "Don't cry. Please don't cry, baby."

I roll away from him. "I can't keep doing this, Bas. I keep falling for you every day. And I know… I know there is no way for this to work. Every ending will be the same. I'll lose you."

He sighs as his hands wrap around my shoulders. "You'll always have me, Cam. Right here." His hand slides down and presses against my heart. "You've taken my heart from me. There is no one else I would rather have hold on to it."

I hiccup as new tears fall. Bastian turns me around

and crushes his lips to mine. He worships my body and with every kiss, my tears start to dry.

We make love. And for the first time I know it is truly that. He told me I owned his heart and he knows he owns mine.

We lie in the dark, wrapped in sheets and limbs. Our breathing steady as we watch each other. I trace my fingers over his brow, down his nose and across his lips.

"I love you," I whisper.

He pinches his eyes closed as if the words hurt too much to hear. But then his hands grip my face, his lips brushing against mine. "You are my entire world, Cam. Love is too small a word to describe it."

He presses his lips to my forehead and pulls me into him as we both drift asleep.

I put my earrings on and stare at myself in the mirror. Flashes of last night flutter through my brain. The way Bastian owned my body. My confession of love. His worship of every inch of me. It's like he needed to touch every part of my body all the way to my soul.

I was devastated when I woke up alone. He left a note that only read, "I loved all the nights with you under the stars." Anger flooded through my veins at the note. It was vague and gave me the uneasy feeling of goodbye.

A foreboding mood runs through me as I take the elevator down to the lobby. All the warnings and words Bastian told me when he came barging through my door fell to the wayside by his touch. But now as this dark feeling sinks into my bones, I'm worried I read last night all wrong. What did Bastian do?

When the elevator doors open, I don't have time to contemplate anymore. I force a smile on my face and meet up with the event planner and my team.

The event gets underway, the rich and famous laughing and having a great time as they gamble and dance the night away. I don't even pay attention to the time until I see Lucas standing along the wall. I grab my phone out of my clutch and see that it's well past nine. Bastian should have been here by now. When we were in Mallorca, he told me he would make an appearance early and then leave. But the party has been going on for hours now. I look around the room, the presence of Lucas making me believe he should be here. But I can't find him anywhere. I make my way out of the ballroom and onto the casino floor. After two loops, I give up and make my way back to the ballroom.

I pass the hall that leads to the restrooms, and Lucas steps out. "Ms. Wilder."

"Where is he?" I ask, panic rising in my voice as my mind tries to put together all his vague comments from last night.

"I think you should come with me."

"Why?"

He places his palm on the small of my back. "Because you need to be sitting to hear this."

My chest tightens at those words, anxiety and panic setting in. "Where is he?" I ask louder.

"We should talk elsewhere.'

"Tell me, damnit," I demand, as tears start to crest my lashes.

Lucas pulls me down a hall that leads to the bank of elevators. "He wanted to tell you."

"Tell me what!" I cry out.

The doors open and he pushes me inside. He doesn't say a word to me as the elevator heads up to the floor of my suite. Not the penthouse.

My breathing is erratic by the time the doors open. Lucas half carries me down the hall. When he gets the door open, he pushes me inside. "Tell me!"

"Bastian was arrested for his part in trafficking and money laundering through Montford Hotels. Interpol arrested him an hour ago."

"No," I cry out. "He wouldn't do that. He told me it wasn't him. He told me..." I gasp for breath as I try to piece all the things he told me together quickly. But there are so many pieces of the stories he left unanswered. "He wouldn't..."

Lucas takes a deep breath. "He lied."

I collapse to the floor, a crying, broken mess.

30

BASTIAN

The party starts in a few hours but instead of getting ready in my penthouse I am sitting in the office on my yacht, patiently waiting for Parker to show up with the file I requested he find.

When he walks through the door, he looks pale.

Good. That means he believes what he's reading.

He hands it over to me and I read through it. The words familiar to me since I've seen them before.

I slam the file in front of me closed. "Fuck."

"I assure you everything in there is true, Mr. Montford. When it was brought to my attention, I made sure to fact check it all. The photos aren't edited."

I slide my fingers along the back of my neck. "Make the call then."

"Sir, are you sure?"

I look up from my desk and glare at my assistant. "Make the damn call."

His hands shake before he shoves them into his pockets. "You know what this will mean."

I clench my fists that are laying on top of the file that will crush my entire world. "I'm not an idiot Parker. Make the call. Consequences be damned. I should have known this would happen."

He stutters, something I haven't seen him do in years. "But you'll go to prison."

I glare at him. I know he can see the anger, the fire, the betrayal burning in my eyes. "I am quite aware of what will happen. I should have known sooner or later I would."

He nods at me and heads toward my office door but stops suddenly before he opens it. "She will never forgive you."

I sigh as my eyes scan across the window to my left, looking over the sea I believed would bring me peace. "She already hates me. But it's time she learned the truth. I would be a fool to think she would give me her forgiveness."

"As you wish, sir."

I don't look at him as he walks out of my office. Instead I look at the sea. At the calming blue of the water. The water that reminds me of her and I know always will. But where it once brought me peace, I know now it will only bring me pain.

As I wait for Interpol to arrive, I think about Cam. The feistiness of her, the woman who pushed all of my buttons, yet for some reason instead of firing her or pushing her away, I dragged her closer to me. She captivated me. She made me feel like I've never felt before. I lost all sense of control when I was around her. From that first wild kiss after an argument to when I fucked her over my desk as I restrained her.

But as I got to know her more, as she started cracking away at the pieces of my heart, I never wanted to let her go. The day we spent on the boat and our night in Pollença was something I'd never experienced. I'd never felt so connected to another person before. And with her, I felt like I could tell her all my darkest secrets without her running away.

And she didn't.

I did.

When it started to get too hard, I made the choice to destroy her, to mangle up her beautiful heart.

I led her on last night. I made her think I finally gave in. Like we could make this work. But I just knew how to play my words right. I am sure she is searching for me right now at the party, waiting for me to sweep her off her feet. In a way, I guess I will be, but not in the way either of us wants.

I think about that night a week ago. When I found her sleeping in my bed. I was sitting in the dark on my balcony, contemplating my decisions, when I heard someone in the house. I saw her peer at the balcony. I wanted to go to her, yearned to touch her. I needed her because she is my cure for everything. But I couldn't do it. Because I wouldn't drag her into this world anymore. When I found her asleep, I curled up next to her. Whispering all the words I wish I could tell her. But like the coward I am, I left before she woke up. Hid in my office.

I heard her call out for me, and it felt like a vise around my heart as I ignored her.

But that had nothing on how I felt walking away from her this morning. I had every intention of her waking up with me wrapped around her like those nights in Mallorca, but when I thought about how much it would hurt her when I didn't show tonight, I knew I had to leave before she woke.

I made love to her for hours last night. Let her confess everything she felt, the good and the bad. And I know she fell more in love with me as I showed her how much I loved her words. But I couldn't say them back to her. Couldn't lead her on more than I already was. I know I am a bastard for doing it. I never should have shown up at her door. I should have let her hate me after I took advantage of her in her office. But I'm tyrannical. Maybe it was as much a punishment to my own heart as it was for hers.

I've known for a week that it would come to this. That I was atoning for all the sins I've made in the thirty-eight years of my life.

I wish I had more time. Another week, another day, another hour with her. Maybe I should have said something last week. But it only would have made this harder on her. On both of us.

I wish I could see her tonight. See her in her element. Charming the rich, entertaining the wealthy, dancing with the famous. I wish I could see her in that dress. The one I wanted to peel off her when the night was over. But all I get is a picture.

I look at the text Lucas sent me an hour ago. A

picture of her smiling, gorgeous, untouchable in that gown. I've never loved a woman like I love her. And it's the reason I'm here. The reason I made one of the hardest decisions of my life. Or maybe the easiest. Because I would give my life up for her over and over again.

My fingers trace over the picture of her on my phone. I think about when we bought that dress and how I wanted nothing more than to slide that dress off her body and make love to her. Or maybe keep it on her as I fucked her against a wall in a hidden alcove of the party. Now I picture her sliding down to the floor as she cries. When she finds out the truth. Or at least the version of the truth I want her to hear. I clench my fists. My heart aching. I am doing this for her. It was my only choice.

I don't know how long I sit there. I can only tell it's been hours as I watch the sun set below the horizon.

The sound of footsteps in the hall does nothing to make me move. Or make me regret my decision.

I don't even look up when the detectives walk through my office door without a knock.

The Interpol agent doesn't say a word to me.

What could he possibly say?

What's done is done.

I stand when he places his hand on my shoulder.

I don't even wince when he places the cold cuffs on my wrists.

"I'm sorry, Bastian. I didn't want it to end this way."

I take that second to look up at Benjamin Cole. The one man whose identity is hidden from most. But I've known all along who he worked for. I kept him close. He was supposed to help me with Matías. Even he didn't expect this of me.

I close my eyes, letting the image of her flash behind them. Her blonde hair flowing in the wind, the curve of her body as she stood on the spot just outside on the terrace of my home in Deià, the sparkle in her eye as she gave me that smile she saved just for me.

I did this for her.

To save her.

Just one more secret I will keep buried.

31

CAM

I sit slumped against the Juliette balcony in my tiny Paris apartment. I watch the revelers in the streets as they celebrate the last days of summer. If I were my old self, I would be out there on the streets with them laughing and drinking.

But instead I've cooped myself up in this tiny apartment for two weeks. Unanswered messages from Tacoma and my sister. Even Parker has sent me a few but I don't have the energy or heart to talk to any of them.

As soon as my contract was done with Montford, I came back here to wallow in my misery. At least I show up for work every day. I haven't been assigned a new client so I've been helping everyone else out with theirs. It helps distract me more. I'm sure if I had my own client, I would be a mess.

I'm supposed to go out looking for apartments today but I just don't have the energy. I don't have the energy for much of anything anymore. I feel like I lost every piece of me that made me who I am when I found out Bastian had lied. My heart shattered into a million pieces and I left them for him in his stupid hotel.

I guess I should say his brother's hotel because Matías was cleared of all charges. I don't know how any of this has stayed out of the press as much as it has. A few articles popped up yesterday about Bastian's arrest and his brother's innocence. My only guess is it has something to do with that group Bastian told me he used to be involved with.

Bastian said he had a price to pay and he paid it with his own life. For his brother's life.

At least I did take one piece of his advice and stopped digging into things. I think I am just too heartbroken to do anything.

Sometimes I worry though. He told me my life was at risk, that it was threatened. I always felt safe in his protection but now that I am back in Paris, I worry something could happen to me at any moment. Maybe that's another reason I spend all my time in my shoebox when I'm not at work.

My phone rings from the kitchen counter but I am too lazy to get up and get it. When it won't stop ringing, I finally get up and grab it off the counter.

"How long are you going to ignore me?" Tacoma says into the phone.

I slump onto my couch. "I wasn't ignoring you."

"I've called you like ten times since you got back to Paris."

"I've been busy," I say nonchalantly.

"I saw the news, Cam."

I bite down hard on my lip, trying to keep in the tears that have been falling nonstop.

"Have you talked to him?"

"T…" I sigh into the phone. "I can't talk about it."

"Why not?" She raises her voice.

I sniffle into the phone. "It hurts too much."

"Shit, you loved him." She pauses. "I knew you were getting feelings but I didn't realize how deep they went."

I scratch at the fabric of the couch. "I didn't want to face that reality. I thought if I didn't tell anyone…"

She snorts into the phone. "Since when does that work. Remember how I was, Cam? Remember how you forced me to talk to you when I ran from Ryder? We both know ignoring our feelings doesn't help fix anything."

"He lied, Tacoma."

She's quiet on the other end. She went through the same thing with her husband before they got back together, lies and broken hearts that nearly tore her apart. But I was there for her every second even when she didn't want me to be.

"You know I'm here, Cam. Whenever you need me."

I wipe away the tears on my cheeks. "I know you are."

"I wish I could tell you things will get easier. I mean… they will but it's going to take time."

I wipe my nose on the back of my hand. "It hurts."

"It's going to for a while."

"This is why I never wanted to fall in love, T. The pain is constant, a constant pressure on my chest every second."

I can hear the sympathy in Tacoma's voice. "I know."

"How did you get through it?"

"I learned to breathe without him."

Her words pierce my heart. But I know them to be true. She learned to live on her own again. Learned to live a life that didn't revolve around the one man that made her heart beat.

And I know I have to do the same.

I promise to call her in a few days and hang up the phone. My eyes are puffy and sore from crying. I crawl into bed. At least when I sleep, I don't think about Bastian.

"Cameron, avez-vous trouvé un appartement?"

I look up at Sophia as she leans against my desk in a red and white polka dot swing dress. Her hair is pulled up in some intricate curls. "No, I haven't found an apartment yet."

"Have you looked?"

Busted. I shake my head.

"Well, good thing my friend is a realtor. She said she will help you find one. In fact, I got us an appointment after work."

I sigh. "Sophia, you didn't have to—"

"I know I didn't but you've been so miserable since you came back from Saint Tropez, I figured it was because you were living in a shoebox instead of some swanky hotel."

"Most likely," I lie. "And the water. I miss the water.

Who would have thought a city girl like me would have liked a small town?"

Sophia scoffs. "Well, it's not like you were in some farm town. Saint Tropez is pretty lively."

I smile at her. That's not the town I miss.

She looks around the office then sticks her hand out for me. "Let's go."

"What? I still have work to do."

She gives me a look that Bastian would bristle at. "La vache! No one is in the office. It's such a nice day out, they are all probably working from a café." She uses quotes when she says working.

"I feel like I need to catch up after being gone for so long."

She pulls me out of my chair and leans down to grab my purse out of my desk. "You don't have work to catch up on. You've been back for two weeks and don't have an account. Busy work is not as important as champagne."

I laugh as I shake my head at her. "You are crazy."

She twirls around, her skirt fluttering high. "I know. That's why we are friends."

We both giggle as we walk out of the building and onto the cobblestone streets of Saint Germain des Pres.

———

I've been in a better mood since I went out with Sophia three days ago. This morning she and Jacques helped me move into the new flat I found. It's spacious and full of history. It's the perfect French apartment and I am in love.

The arched doorways, the gaudy pink striped wallpaper in the living room, and the clawfoot tub. All things that make me feel like myself again. Even though I would never choose pink wallpaper. It has a charm about it I can't deny. It even has a tiny balcony that fits one chair and a small side table so I can enjoy my coffee in the morning.

After they leave, I take a long bubble bath, letting the last few weeks wash away. I am starting fresh again. A new place of my own, a new client, a new outlook on life.

Learning to breathe again, like Tacoma told me.

32

CAM

The next night I decide to explore my new neighborhood in the Latin quarter. It's a perfect location, right near Saint Germain and just a fifteen-minute walk to work.

I find a cute restaurant with a gorgeous outdoor patio. Edison bulbs are strung across the patio, with small lanterns hanging along the posts of the railing, and vibrant fabrics draped around the lights.

I take a table in the corner of the patio and order a martini. After a long day of unpacking and decorating my apartment, a few cocktails are in order. When the server returns with my beverage, I order a few small plates to snack on.

I people-watch as I sip on my drink. Finally feeling relaxed and somewhat okay. I miss Bastian but I don't feel this deep-seated pain anymore. I guess that's what everyone says. Time heals all wounds. But I still feel the cuts he left on my heart. The scars on my soul where I let him in. I don't think those will ever go away. Bastian will always be a part of me. Always live inside of me but I am learning to live with the pain.

I think what hurts the most is I haven't heard anything about Bastian's arrest except for those couple articles last week. Like the whole thing didn't even happen. No press. No rumors. Silence.

It scares me a bit because I wonder if he is even still alive. If Lucas lied to me and told me he was arrested but instead killed. Like his older brother was.

But I think I would have heard about that. I'm sure whatever underground organization he was involved with would have made that information public.

My server returns with the tapas I ordered. I laugh to myself as I think about the fact I found a Spanish restaurant. I guess my heart really does miss Mallorca.

I'm distracted by a couple dancing in the street when I feel a body near me. I think the server came back to check on me but when I look up, I see a man I've never met before. He stares at me, a perplexed look on his face. But before I can say anything, he takes a seat across from me.

"Who are you?" I ask, panicked. I thought after Bastian's arrest I would be safe. That the people he warned me about wouldn't come looking for me. Maybe I was wrong.

"Why did you do it?"

"Do what?" I ask the stranger.

"Put Bastian in jail."

I scrunch my brow, confused. I had nothing to do with

him going to jail. I didn't even know that was his plan. I should have figured it out though. Saw the signs when he came to my room that night. Showed me how much I meant to him, how much he loved me even though he never said the words. I should have known that was his version of goodbye.

"I-I don't know what—"

The man grows angry, his knuckles clenching where he has them laid on the table. "Don't lie to me."

I study him, the tic in his jaw, the dark hair that is unruly, the light amount of stubble against his square jaw. Then I look into his eyes and I see the storm. This one blue instead of gray but I know that look and those eyes. "Matías?" I ask.

He leans forward in his chair, he looks crazed. Maybe he is on drugs like Bastian told me he was on before the raid. "Tell me," he pleads.

"I'm telling you the truth, Matías." He never confirmed his identity but memories flash through my brain of the articles and pictures I saw of him. The man in front of me, not the composed man I saw in the pictures. "The last time I saw your brother was…"

My heart clenches thinking about the last time. I was wrapped in his arms, our chests pressed against one another, I told him I loved him and I never wanted this to end. He called me his little sky and pressed his lips to my forehead. We stayed like that for who knows how long, staring at each other, wishing for a future we both wanted but weren't sure we could have. Then we fell asleep and when I woke up, he was gone.

I look back up at Matías and find him studying me.

He seems to have calmed down now. He's more relaxed in his chair. "You love him."

I don't know what to tell him. I don't know if I can trust him. I go to speak but the server comes back to the table.

"I didn't realize you were expecting a guest, mademoiselle. May I get you anything, sir?"

"Iced tea, please."

The server nods and leaves. I am surprised by his order. From everything I have heard about him, I expected him to order something much stronger.

"I'm not the man the media made me out to be. Or my brother."

I look at him, confused.

"You thought I would order liquor, perhaps a bottle, maybe ask for some coke on the side."

"I—uh—I…" I can't form a sentence.

He waves his hand in front of him. "You shouldn't believe everything you hear."

At that statement, the fog in my head clears. "I don't. I spent two months clearing your name."

"To think someone as beautiful as you had my back when you don't even know me."

"Your brother was my client. It was a job."

He smiles at me in a way that sends a chill down my spine. "Did your job entail sleeping with him? Because that is against company policy."

I don't know what to say to him. I don't want to talk about my and Bastian's relationship. I don't know if I can trust his brother. He is all over the place. And I am not sure if he is guilty of everything or not, I tried to have the media changed. For all I know, he could be working with that group.

He laughs as the server returns with his iced tea. "Bastian always had a thing for young, pretty blondes. He just can't seem to keep his hands off them. Kind of like me."

The chills return as Matías talks. "Oh, don't worry, I won't touch you. I'm not into sloppy seconds anymore."

The fear I was feeling from him quickly turns to anger. "What do you want?"

His eyes turn cold as he stares at me. "I want to know why my brother took the fall for me."

"He what?" I act surprised.

Matías looks over me as if he is trying to judge my reaction. "Don't act like you didn't know."

I shake my head. "I was only told he was arrested. Not that he took the fall for you."

"It was on the news," he says as he studies me. "He was found guilty and I was exonerated."

"I don't pay attention to the news," I lie.

"Hmm."

I swallow down the emotion flooding through me, the tears I want to release. Bastian loved his family more than anything. He would give up his own life for them. I remember him telling me how all he wanted was a family life like his cousins had. And I know this was his repentance.

He slams his hand on the table causing me to jump. "Damnit." He sighs as he rubs his hands over his face and through his unruly hair. "Bastian doesn't always think straight. He was supposed to use you to—never mind. That's not important anymore."

Used me? Was he lying to me the entire time?

I'm quiet as I talk. Not sure if Matías really knows how much he meant to Bastian. "He would have done anything for you, Matías. He loved you. He loved his family. He just wanted you to be together."

He scoffs. "Well, he sure picked the wrong way to do it." He stands from the table. "I'm sorry to have bothered you, Ms. Wilder."

"How... how did you find me?" I ask.

He runs his hands through his hair and it reminds me so much of Bastian I bite back the tears. "It's not hard to find someone." He gets out of his chair and starts to walk away but stops. "I'm not sure what they see in you."

"Excuse me?" I asked, shocked.

Matías looks at me curiously but doesn't say another word. He just turns and walks away. I watch him as he makes it to the end of the street and turns the corner. But I don't take my eyes off the street. Too many thoughts and memories are flooding my mind. Matías' words sending a chill down my spine.

Who was he talking about?

"Everything okay, miss?"

I look up at the server and nod. I ask for the check and then head back to my apartment. Sadness and fear loom over me like a dark cloud.

I jump when I hear a noise behind me and look over my shoulder. I swear I see Lucas hiding in the shadows, following me, protecting me. Like Bastian would have wanted.

33

CAM

It's been a week since Matías surprised me at the restaurant. I haven't seen him since but I swear I have seen Lucas following me around. It makes me somewhat worried that my life is in danger. Not to mention those words Matías said to me have been haunting me all week.

Sophia asked me to go out with her and Jacques tonight but I wasn't in the mood. Something just isn't sitting right with me. And it's my stupid thoughts that Lucas is following me because I'm not safe.

I don't know how Matías found me. I know it wouldn't be hard to find my job or my old apartment. But I literally just moved to this neighborhood the day he found me which makes me think someone has kept tabs on me for the last month, since Bastian's arrest.

I try not to think too much of it. Or about whatever organization Bastian was involved in. He thought his brother became involved and maybe he is. Maybe he was trying to do more than ask me questions last week.

I grip my ponytail as I try not to let my mind go crazy. I seriously think I am becoming delusional. No one is following me, no one is looking for me.

The knock on my front door scares the crap out of me so much that I fall off the couch in my living room.

How the hell did someone get to my front door without ringing the buzzer?

Calm down, you idiot. It's probably a neighbor needing to borrow something.

See, delusional.

I get up off the floor and crack open the door enough to see who is outside. "Kilian?"

His handsome face is creased with worry, and I don't hesitate to open the door to let him in. He surprises me by wrapping me in a hug.

"I was worried about you," he says as he pulls away.

"Me?" I walk us toward my living room. "Why would you be worried about me? It's like everything is normal. Life before Bastian."

Kilian stops and stares at my striped pink wallpaper. "I thought you had better taste than this Cam."

I laugh as I flop down on the vintage pink sofa I bought to match the walls. "It feels homey. And very chic."

He laughs as he sits on the larger couch across from me. "You can have it taken down."

"I also could have just found a different apartment but this place spoke to me." I pause, looking between the wall and Kilian. "Why are you here?"

"Can't I visit an old friend?"

"Bastian wouldn't like to hear that we are friends."

Kilian winks at me. "And how would he know?"

I nod toward the window. "I'm sure Lucas will tell him. The man's been following me for a week."

"Keeping you safe." His voice is serious, not the jovial one from seconds ago.

"Safe from what, Kilian?" I sit up as anger starts to pour out of me. "I thought everything was fine. I thought Bastian took care of things. Whatever stupid crime organization you are involved in was over me. Everything felt fine until Matías showed up a week ago, spouting shit about how Bastian took the fall for him. And all I want—"

"Matías was here?" Kilian asks sternly.

"Yes."

"In this apartment?"

I shake my head. "No, he found me at a restaurant down the road."

Kilian gets up and walks over to the window, looking outside and then shutting the curtains abruptly, making it darker in the room than it was. I'd been using the streetlights as light that night.

"What the hell?"

Kilian's face turns cold, calculated like the man Bastian warned me about. "Have you seen Matías since then?"

I shake my head. "What's going on, Kilian?"

He sighs and sits on the couch next to me. "That morning you left Mallorca, Bastian got a phone call that his brother was stabbed in prison."

"What?" I shriek. "He didn't say anything, he was so cold. He—"

"He didn't want you involved. Why the hell do you think he pushed you away so much? That man fell in love with you the moment he laid eyes on you and he battled with himself daily to push his feelings aside. He didn't want to drag you into this mess. Ruin you. You are too good of a person to be involved with people like us."

I shake my head. "No. Bastian is a good man. Whatever that group is that you are involved with, he got out. He paid his dues. Thiago paid the ultimate price."

Kilian groans. "You know?"

"Very little. He only told me when he thought my life was threatened."

"It still is, Cam." I stare at him, slack-jawed. "And I think Matías led them straight to you."

"No, he... he asked me why I let Bastian take the fall. I had no idea what he was talking about. He just wanted answers."

"Fuck, Cam. I don't want you involved in this. I warned Bastian. I told him to fuck you and forget you. But he wouldn't even do that," he stands abruptly, shouting. "Fuck."

"Tell me what's going on, Kilian."

"Matías fell in deep with The Partners. He owed them a lot of money, information, time. But he never followed through on anything. He let his debts pile up. He was too busy partying and living the billionaire lifestyle his brother afforded him. When The Partners finally had enough, they framed him. Had Interpol raid the hotel. He was arrested on money laundering through the casino, human trafficking, drug charges, as you know. But none of it was true. They set him up then kept feeding information to the press."

"That's why it was so hard for me to bury it. To fix the image. The Partners, as you call them, just kept giving the media more."

Kilian nods. "Bastian didn't know it involved them. He really thought his brother was guilty of those crimes of his own stupidity. Matías and Bastian don't have the best relationship, and Bastian knew Matías' antics. He didn't put it past him that he would get involved in that kind of shit. But when that one article came out about the Montfords being a new organized crime family. Bastian knew at that moment The Partners were involved.

"So he went to them despite my advice not to. He told them to end it all. Make the charges on Matías disappear. He offered them twenty million dollars. But Matías owed them nearly one hundred million. Bastian didn't care; he was willing to pay it. But The Partners found something they wanted more."

"What?" I ask.

"You."

"Huh?" I blurt out. "What the hell do I have to offer? I am just some rich girl from Boston set on proving to her parents she has the brains to work and not be a piece of arm candy."

Kilian pauses as I say those words. "You could never be a trophy wife, Cam. You are too wild for that."

"I know. But please continue your story. Why me?"

"Your body. Your mind. You're a leveraging piece,

Cam. Bastian was still too powerful after he left The Partners. They weren't happy to see him succeed and grow. No one leaves The Partners and becomes better off. They wanted him back. They never wanted to let him leave. But they let him think Thiago's life was enough to pay the debt for freedom. It wasn't. I think they used Matías to draw him in and failed. He wasn't giving in. Wasn't willing to pay them off. Then you happened."

"What do you mean 'I happened?'"

Kilian clears his throat as he walks over to the fireplace and rests his elbow on the mantle. "Bastian has always loved too hard. Despite his business demeanor, when he loves, it's hard for him to not show it. I've warned him about that too. The Partners saw it with his ex-wife. Saw the love he had for her fade. So when you came along, they knew how he felt. They knew you were the way to get him back.

"They changed their price. They wanted you. They told him they would take the twenty million he offered and you. But Bastian being the hardheaded bastard he is, wouldn't give you up. He's not that kind of man. So he took the fall for everything. He knew it would destroy his family, his company, his reputation but he did it to protect you."

"But they don't have him. He is just rotting away in a jail cell—"

"He isn't in a jail cell."

"What do you mean?"

Kilian sighs and then sits down next to me. "I'm not going into detail with how this group works. But if you end up on the bad list, they usually kill you. But if they know you have leverage, they make you do the killing, the crimes…"

"They make you the scapegoat if they get caught."

He nods.

I pull my legs up to my chest and wrap my arms around my legs. "You think they still want me?"

"I'm not sure. With the fact Lucas is on your tail, it's possible. I think they are using Matías to get to you. Bastian should have known they wouldn't just let it all go if he offered himself to them. They don't stop until they get what they want."

I stare at Kilian as I try to piece everything together. "How did his brother even get involved? I thought Bastian tried to keep him away from them."

Kilian sighs, defeat taking over his face. "I'm a bad man, Cam. I'm sure Bastian told you that."

"You got Matías in with The Partners," I say as I piece it together.

"I'm not involved—"

"Bullshit, Kilian. You are involved with them. You and Bas joined together. I know more than you think."

Kilian smirks at me. "So Bastian did spill more secrets than you care to admit."

My cheeks go red when I realize I gave it away.

"I didn't get Matías involved. At least not directly. I got his CFO to dangle the forbidden fruit."

"Davenport?" I ask. "He is involved?"

"Was." Kilian's smirk returns. "He's dead now."

"Who…" I start to ask but don't think I want to know the answer.

Kilian stands and takes the seat next to me. "Don't ask questions you don't want to know the answer to."

"Why did you do it, Kilian? Bastian sees you as a friend. He trusts you."

Kilian rubs the back of his neck. "He barely trusts me. I've ruined our friendship too many times to count. But he always lets me back in. He's a much better person than me."

"You didn't answer my question."

"Again, sometimes you don't want to know those answers."

I know I am not going to get anything out of Kilian on his own motives. "So how did Bastian manage to take the fall for his brother?"

"Bastian is a good piece to have. He's the rook on the chessboard."

I nod, not sure what to say.

Kilian puts his hand on my knee. "Cam, I'm not an idiot. I know you love that man. And that bastard loves you more than anything. Hell, he took you to Mallorca. You know he's only ever let me go to his house once." A smirk crosses his face before he gets serious again. "I am trying everything I can do to fix this. He got out before and he was happy, at least the happiest I'd seen the bastard until he met you. I dragged him into this mess. I'll get him out."

"How?" I don't want to get my hopes up. I'm not sure if Kilian can really do anything. I don't know how deep his involvement is with The Partners and I probably don't need to know.

"I'll figure something out."

"Kilian…"

He grabs my hand and squeezes it. "The less you know the better."

He stands and walks to the front door. I scramble after him, more confused than before.

He turns to me, brushing a piece of hair behind my ear. "What's it like?"

I scrunch my brow, confused. "What's what like?"

"Being in love?"

I bite my lip, not sure how to answer. I stop and start ten times but I can't get the words out, I can't describe it.

"That's answer enough."

"Kilian."

"Don't do anything stupid. Maybe stay out of the clubs. Make sure Lucas can always see you or grab you. And if you see Matías, don't be alone with him. I don't trust him."

"Okay."

He opens the door, his green eyes turning to meet mine one more time. "I'm sorry. For all this, Cameron. Bastian would have a much different life if it wasn't for me."

"You two have been friends for a long time."

He nods, a look of defeat in his eyes. "And it's time I finally give him the kind of friendship he deserves." He walks out the door. "Take care of yourself, Cam."

I let his words soak in. The nightmare that is both of their lives. And somehow has become mine too. My mind thinks about a chess game and my knees nearly buckle.

"Kilian?" I ask before he makes it to the stairs. He

pauses, and I walk down the hall to meet him. "You said before that Bastian was the rook. Then who is the queen?"

He gives me a cocky smirk but I don't miss the grief, the defeat, and the fear in his eyes. "I am."

My chest clenches as I watch him walk down the stairs. I know what he is going to do.

34

CAM

I've grown tired of Lucas following me around, not saying anything. So last week I made him a damn lunch when I went to the park to read and have a picnic.

He finally stopped hiding behind trees and in shadows. He ate lunch with me. I even offered him the second bedroom in my apartment that I turned into a closet. I told him I would take everything out but he declined. He lives in my building apparently.

It's been a month since Kilian sought me out. Two months since I heard from Bastian. Matías has tried to make contact with me but Lucas has taken Kilian's stance and disallowed it. He thinks Matías is trying to lure me to The Partners so he can free his brother.

I don't know Kilian's reach, his power. All I know about him is what Bastian told me. The last time I saw him was the first time he didn't flirt with me. But that is part of his power, his charm, I am sure it can win anyone over and maybe even The Partners.

The phone on my desk rings, startling me from my thoughts. "Bonjour?"

"Ms. Wilder, it's Bernadette. Would you be able to meet us at our offices this afternoon? We need to discuss part of the contract Jacques sent over this morning."

"Qui. I can head over after lunch. Maybe around two."

I can hear Bernadette smiling into the phone. "Perfect. Merci beaucoup."

I hang up the phone and grab my purse. The Maison is not far but since it's nearly one, I should probably grab some food before I head to their offices.

As I exit the building, I sense Lucas behind me. I smile at my feet. The man still insists on lurking instead of accompanying me.

I stop at a small café that has become my favorite. They make the best cappuccinos and the most incredible chocolate croissants that have ever touched my tastebuds.

As I wait for my order, I hear a news story streaming from someone's phone. I grab my sandwich and coffee when I hear a name on the man's phone.

I freeze as I listen in.

"Reports of a yacht capsizing in the Mediterranean along the Amalfi Coast is coming in. The yacht belongs to British billionaire family Bancroft Enterprises. The death toll is still unknown but coast guard officials have confirmed that Kilian Bancroft, one of the heirs to the Bancroft fortune, has perished."

I drop my coffee on the ground as all hope diminishes from my soul.

I hear the café worker saying my name but it sounds

muffled, my vision fading. Someone comes rushing over to me and tries to help me off the floor but I push them away.

I don't need comfort.

I don't need anything.

Because nothing will fix the emptiness inside of me.

A darkness takes over as my last hope for ever seeing Bastian again just died in the Mediterranean.

I'm still blinking, trying to make my vision clear, still trying to find a breath that won't seem to fill my lungs, when Lucas comes storming into the café. He picks me up and I don't fight him. I'll let myself feel like a damsel this one time.

I'm too broken to feel anything else.

35

CAM

I've been sitting at home for three days. My boss was not happy I missed my meeting with Bernadette. We almost lost the contract with the fashion house because of me. But Lucas somehow saved my job. Pretended to be a doctor or something. My memories of the last three days are vague. I've been taking sleeping pills to keep my mind shut down.

I vaguely remember talking to my sister. She told me she would fly out but I told her not to. She barely even knows about Bastian. She doesn't even know we had a relationship. I am sure she guessed but I never said a word to her other than the chemistry was electric between the two of us. But from her concern on the phone, I can only guess she figured out something happened between us. And to my surprise, she seemed consoling. Like a sister should.

She definitely didn't know about the danger I was in. The danger Bastian Montford brought into my life. And if I was still in danger, there is no way in hell I was going to bring her into it.

Lucas walks into my bedroom with a cup of tea. The man has been a saint to me the last few days. I never thought this man with scars on his knuckles and face, his bulking shoulders, and fierce eyes would be such a gentle giant. But he has been. Not that he's said much. We've maybe spoken ten sentences. It's usually him asking me if I am okay or need anything. And I respond with a head-shake or nod.

"I'm going to step out to the market. You are low on food and you are out of tea."

I stare out the window. I can't even cry. My emotions are dead like my heart.

"Do you want anything?"

I shake my head and pull the covers up to my chin as I settle into the collection of pillows on my bed.

He grunts. "I'll be back in thirty minutes. Don't—"

"Answer the door," I finish for him. Ever since Kilian's mysterious death, Lucas has been on edge. When I am lucid enough to pay attention, I hear him on his phone but can't tell who he is talking to or what it's about.

I don't really care though. Nothing matters. I don't even know why I am still in Paris. Besides the fact I can barely move from this bed. I should have left months ago. When my assignment with Montford Hotels was over. When my relationship with Bastian was over. Instead I held on to hope. A fool's hope.

I groan into my pillows then throw my blankets off me.

I need a drink. I need something to calm the thoughts in my head.

I stumble into the kitchen, not sure if it's even a good idea to drink. I think the sleeping pills are still in my system. The dark hole inside of me is eating me alive, destroying me, breaking me apart.

Maybe I should listen to Dolly. But I don't think even she could cheer me up right now. With my luck, only her love songs would play.

I find a bottle of wine and struggle to open the damn thing. My muscles weak from lack of food and energy.

The bottle slides on the counter and falls over, rolling to the floor. Red wine splatters all over the white cabinets, the floor. The bottle rolls to a stop against the pink wallpaper in the living room. And I can't help but laugh. Maniacal laughter pours from my lips as I fall to the ground and sit next to the spilled wine. The mess. Just like my life.

I really do think I am losing it. That I need to be committed.

My laughter eventually dies when I realize I am soaked with wine.

I finally get off the floor and head to the bathroom when there is a knock at the door. I know Lucas doesn't want me to answer it. But what if it's him. What if he forgot to grab my keys on the way out?

Despite my better judgment, I walk over to the door and look through the peephole. All I see is a head of dark hair. The man it's attached to is gripping either side of the door, his head down.

I step back from the door, heeding Lucas' advice.

And Kilian's. I fear it is Matías, even though I have no idea why.

But then the man knocks again and mumbles *merda*. I step closer to the door, the voice too similar. My mind is playing tricks on me.

It has to be.

It can't be.

"Cameron."

I nearly crumple back to the floor at that gravelly voice, the unique accent that takes hold of my aching heart.

I know it's stupid. I know it could be a trick but I don't listen to my head. I listen to my heart and it's telling me to open the damn door.

I undo the locks and come face-to-face with the man I would die for. Or at least I would have two months ago.

His hair is long and overgrown. He has a thick beard on his face. His eyes are sullen, his cheekbones gaunt. But when I look into his eyes, I see those stormy gray ones that I fell in love with.

"Bastian." My words are a whisper.

"Mi cielito."

Tears crest my eyes at his words as he burst through my doorway.

His arms are around me instantly. His body feels smaller. But I can feel his heart beating through his shirt. And it syncs with mine.

"Mi amor, mi corazón, mi vida," he whispers into my neck, his hold tight and strong despite the weight he's lost.

"How?" I manage to get out between tears.

He shakes his head. "I don't know. I don't know."

He pulls back and stares into my eyes. A million emotions pass through them. A million words left unsaid.

But he doesn't say a word. Instead, his lips crash into mine. Burning need overwhelms my body from his lips. I missed this. I missed him.

I kiss him back with a ferocity I didn't think my weak body had. I kiss him for what seems like hours. I hear the click of my door but ignore it. The mumbled apology from Lucas as the door clicks shut.

Bastian backs me up to the pink wall, gripping my ass and lifting me so I wrap my legs around his hips. His kisses turn rough, his teeth biting down on my lip, his fingers gripping hard enough to form bruises.

This isn't the man I fell in love with in the waters of Mallorca. This is the calculated man that stole away my breath with our first kiss. This is the man who keeps his heart closed off. This isn't the man I want.

I push him away from me. But he doesn't drop my legs.

"Bastian, stop. Please stop."

His hand comes up to my jaw. "What's wrong?"

"What happened to you?"

He closes his eyes, this time dropping my legs to the ground. "Cameron," he sighs.

"Please Bastian, I need to know. It's been two months. I haven't heard a word for two months."

"I was in prison."

"No, you weren't," I yell. "Kilian told me it was a lie. He said you weren't in prison. So where were you?"

"Cameron…"

I push away from the wall, storming toward the kitchen. "No, Bastian, I am tired of the secrets. I spent two months not knowing if you were dead or alive. Ever since you didn't show up at the gala and Lucas came and told me you'd been arrested. I-I didn't know what to think. I was heartbroken. I was devastated. Not a word from you. Then Matías finds me and tells me you took the fall for him. Then Lucas started following me, Kilian came to see me. God, Bas... I don't know what to think."

Bastian walks up to me, gripping my shoulders so I stop pacing. "Listen to me, Cameron. Kilian wasn't lying. I wasn't in a real prison. I was stuck in something far worse. And I don't want to tell you what it was like. You don't deserve to be tortured the way I was."

"Why couldn't you reach out to me? Have Matías... I don't know, somehow..."

He pulls me into him, his hands sliding up my neck, then cupping my jaw. "I didn't do what I did for Matías, Cameron. I did it for you. Every second of torture I went through I did it so you would be safe so they wouldn't take you as collateral."

"But Matías..."

"I don't trust my brother. Not right now. The fact The Partners were so quick to spit him out makes me think they don't trust him either. I stopped trusting him long before the raid on Montford. Before I let Interpol arrest me—"

"You let Interpol arrest you?" I shriek.

"Shh. Just let me talk."

I grumble but keep my mouth shut.

"Lucas was keeping tabs on Matías. Which in turn

led to keeping tabs on you. Shit, I didn't even know he was watching you until I found you."

"He knew you were here?"

"I only just ran into him when he left your building. When they let me go, I made contact with him. And he let me know where you were."

I try to make sense of everything he is saying. But I have more questions than he's giving me answers right now. "You came right here?"

He nods.

"You didn't take care of your businesses or your—"

"Cam, there is nowhere else I would go first. Nowhere else I needed to be but right here in front of you."

Tears start to fall down my face again. "Why would you let them arrest you, Bastian? Why didn't you tell me anything when you came to me that night? Why didn't you say goodbye?"

"Cam, there are so many things I wanted to say that night. But I didn't know what my future held. I didn't know if I would ever see you again. I didn't want to leave you with false hope. And I was afraid if I said those words, I wouldn't have the courage to let you go."

"What words?" I ask, my lip quivering.

One hand wraps around my waist and the other on the back of my head as he pulls me into him. "That I am in love with you, Cam. You tore apart my walls. You made me want to love again. But with you, it wasn't loving again. It was an entirely different type of love. One I never experienced before. One I knew I would never have again. You, Cameron Wilder, own my heart and I never want it back."

I want to believe his words. I want to grab him and kiss him and never let him go. But the last few months have been torture. He let my heart shatter into a million pieces and I've slowly been picking them up. Slowly learning to put my life together.

I worry that if I let him in, let him take hold of my aching heart, he will just leave me again.

Know your worth.

And I am worth more than heartbreak, tears, and regret. I am a strong woman. Fearless. I don't deserve this from him.

I wipe my tears away from my face. "No," I stammer. I clear my throat after choking on the word. "No, Bastian."

"No?"

I look up at him, at the defeat written across his face. This man that sacrificed himself for my own life. But for some reason, I cannot forgive him so easily. "How do I know you won't do it again?"

He takes a step closer to me. "Do what?"

"Leave me."

His face falls as his hands come up to my face. "I'll never leave you again, Cam."

I push his hands away and walk over to the balcony. "You can't promise that. You can't. What about your brother, what happens if he comes back for us? Or if The Partners lure you back into their depths? What then, Bastian? You would never take me with you."

He sighs as I hear him sit down on a chair. I turn

around to see his elbows on his knees, his hands in his palms. "You're right. You can't know. But I need you to understand." He looks up at me with such devotion in his eyes, it nearly makes me crumple to my knees in front of him. "I will sacrifice my life over and over again for you, Cam. You are everything that is good in this world. You make me the man I want to be. I've always told you that. And I won't let the evils of this world tear you down, darken your soul, bury you. But know that I will fight like hell for you. To get you back every time."

My heart breaks at his words. At his utter selflessness for my own life. He stands and crosses the room briskly. And I'm frozen in place as I watch the storm in his eyes. The storm I have no way of escaping.

His body cages me in against the wall, his lips inches from mine. "I love you. I love you more than I could ever put into words. Loving you is like looking up at the stars. Infinite, endless, and I never want to stop. I want every single one of those damn nights with you."

He drops one of his hands to my waist, pulling me against him. "I didn't come here expecting your forgiveness. You are a wildfire, Cam. You know your worth. And you would never let anyone treat you how I have without putting up a fight." He falls to his knees in front of me. He wraps his arms around the backs of my knees, pulling me into him. "So I am not going to ask for your forgiveness, Cam. I'm begging for it. I love you. I would have died for you. Hell, I almost did and I would do it again because you are worth it. Your smile, your laugh, your heart, your soul. Every damn part of you is worth it. So I'll beg for your forgiveness because that is the man you have made me become. A man that will never be as worthy as you."

Tears crest my eyes. I don't even try to bite them back. Because I can't with this man. He knew I wouldn't forgive him, knew I would put up a fight. Yet here he is, a man more powerful than most, on his knees begging for my forgiveness.

Maybe I am wild, reckless. But there is only one thing I know to do.

I lean over him and press my lips to his. I wrap my fingers in his overgrown hair. I feel the rub of his beard against my cheek and know I want to feel it elsewhere. I want everything with this man even if it means living the rest of our lives in danger. I'm willing to risk it all for him.

I pull back, my thumbs running over his cheekbones. "I love you too, Bastian Montford."

He stands up, wrapping my arms around the back of his neck. "Let me show you how much I love you."

I kiss him softly then grab his hand and lead him into my bedroom. He pulls off my T-shirt and pushes my wine-soaked shorts to the ground. He raises a brow at me and I just laugh as I grip his own shirt. Pushing it off his shoulders before removing his pants. He kicks them to the side as he pushes me back onto the bed.

He crawls over my body. "I want to spend all my nights with you. Just like this."

"I think we could do that."

He grins at me and he finally looks like the man from Deià. Free. Like nothing else in the world matters except me and him. He enters me slowly, our eyes never breaking contact as we both fall into bliss.

After we make love, he holds me in his arms, promising to never let me go.

"But what happens with everything else? Are you ever free from them?"

He presses his lips between my shoulder blades. "This time I am."

I don't ask questions, I don't worry if he really means it. Because I am happy in our bubble, in a world where it's just me and him.

36

CAM

I roll over and find an empty bed. Panic sets in as the fear of Bastian leaving overwhelms me.

I find my T-shirt on the ground by the bed and pull it on. I quietly tiptoe across the wooden floors, my heart beating rapidly, my breaths short as I expect the worst.

My breath leaves my body in a giant whoosh when I find Bastian on the balcony, leaning against the railing, his head bowed to his chest.

I walk over to him slowly and press my hand between his shoulder blades. He must have felt my presence because he doesn't jump. Instead, he reaches behind him and pulls me around so my back is against his chest. He holds me tight, not saying a word. His beard scratches against my neck as he breathes deeply, as he takes in this moment.

When he begins to speak, it startles me. "I never thought this moment would happen."

"Right here, right now?" I ask.

I feel him shake his head against my back and then shrug. "Maybe. Any of the last hours really. I didn't think I would ever get to tell you how I truly felt."

I spin in his arms and grab his face. "What happened to you, Bas?"

"I told you I don't want you to know."

I run my hands down his arms, my fingers tracing lines over his body. He's lost weight but nothing terrible. I think they did more than torture him. I think they made him do terrible things. At least that's what I inferred from Kilian.

"Did Kilian..."

He nods. "He saved me. For you. He knew I needed you."

Tears crest my eyes. "I need you too, Bas."

The hardened man that usually stands before me lets out a moan. I don't know if he is broken or grateful. But I plan on spending a lot of time finding out. "Come on, you brute," I tease. "Let's go back to bed."

He nods, grabbing my hand as we walk back to the bedroom. He falls asleep immediately and I watch him sleep. Worried that if I close my eyes, he won't be there when I open them again.

I sit on the bathroom counter and watch Bastian as he shaves his beard off. It's been nearly a month since he came back to me and up until a week ago still looked like he was living with a ghost.

I forced him to come to Deià, to spend time in the sun, in the water, looking at the stars.

The first day was rough. His attitude all over the place. Like it was when we first met.

But I forced him to step away from work. To focus on him.

By the third day we were here, parts of him started to come back. The man I fell in love with on this island began to show again.

Then this morning I forced him to shave his beard. It felt like a reminder of his imprisonment, a reminder of his sacrifice, of Kilian's sacrifice. But he decided it was the right choice.

I could tell losing Kilian was killing him. Day by day, he fell apart a little more. This man who wanted nothing more than to atone for his sins let someone else take the fall. A man most might think an enemy to him but deep down I understood their friendship.

I don't think he knows the truth. The words that Kilian told me that would break Bastian even more. Or maybe they would help heal him. But just like the secrets he keeps from me, I will keep this one to myself. Until the time is right.

The sun on his skin helped. The memories he has in Deià helped. And day by day I watch him return to me. The man whose heart is made of gold. The man who would give everything up to make others happy.

He always thought he was a bastard, a tyrant. But when I look at him, I don't see any of that. I see a saint. This man would give up the world to save those he loved.

And someone did that for him. Probably for the first time in his life. And I think he sees it now. He's been atoned.

He looks over at me and smiles. A smile I haven't seen in months and my heart drops to my stomach as the butterflies take over. "I was beginning to think you liked the beard."

I bite my lip and smile. I did like the beard. The way it left a burn between my thighs. The way he would drag it up my body and across my clavicle. The way he was rough with me the last month. "I did."

"But you like me clean-shaven more?"

I rest my hand on his forearm. "Bas, I love you with or without it. Maybe one day you can bring it back but I think you need the reminder gone."

He nods at me and goes back to shaving. The man has come a long way in just a few days. I was worried I was never going to get the man I fell in love with back. I knew he was in there deep down. I just needed to find him. I can't believe it took me so long to remember he said he always finds himself in Deià.

As he swipes away the last of the shaving cream, he looks over at me and kisses me hard, leaving me breathless.

"Thank you."

"For what?"

"Waiting for me."

I pull him into me. "There is nothing in this world that would make me stop."

"I was lost, Cam. I wasn't the man..."

I rest my hand over his chest. "The man I fell in love

with has always been in here. I just knew he needed time to come back out."

"You're an incredible woman, Cameron Wilder."

I press my lips to his cheek. "I'm your woman, Bastian."

"Forever?"

I look into his gray eyes and swear I can see stars staring back at me. "Forever."

EPILOGUE

BASTIAN

Four Years Later

I hang up my phone and walk out onto the deck off the office of the yacht. Cam is laying out on a sun lounger, her tan skin almost as dark as mine. I lick my lips as I watch her sunbathe. Even after four years, I find her as desirable as I did the day she was waiting for me at the marina. And just like then, she is still a spitfire.

"Hey, boss."

I shake my head as I laugh at my fiancée. A few months after I came back into her life, she accepted a job with me as head of public relations at Montford Holdings. I didn't think she would take it since we only argue when we work together. Of course, she threw a fit when I brought it up. Accusing me of controlling her and wanting to keep an eye on her when she was perfectly capable of doing it herself. That argument ended with her bent over my desk again and three orgasms. She resigned from her company the next day.

Ever since she came to work with me, she likes to push my buttons and call me boss. I'm not going to tell her I like it. I honestly don't but more times than not it ends up with us half naked.

"Babe, we're on vacation. Stop with the boss."

She props her hands on her hips. "Stop with the babe."

I raise a brow at her and smirk. "Not happening."

"You're a dick. Why do I even put up with you?"

"Because you love me."

She eyes me up and down. "Mmm. Depends on the day. Today isn't your day."

I pull her into me and smack her ass as I do. "Behave."

She pushes her sunglasses on top of her head. "You are the one that's going to have to behave. You can't be slapping my ass when my parents are on board."

"Maybe you shouldn't have invited them."

Her jaw tics and I think she might actually slap me. "You are the one who invited them!"

I grin at her. "You expected me to let them miss our wedding?"

"Yes."

"Your parents love me."

She grabs a hair tie from around her wrist and throws her hair up into her usual ponytail. "Yeah, because my dad thinks you are a superb businessman."

"I am," I agree.

She rolls her eyes. "And my mom finally got her wish. I'm marrying into society."

"We all win."

"None of us win, if we have to put up with my parents for a week."

Her parents aren't nearly as bad as she makes them out to be. Or maybe it's just she had a heart-to-heart with her mom after I came back to her. Her mom happy she settled down and even happier she did it after finding her own success.

My parents are worse, especially when my dad brings one of his new wives around my mother. Needless to say, this week should be interesting.

"The boat's big enough."

"Fortunately."

"You'll get to spend time with Yve."

She shrugs. She has no idea I flew her friend Tacoma and her husband out for our small private ceremony.

"You don't seem all that happy to marry me."

She shrugs again and I slap her ass before pressing a soft kiss to her forehead.

Her hands wrap around my shoulders and play with the ends of my hair. "I would marry you without anyone around, Bas. You and me. That's all I need."

"As long as you remember that," I tease.

"Still an arrogant brute when I am trying to be sweet."

She grunts and tries to pull away from me but I press my lips to hers. It still shuts her up. She groans into my mouth and pulls me closer to her.

"I like you better when you're sassy." I grab her hips

but instead of pulling her into me like she thought I would, I push her away.

"What are you doing?"

"Before we dock and pick up our friends and family, I thought we could go for a swim." I nod toward the bay behind us and watch Cam's eyes as they light up. She knows exactly where we are. The cove I love so much. The place I tied her up and fucked her hard. The place I fell in love with her.

"I hope they aren't expecting us soon." She dives into the water and I quickly follow her in.

I kiss my wife as our captain declares us married. I never thought I would do it again but with Cameron, I didn't have a choice. She burrowed so deep into my heart there was no hope for us not to be together.

One of the deckhands serves us champagne and Lucas claps me on the shoulder, congratulating me. I look out over the sea, the one place I feel truly free and see a boat far out on the horizon. I lift my hand and wave, unsure if they can see but a friendly gesture nonetheless while we celebrate.

Cam wraps her arms around my middle and rests her head against my shoulder. "Who are you waving to?"

"No one."

She presses a kiss on my arm. "I wish he was here too. You know he woulda been here."

I know he would if it was possible for a dead man. I

squeeze her closer to me and joke. "He would have tried to steal you away from me."

I look down at her as she looks up into my eyes. "I never would have let him. You're the only man that gets my heart, Bas."

My lips crash to hers. The love I have for this woman is catastrophic. Hell, I risked our future and my life to save her, to protect her. And I vow to do that until the end of our days.

This woman lights something up inside of me. Makes me burn with passion instead of fury. She's changed me. She makes me feel like the man she says I am.

I pull away from her but keep my lips within millimeters. "I love you."

I feel her lips smile against mine. "I'll never get tired of hearing that."

I press a quick kiss back to her lips as everyone on the boat cheers and hollers. We pull apart and I watch her as her cheeks turn a light pink. I kiss her temple then pick up my glass to toast with our friends.

I nod my head at Matías, and he nods back. It's been a rough few years for us and for him. We're both finally free of The Partners. At least as free as we can get. They will always watch us. And we will always be ready for them. But for now, we are both at peace.

Later that night, I pull my wife onto the deck of our room. I play the song we danced to the night we ate dinner under the stars. I pull her into me, wrapping her tight in my arms.

"Did you think we would ever get here?" she asks me.

I brush my nose against hers. "I wished for it."

"Me too."

"Mi cielito, the stars brought us together. And now we finally get all our nights under them."

She rests her head against my chest as we slowly sway back and forth to the music. Our hearts beating as one.

The End

ALSO BY TORI FOX

The White Creek Series

Missing Pieces

Broken Pieces

Forgotten Pieces

The Broken Lyrics Duet

The Ghost of You

The Fate of Us

The Partners

Atonement

Other novels

Desolation: A Salvation Society Novel

Burnout: An Everyday Heroes Novel

ACKNOWLEDGMENTS

Two years ago I wanted to write this book but the timing never worked out. But I think it was for the best because the original book I pictured in my head was more contemporary/rom com and I went on a total different path. And I think it was the best decision. I love this book. I love Cam's strength. I love the banter. And I love Bastian Montford. I hope you loved this story as much as I did. And I cannot wait for you to dive deeper into The Partners!

Thank you so much to my partner in crime, the pea to my pod(cast), and one of the best people I've never met in real life. J. Akridge you are an amazing human. You make me laugh every day. You also make sure I'm getting my shit together and not procrastinating all day. I don't know what I would do without you!

This book would not be what it is if not for my amazing beta readers. Autumn, Mary, Athena, and Nicole you made this book so much better. I'm forever grateful for you.

Meghan, thank you to you and your mom for helping me with the French. We will have a girls trip to France one day!

Juliana at Jersey Girl Design, thank you for knocking this cover out of the park!

Ellie at My Brother's Editor, you make my words pretty and put up with my crazy.

Thank you to everyone at Grey's for getting the word out on this book and getting it in more reader's hands!

To everyone that has been on the podcast, you all motivate me daily to write more, write better, and work harder.

This book wouldn't be here if it wasn't for Tom Ford. That man knows how to make a fragrance. And one sniff of Costa Azzura Acqua brought Bastian Montford to life. Thank you Mr. Ford.

To my husband, thanks for believing in me and offering to bring me lunch or cook dinner whenever I was deep in the cave. You'll always be my biggest fan.

Thank you to all my readers. There wouldn't be books if it wasn't for you. I cannot wait to share more stories with you!

ABOUT THE AUTHOR

Tori Fox is the author of romantic suspense and contemporary romance with a little bit of angst and a whole lot of sexy. When she isn't writing, you can find her listening to true crime podcasts as she tends to her plants or singing along to pop songs as she drinks champagne. Tori lives above the clouds with her husband and dog in the Rocky Mountains.

You can find Tori on Facebook, Instagram, and Twitter @ToriFoxBooks

For the latest news and releases visit torifoxbooks.com